A Gathering of Loves

Horace Belvins Helmick

ISBN 978-0-9895100-2-8

PROLOGUE

Spit. Caught and carried by the wind, the white glob lands on the sand out ahead. Sand, rocks, a few scraggly plants. Any other signs of life? Yes, infinite signs of life, small life, smaller than the snakes and toads, much smaller than a coyote, smaller even than the armored bugs and tiny flowers. Spitting on the desert in a dream.

Caught and carried by the wind, the dreamer lands on the sand out ahead. Shaken but not hurt, the dreamer rises from the sand and rocks and sees the wind, rolling and turning, fluid, alive and willful. Big life. Not fickle at all. Enduring. The dreamer believes that the wind knows more about the dreamer than the dreamer knows about the wind. If everything seen is a reflection of what the seer already owns, what is the wind?

Floating away, bing, bing. A human with no where to go, with no *from here to there to see you*. She awakens, sits up, looks around, up and down, side to side. The sky is still up there. The earth still waits under her. To the right, a tree. To her left is the path she followed here. Piled in front of her, between her and a bush, are her possessions. Beyond the bush is a river or a large stream. Behind her, a rugged, nearly vertical, somewhat overgrown cliff blocks out the morning sun. Another dream.

She awakens, sits up, looks around, up and

down, side to side. The morning sun is shining on the skylight above her. Her bed is in disarray. The door to the hallway stands open. Out the window her flowers are blooming. She sees herself in the tall mirror. And behind her, the smooth, quite vertical, somewhat decorated wall of her bedroom blocks out the neighborhood. Another dream.

COULD I TOUCH HIM

"Dreaming is a dream. Yes. Of course. You and I both know that."

Not many steps ahead of them, the concrete walkway split gracefully into two narrower walks, like the pale body of someone lying on the ground with his or her legs thirty degrees apart. Nubbel shook his head in doubt. Noticing where they were on the walk, he smiled forgivingly and indicated with a curving away motion of his hand that he needed to follow the cement thigh that led off to the right. "Then why do we think that we dream, Dan?"

The woman walking beside him asked him right back, "How else might we strip away our immortality?"

Nubbel grinned and reached out his hand to briefly touch the woman's sleeve just before he veered away from her at the splitting of the walkway. "Is that what you think dreaming is all about, mortality?"

"No, Nubbel, that's what *thinking that we are dreaming* is all about." With a nod of her head and a wave of her hand, the woman went the other way, taking the cement thigh on the left. "We are shaping ourselves into mortals."

And when they each reached a knee at the same time, Nubbel called to her over the freshly mowed grass, "Next you'll be telling me that depression doesn't exist."

Thighs, knees, shinbones. Nubbel's paved shinbone would carry him all the way down the north side of the line of buildings, while the woman's lower leg of concrete quickly reached its foot on the south side at a circle of bicycle parking racks. *Depression? What's that? A hole in the earth?* She slowed her pace and came to a standstill at the center of the circle of racks.

She snorted at the fix she found herself in. Turning slowly around, clockwise, she glanced at each and every bicycle. *Why did I come this way? Do I have one of these…these gimmicks chained to one of these racks? Hmm.* She couldn't remember riding on a bicycle, not for a long time anyway. *So what am I doing standing here checking out the selection? Am I a thief?* She consulted her memory again. No, she had never stolen anything, nothing anyone would ever miss anyway, an occasional grape in a grocery store or a glance or two at a particularly interesting man. *So why are my hands hidden deep in my pockets and why oh why am I acting ever so innocent? If my dumb pose and cute pretense mean I am guilty, I am guilty of what? Of liking the sun? Of being alive? Oops! There I go, playing the innocent again.*

"Dan!"

She cut short her introspection to attend to the sound of someone calling out. A particularly interesting man strode up behind her and stuck the first joints of the fingers of one of his hands in her back pocket. Her turning around to look at him necessarily pulled him and her very close together. "Dan," he said again, locking in on her eyes. He smiled softly, deliciously.

"You must have the wrong number. My name is not Dan."

The man frowned, then grinned, then smiled

broadly and cocked his head. "It was, this morning. Remember breakfast? I called you *Dan* maybe four or five times. And you never once hesitated before responding."

"You present a convincing argument, yes. And what would your name be?"

"During that same breakfast, you addressed me by name two or three times."

"Then you must be Terry."

"That is who I am, all right."

"Then maybe you can tell me why I'm gawking at these bikes."

"That is a problem. I don't know if I know the answer. Would you like to have a bike, Dan?"

"I don't think I have any abiding interest in bicycles." Dan shook her head sincerely. Then she nodded her head. "By the way, that's a nice looking shirt you have on."

"Thanks. You bought it for me."

Oh, I don't think that I did, no. I'll have to think about that. "Tell me, Terry, how do I get out of here?"

"That's easy enough. Come with me." Terry promptly led her out of the circle of racks on a little well-worn path she hadn't noticed.

He certainly has pizzazz. Following close behind Terry, Dan admired his carefree walk. *His muscles work smoothly. Not one of them goes unused. And his shoes… What about the shoes? Yes-s-s, I remember those shoes! They were purchased the same day at the same store as the shirt he has on. And neither the shoes nor the shirt were purchased by me. I was straggling along somewhere behind Terry in the store that day, looking for something to look at; I gave that shirt a casual eye, just the briefest glance, and Terry immediately appeared beside me and snatched it off the rack. "You like this?" he asked, neither looking at me nor expecting an answer. The shirt, the shoes, underwear and a vest: he bought them, not me. And by the way, where is he taking me?*

"To lunch," said Terry back over his shoulder.

Maybe I didn't hear correctly. Did he just answer my unvoiced question? "What did you say, Terry?"

"Lunch, to keep you fit." He sighed. "I think you would literally starve to death, Dan, if I didn't keep watch over you." He peered back at her mouth.

To see if I still have one? Fools and their mouths are soon parted.

Arm in arm they entered the filling center. Terry stood in line while Dan meandered around running into roof-support columns. Dan slapped a couple of backs, tripped over a chair, had a talk with Milosh. Terry whistled. *That can only mean that Terry wants my opinion on what he should have to eat, since he never has any problem picking out what I will enjoy eating.* Dan helped Terry make his choices, and they carried their food to a table and sat down, just the two of them.

"Eating," said Dan as she untrayed the three dishes Terry had selected for her. "Honesty of form." She arranged the dishes before her. "The true appearance of the eater while eating."

Wisely silent for the moment, Terry just nodded and waited.

Dan had not yet taken her first bite. "Shall we be pigs or cranes, Terry? Mice or hippos?"

"I will be me today, Dan. I feel like staying inside the cultural structure and playing by the rules." Terry's tone was friendly but, in sharp contrast to his words, noncommittal. "You could pretend you are doing that, too, if you want." He opened his napkin in his lap.

"How?"

"Just arbitrarily pick someone nearby and copy their style."

"I can pick anyone?"

"Anyone but me, Dan."

"And how close must I mimic someone besides you, Terry?"

"If no one turns to stare at your face or hands, you're doing OK."

Dan picked the someone sitting over next to Milosh, which seemed a good choice--Dan had a clear view of her, etc.--except the woman soon stood up and left the center. Dan didn't think that Dan's looking at the woman had had anything to do with the woman's leaving. *But who knows.*

"I have a question, Terry."

"I believe I am ready, Dan. Shoot." Terry had started eating.

"It is an I-don't-know-what's-going-on question."

"Yes?"

"You just said that you feel like playing by the rules today. Right? Does this mean that for the time being, at least, we are treating the 'cultural structure,' to use your words, as a personal add-on that we can make use of or not according to our whim?" Dan found a napkin on her tray and laid it in her lap. "Or, if this *does not* mean that, are we to look upon it, the 'cultural structure,' as a basic and ever-present ingredient in the production and maintenance of the animal?"

"Ouch!" Terry laid down his fork so that he could slap his jaw. He didn't hit himself very hard, but his slap was solid enough to make the distinctive sound of a slapped face. "Was that really just one question?"

Dan pressed a hand's worth of her knuckles up under her chin.

Terry started to pick up his fork but, instead, touched his index finger to his chest. "In my case, whether I play by the rules or not, Dan, the cultural structure is probably always the latter, a basic ingredient." He turned the finger to point at Dan's chest. "In your case, it's probably always the former, an add-on." He picked up the fork. "Why don't you take a bite of your food every now and then?"

"Ah, for you it's a basic and for me an add-on." Dan tilted her head at Terry. "Does that make you one of many eggs under a warm chicken and me the egg that for some reason rolled away from the nest after the hen pooped it out her butt? Yea?"

Terry smiled enigmatically. "Yeah, for the time being."

"Did I really? Did I really hear that? Did you actually say 'Yeah, for the time being'? Haven't you told me many, many times, Terry, that events like that don't change, that they are cast in stone or a stone substitute forever?" She did. She took a bite. It was good. She forgot to look to see what it was before she put it in her mouth.

"I'm coming around to your kind of thinking, Dan." Terry laid a hand momentarily on Dan's forearm. "Not on everything, mind you. But concerning personal history."

Dan grinned. Her eyes twinkled as she leaned toward Terry, keeping her back straight. "If I turn my head away and then turn it right back, can I expect to see a pitch black raven or a spotty panther sitting there on your chair?"

"Not hardly. I only meant that I can see now that everything is how one interprets it. And it is nothing more or nothing less than the interpretation. And the interpretation can and should and does change with time."

"That sounds like a big step for you, Terry."

"Yes, it is, was."

"What brought it on?"

"The willy-nilly way that you act, madam. It finally got to me."

"Do I act differently than you?"

Terry waved his head and rose an inch or two above his chair in disbelief. "Be serious!"

Dan raised her palms to the ceiling and shrugged.

Terry wanted to dismiss her question but didn't. "It's clear to most everybody after their first five minutes with you, Dannie, that you are not deranged. Then a bigger number of minutes must pass before whomever you are talking with can feel safely certain that you aren't just game-playing with them or only clowning around. The third question, however--I see it at least once on every single face--is the toughie that takes more than mere minutes: If you are neither unbalanced nor primarily joking, why does just being around you make the world appear totally unpredictable?"

"And what is the answer?"

"You don't know, Dan?"

"Nope. Haven't the foggiest notion, Terry. For me, it's *your* presence that makes the world appear totally unpredictable."

"Is that for real?"

"It is. The world goes fuzzily every which way whenever you are near me."

Terry closed one eye. "Does your pretty underwear dampen, too?"

"Sometimes."

"Right now?"

"Yes."

"Can I help you prove that to me, Dan."

"These tables afford little privacy."

"OK. You're right, woman. I will just *think* about the world inside your panties."

"And I too will quietly worship the areas around *your* various sex organs."

Terry and Dan were relating to each other with their language tool. They were experiencing a meaningful social relationship. People use their tools. It was to herself, however, that Dan wondered what would happen (1) if she and Terry ceased talking

intelligibly to each other and (2) if Terry then forgot
about her altogether and (3) if he then forgot about
everyone everywhere. Would his need for tools
gradually diminish until every word that he knew had
dipped into the deep water of symbol-less-ness? Until
words became at best music? Or would he just carry on
an internal monologue forever? *Like a thrown stone
skipping over the water.*

"Water?" asked Terry.

Huh? Why does he keep doing that? Terry had
spoken again as if he had heard Dan's thoughts and was
responding to them. *Or, I ask myself again and again, am I
merely hearing from him what I want to hear?*

With a maybe-talent of Terry's on one end and a
maybe-idiosyncrasy of Dan's on the other, their teeter-
totter hung for one long moment in perfect balance.
Terry didn't acknowledge the situation, Dan didn't tell
him her suspicions. Terry turned his head to look
across the room. He returned his head to stare into
Dan's eyes. "Do you want some of my water or not?"
he asked. "You have drunk all of yours."

When they had finished eating their food, they
stood up to hug, kiss, and touch goodbye before taking
off in opposite directions, Terry to some conscious
destination and Dan to nowhere she had in mind. She
paused beside a human-made creek to watch the
goldfish. *And the grey fish and white fish and a blue fish. Are
there any green fish out there anywhere in the wide world?* As if
in answer, a frog jumped up onto the toe of her shoe. It
wasn't a big frog, and it fit on the shoe with room to
spare. *You're almost green but not a fish.* Just then a tall dog

came trotting by. The dog halted in her tracks and came over to investigate Dan's shoe. She looked up at Dan and back down at the frog. She wanted to do something about that frog, but, no, she blew air out her nose, threw back her head, hurried away. No longer in need of Dan's protection, the frog leaped to the earth and hopped away. A breeze came up. The leaves overhead rustled in anticipation. Dan heard their song. Like her, they liked the sun shining down on them and the water bubbling by and the fresh air all around them. She climbed the nearest tree and sat up there making soft leaf sounds.

· · · · ·

Beneath the tree stood a woman looking up. She said something.

Dan cupped her ears.

The woman below repeated herself. "You had better come down."

That bulky, formal costume she's wearing most likely signifies this person is an empowered representative of a group granted a certain amount of authority over the doings of people like Terry and Milosh and me. Dan jumped down and greeted her. "Hello."

"Don't climb in the trees."

Since Dan couldn't say OK or that she wouldn't ever climb a tree again, Dan said nothing. She and the woman looked each other in the eye. Until the woman hurried away, like the dog. *Like the frog too. Dog, frog, woman in uniform. An equilateral triangle.*

Dan turned clear around in a circle, counterclockwise this time. *Now which way should I go?* Since upstream is where she had just come from and straight away from the creek was the direction the woman had taken and behind Dan was the stream itself, which in all likelihood she was supposed to cross only at designated bridges, Dan reckoned she should take up where she had left off following the water downstream.

The creek cut a blocky *S* through a denser planting of trees (a new backwoods?) to then flow right up against a concrete building. To continue downstream without jumping or wading the creek, Dan would have to leave the waterway and walk all the way around the building. She started around; but when she reached the front of the massive, three-story edifice, she decided to go inside to see what the place was used for. The ground floor was broken up into many small offices. Looking in through book-size windows in the doors, Dan saw people bent over desks. The second floor had fewer doors. These doors had no windows cut in them. And the top floor had been divided into four art/craft studios. Unlike the lower two floors, where all the doors were shut, on this floor none of the doors were completely closed. Peeking into the large, triangular rooms from the centered stairwell, Dan observed that each of the four art spaces faced one of the cardinal points and that the outside wall of each studio was mostly glass.

"Hi, Dan. Come in."

The fourth door was standing wide open. *So this is where Willa works, facing north.*

"Hi ho, Willamette." Dan stepped over the threshold into Willa's world.

"And a hi and a ho to you, Danielle."

The first table that Dan came to was covered with red clay dust. She moistened the tip of one finger and wiped up a short strip of the dust to paint an earthy dot on the end of her nose. "My *Dan* is not a shortening of *Danielle*. It stands for *Dandelion*, which is long for *Danakil*, which is long for *Danaos*, which is long for *Dan*, an archaic title for deities and poets. If you are at all interested."

"I am!" Willa waved Dan over to where she was working close to the big window. "I find you fascinating." Willa was a healthy looking woman with dark, black-to-rust-colored skin and naturally red-orange hair. "And your string of names!" Willa shook her head and chuckled. "So which is you today?" Willa knew the words. "A common flower come to my door? A remodeled Ethiopian? A long dead king? Or maybe a butterfly colored like me? Or a god or a rhymer?"

Remembering Terry's reply to a similar question, Dan answered, addressing Willa's hands, "I will be me today. Just plain Dan, at home within the cultural structure." Dan looked up from Willa's hands at Willa's face.

At first Willa appeared to be seriously surprised. Then she roared with laughter, slapping the table before her. This table was covered not with clay dust but with paper cutouts. Willa caught her breath to say in spurts, "You really...really...really are a jokester, just plain Dan! Just plain droll Dan!"

Someone was rolled up, apparently asleep on a bed pinched in the east corner. Curled up like a napping cat, it could have been a man, woman, or big child.

Willa noticed Dan looking over at the bed. "Don't worry. We won't disturb him. He sleeps very soundly. Feel free to do and say whatever you need to."

"Could I touch him?"

"How would you touch him, Dan?"

"I'd just point my finger and move it toward him until I make contact."

Dan had made Willa nervous with this request. Willa ran the palm of her hand up her forehead and back over the top of her head. Dan did the same with her own hand and forehead and top of head. Willa cautiously smiled. Dan crossed her eyes and stuck out her tongue at Willa. Willa grinned and gave Dan a big, palsy-walsy slap on the shoulder.

Willa shuffled some stuff on the table. "So what brings you up here, my friend?"

"Can you see the creek down below?"

"Sure. Just barely." Willa drew Dan to the window and pointed down.

When Dan pressed her forehead against the glass, she could see maybe half the width of the creek. "Does the water's being forced against the building bother you?"

"Now that you mention it, Dan, yes, it does. They could have at least put a walkway between the building and the stream."

"I thought so, too. That, if there is a single

reason for my coming into this building, is it."

2

SKIN GROWS TO COVER THE WOES

Terry's eyes rose slowly, thoughtfully from his book. Dan rose quickly to leave the table. Terry cut off Dan's getaway. "Sit down, kid." Dutifully Dan dropped like a chimp to her chair. Terry smiled, pleased that she had actually obeyed him. "Please sit down again for a minute, Dan. I have a question I want to ask you."

"Is it a question I will want to answer?"

"I don't think so. But I am going to ask you anyway."

Terry laid the book and his hands in his lap. "Can you adapt to anything you can imagine?"

"Is that *your* question or one you just read, Terry?"

"I changed a statement that I read in this book into a question."

"How clever of you." Dan watched to see what effect her flattery would have on Terry. *Yes-s-s, that made him smile. Why do people always smile at pleasing stimuli? But I doubt that I've distracted him sufficiently or even blunted his attack.*

Terry snickered, twirled his head, and continued. "The book claims that everyone can somehow adapt to anything their imagination can cope with."

"*Cope with,* Terry?"

"Yes, *cope with.*"

"Is that a psychology book or anthropology?"

"You're avoiding my question, Dan."

"Yes, I am." Two curls in the grain of the wood

of the tabletop between Dan's hands formed a *69*. She picked for herself the curl on the left, the *6*, weak-strong as compared to strong-weak, so that from Terry's vantage point across the table she would be a *9*. "Tell me first why you asked it."

"I have always secretly subscribed to the old-fashioned notion," told Terry, while his eyes scoured the not very large area of the tabletop that Dan had just stared at, "that the more talented a person is, the more adaptable she or he is. But when I read this statement a minute ago, it made me wonder. Now, of course, I understand that the more talented person would certainly have more to adapt to."

Dan laid her hands in her lap and mirrored Terry's sitting posture. "I don't understand the *cope with* that you said is in the book." Little by little she fell forward until her arms pressed against the edge of the table. "The book may not be saying that everyone can adapt to *anything they can imagine*, which apparently is how you read it. But in answer to your question, no, I don't think I can adapt to everything I can imagine."

"But if you can't, how could anybody?"

"How would I know, Terry?" Dan was counting the hooga-booga beat of a blood vessel in her right arm just below the table's edge. "For all I know, we each and all live our lives inside the same size of balloon."

Terry scrunched his eyes. Dan's statement had stopped him cold. He watched Dan sit up straight on her chair. He scratched his neck.

A slight whistle could be heard in his voice for the first few words he said. "And when someone, some industrious individual, pushes outward against the skin of his own personal balloon to increase his allotted space," asked Terry, tentatively, "his balloon contracts equivalently behind him, so that, despite all his effort, the balloon remains the same volume as everyone else's? Is that what you're saying, Dan? Are you agreeing with the book about everyone being more or less equal in the long view? Are you agreeing with that, while disagreeing with what it says about everybody being able to adapt?"

"I don't know what your book is trying to say, Terry. I don't even know the name of the book or its author. I do think, however, that there is a good chance you have seriously misconstrued what you read. Me? I am not really saying anything, except that I have a whole lot of trouble seeing anybody as more talented or more educated or more imaginative or smarter or kinder or nicer than anyone else."

Terry's eyes fell like deflated balloons to the tabletop. "Well!" he mumbled. He raised his hands from his lap, curled them into *C's*, set them a foot apart on the table to frame the area on which his eyes had landed and stuck. The book remained in his lap. "It must take incredible strength to maintain a position as ludicrous as that. For any amount of time."

His eyes don't appear to be focused tightly enough on the wood between his hands for him to be picking out hidden images or symbols, like my 69. "Which ludicrous position are you referring to, Terry?"

"Your refusing to see yourself as a special case."

"Is that what you heard me say?"

"That's what I heard, Dan."

Dan didn't say anything back but went right on watching Terry while he went right on staring sharply downward.

Then Terry began tapping, repeatedly tapping the nail of his right index finger on the hard shine of the wood. "Even so, I must tell you, Dan, that I myself have detected some very shadowy souls slipping by me out there." Tap, tap. "You, then, must see that same darkness in everyone." Tap, tap, tap.

Dan didn't respond this time either.

Terry looked up at her eyes without raising his face. "Well? Do you?"

"Are you recording this?"

Either surprise or anger flashed into and out of Terry's eyes. "No! I wouldn't do that to you, Dan."

Dan raised her hands from her lap to press them flat together palm-to-palm in front of her nose. "Can I be excused from the dinner table now?"

"Why do you always duck and run whenever I try to investigate your mind?"

"It works just like yours, terrific Terry."

"That's what you say. I don't think so."

"Could you say that again?"

"That's what you say, Dan. I don't think so."

Dan pushed back her chair and stood up. She raised both her arms straight above her, clenched her fists and stretched her back as she turned away from the table. "And again, Terry?"

"That's what you say, smarty ass. I do not think so!"

Dan didn't lower her arms when she was finished with her stretch. Looking across Terry's cozy living room and out over the big white card propped up in the front window, fixing her gaze on the row house directly across the lane, Dan saw in the front window of that other house a jacket or something thrown over the back of a chair, a padded chair positioned under a lit floor lamp. The big white card? Terry would stand the card in his front window whenever he wanted Dan to come over. Usually it was to share a meal. *I haven't said anything to him yet about our having breakfast, lunch, and dinner together all in the same day, today, but it strikes me as a bit mysterious.* Perhaps Terry was constructing a story about Him&Her, and Dan hadn't realized it yet. "I don't recognize that jacket."

Terry stood up to look where Dan was looking. He grinned. "That's not a jacket, beanie brain."

"What is it then?"

"I don't know for sure. I think it's either a shadow or one of your black shirts."

Dan lowered her hands to the back of her head but did not move otherwise. She remained standing beside her chair, staring quietly out the window like an insentient being, her bent arms outlining elephant ears.

Terry rushed around the table to Dan and pancaked his body against her back. He wrapped his arms around her and locked his hands together in front of her. "Let's go for a walk, Damsel Dan."

Terry did not let go of Dan or even loosen his hold on her when she started for the door. It was an odd, awkward, tailless, four-legged critter that escaped the house into the cooling evening air. The full moon was up watching over the neighborhood.

● ● ● ● ●

"Who are you talking to?" Tripping along behind Dan with his head tipped so far forward that his nose was buried on her shoulder, Terry could not see the moon and, hence, had no way of knowing that what he had heard was Dan paying her respects to the circle of silver.

She answered him, sobbing like a dove, "Round hole in the sky."

"A spaceship?" With his upper lip immobile on Dan's shoulder, Terry talked funny.

"No, not a spaceship."

"A satellite?"

"Not a satellite."

"A planet?"

"No, not a planet, Terry."

"A star?"

"No-o-o."

"There are no clouds up there, are there?"

The four-legged, four-eared, two-mouthed critter clomp-clomped inexpertly along.

"No clouds."

Terry started humming, Dan started humming. She felt his head separate from her shoulder. Clomp, clomp. "It's the moon," he sighed. "It's the moon," she sighed. "It's the moon," they sighed.

At long last Terry let go of Dan. He fell behind

her a couple of steps when he stopped to wave his hands at the sky--"Hello, moon!"--but he quickly skipped up beside her and pushed and shoved against her arm to force her off the walkway and back up against a tree. "Want my body all over your face," he said in a low, gruff voice, nearly a growl, as he crushed his warm front against hers.

While he made those hot breathy words sound like an order, he will permit me to treat them as a request. Instead, I will hear them as a question and answer them with a question. "Might I start with your ambrosial neck and work down to your tart toes?"

"My toes are tart?"

"Never met a toe that wasn't." Dan slipped her mouth under Terry's chin and parked her lips against the skin of his neck.

"Tell me about the other toes you have tasted, Dan."

Dan withdrew her lips from their snug harbor. "I thought we had a more pressing matter to deal with right now."

"I *am* pressing you with my male matter right now."

Up the sidewalk came another woman in uniform. *Nope, it's the same one, the leg of an equilateral triangle that's not a dog or frog.*

Involved completely in what he was doing, Terry did not see or hear the woman approaching. The woman stopped on the concrete behind him and reached her stick across the strip of grass to rap on the back of his shoulder. Terry jumped in fright and jerked his head around to see behind him. His grip on Dan had suddenly grown so tight it would probably leave red marks on her skin for an hour.

"What do you want?" he demanded of the woman in a high quaking voice.

"You can't do that sort of thing in the public areas."

Terry looked back at Dan, then back at the woman.

Raising his fists to the sides of his ribcage, he turned his whole body to face the interloper. "Where would you suggest I have sex with this gentlewoman?" The way Terry pronounced his words made Dan think of and then see huge bluish brown beads of rat poison.

The woman wrested a hand-sized gadget from her belt. "Tell me your name, and I'll escort you and your gentlewoman to your place of residence." She glanced away from Terry to give Dan's face a quick brutal squint.

Terry barked, "Not a chance, toots."

"Don't step over the line, mister."

"What happens if I do?"

"If you're lucky, I'll call for a cart to take you to headquarters."

"I don't believe in luck."

"Then you don't want to know what happens next."

"I do!"

"Believe me, mister, you don't!"

"Yes, I do!"

"No, you don't!"

Tired of waiting for the two to resolve their do's and don't's, Dan roamed off into the night.

Ere long Terry caught up with her and took her arm. He didn't say anything, and they kept on walking. He just started humming again. He wanted her to bring up the confrontation.

"How'd it go, Terry?"

"Are you referring to Gawkabit Howlsey, Dan?"

"Is that her name?"

"Actually I think her last name is Chickentruck."

Dan shook her head. "You enjoyed that, didn't you?"

"You bet," said Terry, swaggering along beside her. "I was hoping she would try to use that stick on me again."

"What would you have done if she did?"

"What would I have done? You have to ask? I would have screamed for you to come back." Terry laughed nastily as he bit the sleeve of Dan's shirt. "You would have come back, wouldn't you?" He waited a few seconds for her to answer. "But Lousy Chickentruck totally wimped out; so I didn't need your help."

"You never thought you would."

"I never thought I would *what*, Dan?"

"You didn't ever really think you would need any help, Terry. Or you would not have started that mess."

"Hear me now! *She* started it with her stick."

"I guess that is as good a way as any to look at the event."

· · · · ·

Dan never did learn during her visit with Willa
whether the person on the bed, whom Willa had
referred to as "he," was a man or a boy or somewhere in
between. He didn't wake up while Dan was there, and
Willa's only other mention of him was obscure, to say
the least. "Greying undies," she had deadpanned when
she noticed Dan peeking over at him again. *Greying
undies?* What was Willa talking about? All that Dan's
memory coughed up for *greying undies* was "old secrets"
and "white underwear washed with the colored clothes."
Or something else.

· · · · ·

Home alone, thinking she is dreaming, thinking
she is getting up out of bed to see who is at her door,
thinking it is someone she doesn't know, thinking,
whoa, it just might not be a man or a woman or a man-
woman or a woman-man after all, Dan reached out her
hands in the dim light. It had hands, too, and eyes. It
gave Dan something. It set a package, a flattish box
loosely wrapped in crushed white paper, on Dan's
hands. Dan said, "Thank you."

· · · · ·

"What's this!" Dan was brushing her teeth when
she spotted Terry in her mirror. He had to be standing
in the planted area just outside her bathroom window.

His face was quite close to the window, and he seemed to be looking in through the glass. *He appears to be staring unblinkingly over my shoulder at the mirror over the sink, as if he's standing out there gazing in here at himself.* Dan nodded a good-morning to the new face in the mirror. The expression on the face did not change; nothing changed as a result of Dan's action; Terry moved not at all, except to sway the slightest bit left and right, which he was already doing before Dan nodded. *Maybe it only looks as if he's watching either himself or me in my mirror. Maybe he can't see in here at all; maybe he can't see past the reflections on the outside of the windowpane. If I sneak out the back door to surprise him, I just might find him still standing facing the window, totally unaware I have left the bathroom--if he's even aware I'm in here now. Come to think of it, how did he get to the back side of this row of houses from his row?* Would he know if Dan asked him?

She turned off the water and stepped to the window. Terry did not react, not in the least. But when she unlatched and raised the lower pane, he immediately squatted down. They kissed through the opening.

"Hello, baby."

"Morning, Terry. Do you want to come in? Or I will come out there."

"Me in." He left at once for her back door.

Dan sprinted to the door and threw open the latch not one second before Terry turned the knob. Dressed up, for him, he had on a dark blue shirt, a black braided belt that held up a pair of pleated, translucent trousers that shone like some new semiprecious alloy, and his tweed jacket, unbuttoned. His satchel hung at his side.

Terry caught Dan looking at the satchel. He flopped it on the kitchen table. "Two meetings today. Possums and silver bullets."

"Whatever that means." Dan rolled her eyes heavenward (to the ceiling) to accentuate her ignorance as she danced backward away from Terry. "Better to not ask." Her fancy steps stopped when she ran into the kitchen sink.

"Clap." It was not to applaud Dan's wacky performance that Terry raised his hands and clapped them together. No, he brought his hands together just that once. He then drew himself up into readiness and waited, as if for a starting gate to be raised. Dan thought and thought and then slapped her hands together one time. Terry hopped like a bunny across the kitchen to her, to her person, to her body. "You can ask, Dan. But it's absolutely nothing that would interest you." He slid both his hands up under her shirt to fondle her stomach and breasts.

She would have done the same for him except his beautiful blue shirt was all nicely tucked in. And it didn't button up the front.

"If you squeeze my butt," Terry promised, "I'll be your friend for life."

Squeeze his butt? Dan could do that.

She did.

"Oh-thanks-so-much," he moaned with feeling and asked if he could repay her by fixing her some toast.

"I already ate breakfast, Terry. And brushed my teeth."

"So did I, my child. Will you walk with me then?"

"Where to?"

"To my office first. For a short while." Terry returned to the table for his satchel. "You and I will part company there--" Noticing the whitely wrapped box lying near the center of the table, Terry leaned way out over the tabletop to examine it. He refrained from touching the box, though. Rotating his head without straightening his back, he batted his eyes at Dan, trying to intimidate her into explaining the package.

"I think I will get another shirt to put on over this one," she decided.

Terry smirked at her. He was still leaning out over the table. His eyes sparkled. "Evasion. And that spells trouble."

Pressing the heel of his hand against the back of his hip, Terry straightened up as slowly and achingly as an overworked field hand. Nay, Dan thought that he was pretending he was very old and crippled. He hobbled toward her, rocking from side to side.

Dan offered her assistance. "Might I give you a hand, grandfather?"

"Yes, yes, sunny girl, do help your grandpappy. And while you're at it, you could give his old backside another handshake or two."

Observing and discussing the faint streams of blue smoke hugging the ground and slithering slowly between the rows of houses like wary predators, Dan and Terry bumped into each other a good dozen times between Dan's front door and her address post at the edge of the lane. It took them a full minute to stumble that short distance. Then they had to stop at the post because Dan couldn't get the sleeves of her outer shirt buttoned and had to ask Terry for help. Terry too had trouble with the shirt's buttons. That took another minute or two. When at last they ventured forth--the very instant that D&T stepped out onto the lane they dropped their bungling, ceased talking altogether, and became a precision team. Treading the lane side by side, silently speeding up or slowing down as needed when someone came out a door, leaving the lane to the other workers and taking a shortcut across a dewy expanse of evenly trimmed grass, following a curving line of freestanding flowers up and over a knoll, reaching the first cluster of storied buildings, curtseying to the door as it opened for them, striding into the bronze and blue pyramid and voluntarily taking the stairs instead of either of the crowded elevators, they arrived at Terry-berry's office.

His office was a mess. Everything in it was upside-down. The office did not look like someone had gone through it searching for something; it looked as if someone had come in and turned everything over, had roughly but methodically turned everything, from books to his desk, completely upside down. Terry said, "Wow!"

• • • • •

The text, handwritten in pencil along the lower edge of the mat board of the last 8x10 print mounted on the wall before she reached the lobby's exit to the outside world, read "*Diverting the River*, the California gold rush--Oroville, circa 1852."

"I didn't know you were interested in history, Dan." Milosh stepped up next to her to study the picture, too.

"History?" Dan hardly glanced at him. "Oh, yes, I remember 'history.' No, I was looking at this because I've been there."

"You've been to 1852?"

"I've been *there*, Milosh." Pointing a finger at the photograph, Dan declared, "On that rock by that river."

"It's never the same river, Dan. Or so I hear."

Noticing, barely, that Milosh stood shorter than ever beside her, Dan surmised he was wearing flat shoes today instead of his normal heeled boots. She didn't look away from the photograph to see if she was right. "That can be said about anything in anyone's life."

"Ow!" Milosh laughed. "I think we just got caught in a loop." He pressed closer to her side, looking back quickly over his shoulder.

Over her shoulder Dan saw one of Milosh's workmates holding the elevator door open. "Let's go, Milo," the waiting blonde man called. "Hurry up. It's time to meet our maker."

Milosh pushed his hand deep into Dan's front pants pocket. "I gotta go, Dan," he whispered at her ear.

"Oh."

"Nice reply," he quipped as he drew his hand up and out of Dan's pants and backed away from her. "I'll see you later, maybe at lunch."

"Maybe."

That was not exactly a witty reply, either. Dan was in no mood for talking, not even to simply say goodbye; she wanted to know what Milosh had left in her pocket.

Milosh and his companion stared out at her from inside the elevator as the door closed.

• • • • •

The door closed. All by itself. The window across the office opened, all by itself. Fresh music trickled from the speakers. The lamp over Dan's desk clicked on, and her desk chair rolled back to give her room to sit down. Her hand was Milosh's hand slipping down into her pocket. Then--*yow!*--for one quick moment her hand was Milosh's hand slipping down into *his* pocket. What is this? thought Dan when she had the long, slender, seamless thing out in the air. *Long and round. And warm.* Twice as long as her middle finger and just a bit bigger around than her thumb, it was warm to the touch from being in her pocket pressed against her thigh. Perfectly straight and symmetrical, it was made of pale, almost colorless metal and weighed next to nothing. While it was remarkably light, it did not seem to be hollow. Both of its ends were smoothly rounded off. It definitely looked machine-made.

• • • • •

Noon, in the filling center. Milosh was nowhere
to be seen. Dan looked around for the bossy blonde
guy who had held the elevator for Milosh. Dan was
about to leave the building when the woman from the
office across the hall from Terry's office walked in. She
saw Dan and came over to deliver a message. Terry had
to leave. He would be gone for two days. Dan should
help herself to anything in his kitchen that appealed to
her.

• • • • •

Dan carefully removed three short pieces of
tape, which she pressed against the edge of her kitchen
table just in case she wanted to reseal the package. She
opened the crushed white wrapping paper, lifted off the
top of the flat box and set the box top aside. Dan was
not at all surprised to see lying in the bottom half of the
box another metal rod. She did not pick it up. It
looked exactly like the one Milosh had deposited in her
pocket, except that Milosh's--which was still in her pants
when she checked to be sure--was a pale cream color
and the rod in the box was slightly rose colored. The
box was lined with black felt, and the smooth metal
thing beamed up at Dan from the leftmost of five
identical recesses. The other four recesses were empty.
She checked the box top and found that it had matching
recesses and was also lined with the felt. She withdrew
the metal object from her pocket and arranged it beside

the one already in place. Milosh's present to her fit perfectly into the second recess. She closed the box and folded the paper back over.

• • • • •

"All morning long I roll on, thinking I am alive and functioning normally, if not a touch better than normally, etc. Then, middle of the afternoon, you saunter into my space. Zip zip! Within two and a half seconds, I'm in an event. The world is turning, Dan, and you and I are the motor driving it."

"I'm glad to hear you say I have a positive effect on you, Willamette."

"You do. You do."

"I would like to see the person who was sleeping over there when I was here yesterday."

"You can't. And how about we keep it as *Willa*? I have never been able to view myself as a Willamette. Or as a Will or Bill or Billie or Willie." She ran her fingers up over her ears to lock back her orange hair. "He's gone. Where to? I don't know that, Dan. And I don't know when or if he will be back. Has he taken on some kind of meaning for you since yesterday?"

"I don't know that yet." Maybe he had, but Dan didn't know that yet. "I couldn't see him very well. How would I recognize him?"

Willa paced a small circle while pressing the back of her hand against her mouth. She quit the circle to stand nose to nose with Dan. Her eyes were at the same elevation above the floor as Dan's. "Are you thinking you have seen him somewhere other than here?" she asked in a dusty voice.

"I don't know that yet, Willa. Maybe."

"Nighttime or daytime?"

"Probably it was nighttime."

"Probably?"

"I was not aware of the time then."

"Well, what did he look like then, Dan? At that *non-time*. If it was him."

"I couldn't make up my mind. I couldn't describe him to myself then, I cannot describe him to you now. I am saying *him* or *he* only because you are. I was not in any way sure of maleness."

Smile, Willa, smile. What did Dan say that tickled Willa so?

• • • • •

That night. Dan was in bed again. She did not hear a knock. She got up and went to the front door. The deliverer of the rose rod was not waiting, patiently or otherwise, on the other side of the threshold.

Dan stepped outside. It must have been really late at night, for all the houses up and down the lane stood dark. Terry's house too. But his had been dark all evening. Dan had gone over there earlier, and Terry was not at home. *Why isn't the moon shining? If the moon does work the way it is said to work, in cycles/periods/phases, it should be up and still close to full.* See him in time, Dan, had been Willa's answer in her studio that afternoon. "If you are fully conscious of the passage of time when you see him, you will recognize him." Dan held herself painfully erect in the dark on the stone walk that led from her front door to the lane. She was standing in time, conscious of rivers of time, oceans of time, star beams of time. Make something appear, she told herself. She walked on out to the lane to face down between the rows of houses. She concentrated. Eyes, ears, nose, heart, fingers, lungs, every muscle in her body: they were all concentrating. Something started to appear.

It's a man. This time I know it's a man. I have no doubts.

The woman in uniform walked right up to stand nose to nose with Dan, like Willa had but with a different feeling. "You have no business out here at this hour," she informed Dan at not much above a whisper. A hissing whisper. "Get in your house."

3

NO TAKE NO TWADDLE

In her house, back in bed, her eyes up on the dark, vague ceiling, Dan saw Terry. She had no idea where he was. Wherever he was, it was nighttime there too; he was looking out a window at the velvet darkness of a broad starry sky. There was someone else, someone near him, physically, whom Dan could not see. The two didn't seem to be talking.

Suddenly, feeling an urgent need to move her consciousness away from the ceiling, Dan dropped her eyes to stare out over her ten toes at the dim far wall. The door on that wall opened and someone came into her bedroom.

Dan sat up in the faint light. It was a real person walking toward her bed. She didn't know what to do. Should she speak? Should she run away? Could she run away?

In a flash of wit Dan realized her nipples were sticking out hard. She had no further doubts. This time she knew "it" was a man.

His robe dropped to the floor. She recognized him. Yes, the "greying undies" asleep in Willa's studio was also the who-or-what that had handed Dan the white wrapped box at her door. She lay back as he lay down beside her on the bed. Shoulder to shoulder, arm to arm, they lay silently on their backs looking up at the ceiling. Dan didn't see Terry or anyone else up there now; for the ceiling had become, for her anyway, a swirling, churning panorama of thousands and thousands of tiny, faraway rays of light. The man's skin felt strangely neither warm nor cool against her arm. The touch of his skin was anything but neutral, however; it was so *there*. Dan closed her eyes and immediately saw into his skin. She could see a good five fathoms into the underwater caverns of his skin. Her eyes opened to an opaque, bright white ceiling in a room filled with long rays of light. A wet spot and nothing else waited on the sheet beside her.

· · · · ·

No bodies lay on the floor. No bodies slumped in the shower. No bodies were out in the kitchen fixing breakfast.

But look over there! Dan gaped out her front window at the white card standing in the window across the lane. She jumped into some pants, pulled on a shirt and jogged over there. Knock, knock.

Terry! Terry himself looked out the window to see who was at his door. He waved for Dan to hurry inside.

She had scarcely stepped in and closed the door behind her when Terry grabbed her, pronounced her name with feeling--"Dan!"--and squeezed her hard against him. The squeeze slid right into their biggest, deepest, longest, most passionate smooch ever. Tongue and groove, tongue and groove, tongue and groove.

Warmly wrapped in each other's arms, he had her attention and she apparently had his. They smiled grandly at each other. But the robust erotism that had stirred Terry so deeply quickly drained away, as if his heat were not in truth what it had seemed. He let go of Dan and lowered his eyes. "Was it yesterday that you walked me to my office," he asked, all jittery all of a sudden, "and we found everything upside-down?" His smile had already faded to a shadow.

Somewhat reluctantly, Dan let go of him. "Yes, Terry." His arms hung limply at his sides. She let hers do the same.

"And you haven't seen me since?"

Dan didn't know how to answer that question; so she raised her right hand and tenderly laid it over Terry's left ear. She had never seen him so nervous.

"Ask me where I've been since yesterday morning, Dan."

As best she could remember, Terry had on the same clothes he was wearing the day before. "Oh, where have you been, charming Terry?"

"I can't tell you."

Dan grinned carefully and lowered her hand from his ear. "Thank you. Should I go now?" Was she being earnest? Did she seriously feel personally threatened? Or was she just subtly jesting, trying to offset Terry's gravity?

"No! It's not that kind of *can't tell you*." Terry rocked up onto his toes. He dropped back down to stand flatfooted, to stand hunched over his clasped hands. "I can't tell you, because I don't know."

He doesn't know where he's been? Is that why he's so...can I say overwrought? "How long have you been home, Terry?"

41

Terry stared at Dan's lips. "I just got here. Just now. Just a few minutes ago. I set the card in the window and, bang, you knocked on the door." His eyes dipped below Dan's mouth. Down and down his gaze sank into the slim space between them until his eyes came to a stop at the open zipper on the front of Dan's pants.

Dan nodded at nothing. "Yesterday noon I was told you had to go somewhere and that you would be gone for two days."

"Who told you that?"

"The woman who works across the hall from you. I don't know her name."

Terry looked blankly at Dan's face. Dan said yoo-hoo. Terry blinked. He pushed his pinkie against his lower lip. "Sort of tall? Sort of skinny? Dark skin and hair? Lighter freckles?"

"That's probably her, Terry."

This time it was Terry who nodded at nothing.

Dan watched him closely.

"That's Diane…her name is Diane."

Dan didn't reply, didn't interrupt Terry. He wasn't finished.

He furrowed his brow. "How did Diane know what I didn't know?" He spoke more to himself than to Dan. "Even if she was wrong about the two days."

"She didn't say how or where she got her information. I just assumed you asked her to tell me, Terry, if and when she saw me." Not really. Dan realized after saying that that she hadn't assumed any such thing. "Where did you go?"

"I told you! I don't know." Terry glanced tensely over his shoulder as if to look out the window. "I don't know that. I don't know that!"

"Did you think you were going somewhere for some reason when you left your office, Terry?"

"As far as I know I never left the office. After you and I turned everything back upright," he was having trouble saying every fifth or sixth word, "you took off and I sat down to check my mail. I don't remember ever getting up from my chair. I was checking my mail when--"

"When?"

"I was reading my mail, Dan, and then I was walking down the lane toward home. It seemed earlier in the day to me. I looked at my watch--it was the *next* day! My watch said it was a couple of hours earlier in the morning the following day. The clocks here say the same thing. I called the master clock. The same."

We have heard from the clocks and they are (all) in agreement. Dan rubbed the palm of her hand on the point of Terry's shoulder. "When you found yourself walking down the lane and you looked at your watch, was your mind foggy or clear?"

Terry thought about that. "I would say…somewhere in the middle."

By the time Dan figured out that Terry was gradually leaning his head to the side to rest his cheek on the back of her hand, it was already too late for her to replace her hand on his shoulder. "Do you feel a weight?" she asked him.

"What kind of weight?" He left his head leaned

way over, nearly touching his shoulder.

"A grey mound. A heap hidden over in the corner of your mind." Dan stomped around in her own brain. "A veiled bulk that, if uncovered, might prove to be memories of the hours you seem to be missing between yesterday and today."

Terry raised his head. He perked up just the tiniest bit. He straightened his body, lifted his chin. His eyes almost cleared. "I should calm down more before I try to answer a question like that. I might be looking right at what you're talking about and not seeing it."

"Are you tired?"

"Yes. Very. Sleep might help. Will you lay down with me, Dan?"

"No, me gotta go."

"Where to?"

"To finish getting dressed, for one thing." With a stroke of her hands Dan called Terry's attention to her clothing. She saw the hairy, gaping hole herself and closed her zipper. "Then to my office. Or maybe to your office first, Terry. Perhaps to find the/an answer to your puzzle there."

Terry abruptly stepped back away from Dan and sang to her in his fullest voice, "I might be gone when you get back."

Suddenly thrown off balance--by the volume of Terry's voice as much as anything--Dan could only think to say, to mutter, "I don't remember that song."

Terry gave her a piercing look.

Dan asked in an unsteady voice, "What depth of *gone* are we talking about?" She looked swiftly back into the night, to when she saw Terry on her bedroom ceiling. He was staring out a window at a dark, starry sky. Someone was sitting or standing nearby, someone that Dan could not see. Terry and that someone were still not talking to each other.

"That's another question, isn't it, Dan?"

· · · · ·

Be those chalk marks? She stopped to examine the white on the walkway. *A heart…a carefully drawn heart with writing inside of it.* She squatted to read the white words finely chalked within a heartshape smaller than the palm of her hand. "Whenever I'm by the sea, I see my body as independent of me."

On down the walk some thirty feet, the white of another heart glowed in the morning light. Dan couldn't resist. She took herself straight to it. "I'm a tree standing alone on a high ridge, with no friends, no one to talk to."

One more? Another heart could be seen about the same distance ahead of her. The third one said, "I live in a fairly large, well used compartment of this here society, and I now understand that I am of no special interest to the general public."

· · · · ·

"To de-select an item in a group of selected items, go directly to that item and step on its head." This sweet missive was not nicely inscribed in a chalked heart on the paving but was scrawled with some kind of permanent black ink all over the outside of Terry's office door. Nor was this glad news written by the same person as wrote in the three hearts, unless the hack who composed the message on the red plastic door wrote that message with one hand but wrote the lonely lines in the hearts with the other, more favored hand. Dan's guess was that the works in chalk had been executed by a man and the ink by a woman. *A sad man and a mad woman?* The one thing Dan could be certain of was that the fascist suggestion on Terry's door had been installed since Dan stood with her hand on that doorknob the morning before.

Surprise. The door opened. It wasn't locked. Dan stepped inside.

Well, everything seems in order. The office looked pretty much like it had when she left Terry alone there the day before. She sat down in his chair. Maybe five minutes passed while Dan waited in silence. Nothing unusual happened. Next she tried to call up his mail. She gave up after a few tries and went and knocked on the blue door across the hall. No answer. And that door was sealed.

Swoosh. A sudden sound made Dan's head jerk around. Down at the end of the hall, the elevator door had just opened. In the eerie light inside the lift stood Milosh, dressed for work. With a tight pulling of his hand, he motioned for Dan to join him. Somehow Dan knew she was supposed to not say anything. She was supposed to just go and get in the elevator. Not a single word of greeting did they exchange. Without touching one another or even once looking at each other, Milosh and Dan rode to what Dan assumed was Milosh's floor. Dan is never able to tell which way, up or down, the elevator is moving; so she glanced at the floor number indicator above the door just before she stepped out of the lift. *I think I have never been on this floor.* Mum Milosh led mum Dan down the hall and into an office. Dan glanced around for something that would identify the office as Milosh's. *Aha, I recognize that sweater over there as his.* Milosh closed and locked the door behind them. Save a few personal touches, Milosh's office looked exactly like Terry's. Milosh pointed to a chair for Dan and guardedly sat himself down on his work chair. *He does look most handsome today.* Milosh's brown hair had been slicked back; he had on higher than normal heels; he wore trim grey pants and a flowered, button-up-the-front, not-tucked-in shirt. From his desk drawer he took a piece of white chalk. He pursed his lips and raised the chalk for Dan to see. Dan nodded her head. One word at a time, erasing each word as soon as Dan had read it, Milosh wrote on the palm of his hand: "Stay away from Terry." Dan sent Milosh a question mark with her eyes. Milosh got up from his chair and stepped over close to her. A light but significant kiss on her cheek and a gentle tug on her arm told her he wanted her to leave now. Milosh let Dan out and then waited in his doorway, watching her until she was down the hall and through the door to the stairs.

Dan did not fall into her usual, deliberate pace while descending the countless steps of the bronze and blue pyramid. Today she trotted. She trotted the whole way, not once stopping or slowing down. And the same medium-fast gait took her outside the building, around the elaborate fountain, and across the plaza to the pink and silver fifteen-story rectangle on the northeast perimeter of the cluster. That bit of exercise didn't clean out Dan's mind sufficiently; so she broke into a run. She ran full tilt up the stairs to her office on the twelfth floor. That did the trick. She flopped on her chair like a thrown coat.

· · · · ·

In through her open door walked Willa, bright-n-shiny.

I've never seen Willa in this building before. But didn't I pop into her unfamiliar workplace unannounced, too?

Willa gave the yet-flopped Dan the once-over. "You look out of sorts," she informed Dan as she plopped herself down on the other chair. "What's the matter?"

"I don't know what to make of things, Willa."

"Life can be explained quickly and quite easily, Dan. If you open your eyes, the sun is shining; if you close your eyes, it's dark."

"Uh-huh. That's a tidy rule that can be applied to just about any situation. Yet I do remember times, Willa, when I found it quite difficult to tell if my eyes were open, shut, or somewhere in between."

"Ah, good point. Even if life is easily explained, it is not simple."

"We may live in the dark, but everything new

comes to us as light."

"Are we swapping aphorisms now, Danaos?"

"You have a memory for names."

Willa let just a speck of self-pride shine in her grin. "You're right. I do, Dandelion."

The grin went elsewhere. Willa stared solemnly at the floor. "After sifting through those four names you hung on yourself, I think I prefer *Danakil*. It has a wild sound. Like *Dan-a-kill. Dan is a kill? Dan will kill? Dan did kill?* You get the point?"

Did Dan get the point? If Willa was doing anything more than just playing with words, no, Dan did not get the point. Dan could not pick out one sinister wrinkle on Willa's charismatic face, but Dan kept thinking Willa was telling her something most unpleasant. And if that is what Willa was doing, why was Dan not connecting with the masked message? Was Dan not hearing it by her own choice, or did she just not have enough info to make sense of what Willa was implying? This right here is an example of Dan's not knowing if her eyes are open or shut.

Willa got up from her chair and strolled over to the window that doesn't open. Looking out the glass and down, probably down into the trees on that side of the building, she waved.

Dan forced herself to ask Willa who she was waving at twelve stories below. No one, Willa said. Just someone she knew.

• • • • •

Out the door went Willa, in the door came Roy. Always effulgent, Roy whizzed into Dan's office to position himself, standing on his heels, squarely in front of her chair. "Roy is here! Hi, spry fry!" He had either ignored Willa or not noticed her, though they nearly collided in the doorway. Roy was Dan's work neighbor from across the hall and down one door.

Still draped like thick cloth over her chair with her back to her desk, Dan could see Willa out in the hall waiting for the elevator. Willa glanced back at Dan. Dan watched Willa till she entered the elevator.

"You look terrible, Dan."

"Thanks, Roy Al."

"What? Where in your brain did you find this *Roy Al?* Please don't call me that. Not unless you also attach a *We* at the end." He shifted from standing on his heels to standing on the balls of his feet.

"Agreed."

"How about we have lunch together in The Tower later on, Dan? I woke up this morning feeling rich."

That would have been a far less confusing way for me and me and me to wake up. Having thought that, Dan told Roy that.

Smirking knowingly, Roy slinked around behind Dan and sat down on her desktop with his knees spread wide apart. "But aren't your days always full of loose ends and unanswered questions?" he singsonged. With one foot he spun Dan's chair around to face him. He wore a plaid shirt, green pleated pants, natural sandals. "That's normally how you look to me, anyhow." He dove into Dan's eyes for a leisurely two-minute swim that had Dan feeling much better by the time he climbed out and toweled off.

Oh, he asked me a question, didn't he. "Aren't your days always full of loose ends and unanswered questions." So that is how I appear to Roy. I have often wondered. He is always so upper-than-up that I seldom know what he is thinking.

"A week ago I might have answered, 'Yes, yes, maybe so, Roy; maybe that's how things are with me, normally.' For the past day or two or three, however, all those loose ends and floating questions have been promising resolution, as if some terrible picture were about to finally come clear."

"A terrible picture, you say?"

"Right. Something feels very wrong."

Roy raised his sandaled feet to the arms of Dan's chair, resting one sandal sole on the bend of either arm. "And you have no idea what the something is?"

"The flow seems to go every which way."

"You're not dipping into the monthly bout of paranoia that's customary around here, are you, Dan?"

"Are my eyes open or closed?"

"Well, they look open. But not all the way open."

"I was afraid of that."

Roy kept his bottom planted solidly on Dan's desktop so that his feet, still resting on the arms of her chair, would not push the chair away as he leaned well forward to get his head as close as he could to Dan's head. "How about we skip the boring work this morning and take a long walk to the river? I will pay for a fancy lunch on the way back."

Suddenly Roy's eyes flew away from Dan's face. A chill ran up Dan's back. Remember: Roy had spun Dan's chair to face away from the open door.

From behind Dan came Terry's voice. "Can I come in?" Terry appeared next to Dan. He stood close beside her and laid his hand on the back of her neck.

"Hi," said Roy, addressing Terry no less brightly than he had greeted Dan a short while before. With Roy leaning out toward Dan and with Terry standing right next to her, the three sets of ears involved were well within whispering range. Roy lowered his voice. He tamed his voice without filtering out the lively ripples running through it. "I was prescribing some therapy for Dan's down."

"Is that why you're showing her the inside of your pant legs?"

Roy didn't smile. "No, that is therapy for me." He sat up, straightened his back, withdrew his feet from the arms of Dan's chair to limberly fold his legs up under him. His toes then pointed at Dan from just above the edge of the desktop.

Dan asked Terry if he was feeling OK now. Terry nodded his head and stared down at Dan's lap.

"Dan and I were considering a major walk. Want to join us, Terry?"

Terry did not look up from Dan's lap, but Dan definitely felt a strong force leap from Terry's chest to smash against Roy's chest. Dan took that as a *no*. So apparently did Roy. Roy lowered his feet to the floor, stood up sublimely straight, and stepped to the other side of Dan's chair, opposite Terry, facing Terry. Locked in the middle Dan was. So she closed her eyes.

She felt three fingers under her chin. She opened her eyes. Roy was boosting her chin to look her in the eyes. "Be careful, my gallant maiden," he softly said with a quaint smile before leaving the room.

• • • • •

"I am often asked, 'But what do you think you're doing?' What do I *think* I am doing? What do we *think* we are doing? What is thinking? For me anyway, thinking is not the soliloquy I sometimes hear running with me. I know when thinking is happening, I know what it is focused on, I see the results of its work, yet from my first day to this day I have never really and truly witnessed thinking. Admittedly, I have on occasion convinced myself that finally I have a good grasp on it. But when I open my mind's hands to take a look…"

Terry snatched back the red and green sheet, the

thick, coarse paper folded up tightly into a much smaller rectangle. "Do you recognize those words, Dan?"

"I recognized every one of the words. Yes, I have heard, read, and used them all."

"That's not what I meant, and you know it."

"Then I would say no, Terry." Dan hung her arms over the arms of her chair. "I do not remember having heard, read, or said those words in that exact order before."

"It's an excerpt from comments by the playwright Wilkan Xeniat on his final play, *Koben Quintus*." Terry unfolded the heavy paper so that Dan could see more than just the one paragraph. It was a poster, a poster-sized advertisement announcing the staging of the play Terry had just mentioned. "It's opening in our Little Theatre tonight. It's based on the life of a painter who died most mysteriously just as his work was becoming known."

"What made you think I would recognize an excerpt from comments on a play I had never even heard of before now?" *He had to have already had the poster folded up that way before he came in here.*

Terry was no longer pouting. Enough time had passed since Roy departed. He, Terry, had pretty much calmed down. His swish was returning. He had sat down on Dan's desk precisely where Roy had sat, facing Dan. "The painter died or was killed some fourteen years before Xeniat wrote the play. And Xeniat himself died in a blaze of gory (sic) two years ago."

Dan had not been up, standing on her feet since she ran up the stairs from the ground floor and threw herself down on her chair. Her sitting posture had changed somewhat, but she hadn't been out of the chair since before Willa arrived and left, before Roy arrived and left, before Terry arrived and appeared to be staying awhile. "So what?" she asked.

"The timing!"

"What about the timing, Terry?"

"Koben Gissing Quintus could be Wilkan Xeniat. And Wilkan Xeniat could be you, Dan. Or, to put it another way, Wilkan Xeniat could have been Koben Gissing Quintus and you could have been Wilkan Xeniat."

"Zingo!"

"And just what do you mean by that?"

"All this time I thought I was you, Terry."

One of Terry's hanging legs deftly swung out to shove its shoe sharply between Dan's legs, without actually touching her. "If you're making fun of me, I just might have to bite off your sweet tips the next chance I get."

"Really, how could I be this Mr. Xeniat if he died only two years ago? Talk sense to me. Forgetting for the moment that you say he was a man."

"You have been here less than a year, Dan."

"Oh."

"Can you remember being a little girl?"

"My memories don't include relative sizes. You and I have talked about that before, Terry."

"Do you remember times when you were supposed to be a little girl?"

"No. We have also talked about that. I don't

actually remember people relating to me as if I were a small child."

"See, you've always been what you are right now, Dan. Right?"

"In a way you're correct. Yet the names and numbers I was made to memorize say you are wrong."

Terry gaped at Dan. His mouth fell open. Slowly his mouth closed. Its ends turned up. He grinned widely and said, "You're repeating yourself, Dan-n-n."

"Huh?"

"Your last two sentences are word for word from the play. Not the *huh*. The two sentences before that."

"I don't believe you, dear."

"That… That is…" Terry was thinking fast. "Yes! That is easily taken care of."

Terry's hands fluttered like hummingbird wings, he was so excited. "You and I will go to the play tonight, Dan, together, to the opening. We will sit right next to each other; and when the actor says those very sentences, you will lean over to give me a grateful buss on my lips before you run up onto the stage to confess in a loud voice so that everyone in the audience can hear who you really are. OK?"

Terry had Dan so solidly trapped she couldn't reply. Even if this whole *play* thing were no more than Terry's revenge for Roy's walk-for-therapy, Dan had absolutely no options she could tolerate. She jumped to her feet in a huff. Terry started laughing and biting the sleeve of his shirt like a rabid coyote.

• • • • •

Once upon a time problems were faced and solved by groups of people, and any plight that had to be dealt with by an individual was looked upon as not really real. Those times have become these times, when individuals must take care of the actual problems and group-type dilemmas are regarded as mass delusions. Or so Dan had heard and had come to understand. But is it true? Did this significant shift in emphasis actually occur?

-4-
SELF-BALANCING WORLDS

The actor in dark garb raised one whitened hand beside his pinked face as if to wave to someone other than the gleaming actress he was addressing. Then, much to Dan's chagrin, the actor said in his best loud-and-clear voice, "In a way you're correct. Yet the names and numbers I was made to memorize say you are wrong." The actor left out none of the words, added none, said them all in the exact order that Dan had said them to Terry. Dan's eyes tumbled from the stage.

Her falling eyes landed in her lap where a thin booklet, the fastidiously printed program of the evening's performance, lay opened to its highly decorated first-page. Though Dan's eyes stuck to the lone block of text centered on the page, she did not read the words. No, she had already read them twice. The words said that shortly before he died a man named Wilkan Xeniat wrote this play about another man, an already dead man, a man Xeniat had never met, a painter named Koben Gissing Quintus. *I told Terry no. I told him repeatedly, "No! No! No! I am not either of those men."* Dan spread her legs, and the program dropped to the floor. *But he held on. All day long, no matter how many times I contradicted him, Terry stubbornly threw his completely nutty, totally bizarre assertion in my face like a bucket of urine every time we got anywhere near each other. And now, tonight, sitting here beside him in the theatre, I feel ridiculous...utterly ridiculous. I should never have denied such an absurd idea. I should have just laughed as if it were all a joke and rubbed*

Terry's ears till they superheated. But! If I had not seen or read this play before, before Terry brought it up this morning--which I certainly had never!--where did I pick up those two sentences? Where indeed! It could have been anywhere, couldn't it? Maybe a flyer or something about the play passed unnoticed before my eyes. Who knows! Dan took a deep breath, had second thoughts. *Yet how can I argue with Terry now that we have heard the actor? We both heard him. I heard him, and there's no chance Terry didn't hear him.* Now Dan couldn't just say no; she knew it was up to her to prove that she was not nor had she ever been Xeniat and/or Quintus. *Woe unto me.* Dan didn't know how or even *if* that sort of thing could be proved. Or, rather, if or how it could be disproved. Terry squirmed with pleasure on his seat. Dan hoped he didn't actually expect her to actually hop up on the stage and confess. *Confess to what? Two people say the same thing all the time. Yes, I can remember...* Dan had vivid memories of people saying to her the exact words she had said, words she had said while conversing with someone else somewhere else. *And just because people came up to me and said words that they could not possibly have heard me say first, that certainly didn't make them me!* Or did it? Equally vivid in Dan's memory was her thinking, upon hearing her own words come from someone else's mouth, that something very weird was happening. *But that isn't the same thing! Not at all. Wilkan Xeniat wasn't standing in my office hearing me say his words to Terry! If they are his words. Hearing one's words repeated may be upsetting, but when the two people involved are years apart and in whole different parts of the world and one of them is even supposed to be dead?* Turning to swim upstream in her thoughts, Dan all but lost contact with the Little Theatre. *Why does hearing my words come back to me always sound so strange? And why doesn't that sort of thing happen more often? If there are only so many commonly used words and only so many ways to combine them, why don't conversations quickly degenerate into repetitive trash? Some conversations do, of course, but why don't they all? It would seem that the only thing supporting language--the only thing supporting all conversations everywhere--is each person's sense/illusion of her or his uniqueness. And that's a pretty flimsy support system. Flimsy as it is, it may be the one brass hook upon which not just language but the whole of culture is hung. A person's need to feel unique and at the same time to feel not in any way different from everyone else--*

Two whittle words broke Dan's chain of thoughts. Terry whispered, "So what?" The chain broke, but Dan's mind raced on.

--Why does he keep doing that? And how? How does he respond to my thoughts? No, no, no! Those are the wrong questions. The correct question is simple: Does he respond to my thoughts? Suddenly Dan hollered out loud, "So what *what?*"

Terry patted Dan's hand. He patted Dan's hand that was tightly gripping the armrest between them and asked again, a more complete question this time. "So what do you have to say now about your past?" His upper chest, exposed by the deep circular neckline of his close-fitting turquoise-to-orange shirt, glowed with light from the stage. "Doesn't that man's life seem somehow familiar?"

"Which man's?"

"The painter character in the play. The guy up

there cloaked entirely in black. You heard him, I know you did."

"All characters in plays are somehow familiar, Terry, or people wouldn't go to see them."

"Granted, Dan. Now answer my question."

Dan's one and only heart was saved by the woman sitting beside her. This round person gave Dan and Terry the time-honored *sh* with a finger pressed to her lips. The bony couple sitting over next to Terry nodded their heads in agreement. If Terry had set up this whole event to entrap Dan--*yes, Terry could do such a thing*--apparently the three playgoers closest to them had not been clued in.

For days now every unexpected turn of events has been followed posthaste, if not sooner, by another of the same color. It's hard to believe that one person could pull all that off onto me all by himself. Terry hid his mouth behind four fingers. "We are *all* on your side, Dan." *There he goes again! Speaking as if he just might have free access to my deepest places!* Slamming closed her eyes, her mouth and nose and ears, Dan finally got the point of that old fable in which a sparrow perching in a tree was in the blink of an eye turned into a mouse running in the basement.

• • • • •

This led to that and that to those and from there back to them, D&T. She, D., lay flat on her back on her bed staring up at the ceiling. He, T., lay stretched out on his side beside her, staring at her facial profile. She could smell his sex drive rising again. He elevated his head and propped it up on his arm to gaze down on her, to examine her eyebrows, her chin, her chest, etc. Her eyes stayed stuck to the ceiling. He was well equipped for his chosen hobby, if sex can be called a hobby. Without fail his body made her body whine and bay and sniff every time she saw him unclothed. And that is why she was looking straight up at nothing, letting her eyes wander no farther than to the dark skylight every so often. Scraps of images began to replace the ceiling. She fought to make them go away. But soon she relented and allowed the images to increase, to expand, to develop.

Terry jerked, jumped, screamed. "Stop that!"

How much more proof can I want that he reads my mind? Trying to sound nonchalant, Dan asked, "Stop what, dearest intruder?"

"Stop wiggling your nose! It's giving me the creeps."

"I am not wiggling my nose."

"You aren't now, but you were. Like this." Terry grabbed Dan's nose and jerked it left and right, up and down.

Dan thought she was going to sneeze all over Terry and the bed. *It would serve him right if I did.* "Pardon me, sir. I must have been a playwright or a painter in bed with someone with gentler hands, for I didn't feel my nose move independently at all."

"You can forget them now."

"Forget who?"

"Wouldn't that be 'Forget *whom*?'"

"Point taken, Terry, for what it's worth. Now

answer my question."

"Wilkan Xeniat and Koben Quintus."

"How could I possibly forget mine own ancestors?"

"The ruse is over, Dan. I am tired of it now."

"You were just playing with me then?"

"You can fly over my head with your personal freedom flapping elegantly in the wind only so many times, Miss Highandmighty, before I have to bring you down. At least you are still alive."

Is that what Terry said? "At least you are still alive." That is exactly what he said. He laughed haughtily while saying it, but he didn't blink his eyes nor blush his cheeks.

A ruse is not merely a simple trick. A ruse is used to divert attention from the truth. The truth in this case might amount to nothing more than what I first thought it probably was: finding Roy in my office this morning upset Terry and set his quick-witted wheels to spinning. What else the truth might amount to, Dan couldn't even guess. *The actor in black might be able to tell me something.*

• • • • •

He did. Although not with his mouth.

The next morning Dan found out who the actor was and where he lived and went there to talk to him. Dan found the man in his mime mode.

The actor listened carefully while Dan explained the troublesome situation. When Dan grew quiet, the actor rose like a cat from his chair and took himself over to a pile of scripts on a table. He carried one of the scripts back to Dan's chair. He laid the script on Dan's lap, then stood behind Dan and turned the dog-eared pages until he located the page he wanted. The man pointed to a line on the page. Dan read the line and remembered hearing the actor say it the night before. The actor pointed to his next line, then stepped out in front of Dan and had Dan watch him. The actor stood on one foot and held one of his hands floating out in front of his chest with its straightened fingers aimed just to the right of Dan's face. The actor pressed the side of the index finger against the side of its thumb. He separated these two digits to insert a piece of paper between them. He stood on his two feet again and bowed his head and shoulders as he handed this unforeseen sheet of paper to Dan. He helped Dan up from the chair. He shook Dan's other hand goodbye.

Outside.

In the fresh air.

Dan's head rolled forward and her shoulders slouched, as if she were unconsciously, poorly mimicking the actor bowing his head and shoulders. *Yah yah!* On the paper-from-nowhere were the two sentences that Dan had said to Terry and the actor had said to the crowded theatre. *The very words.*

The words had not been written by hand. The words had been printed on the paper by a machine. They had not, however, been printed by the same machine that produced the script from which Dan had just been coaxed to read. Plus, the sheet in Dan's hand was whiter and of a lighter weight than the script's paper. *Terry uses this kind of paper. But so do I. So does most everyone; it is generally available.* Dan reminded herself that not everyone had heard her say those words. She walked a short way trying to remember all the printers available to Terry. She stopped again to examine more closely the individual letters on the paper. *No, these weren't printed by any of the machines Terry might have used, none of the printers that I know of, anyway.* A puff of wind in her face made Dan glance up from the paper. As she looked up, she saw the world change; everything shifted a notch or two to her left. *Has this ever happened to me before? Yes, I think so. A number of times.* Suddenly Dan felt like a dummy. *No, I'm too stupid even for a dummy.* She tossed herself down on a grassy swell to glare up at the sky. Her eyes drifted toward the sun. *Terry has played a nimble trick on me, yes; but here I am trying to make a major conspiracy out of it, to account for all my confusions. And furthermore, he can no more read my mind than he can count the freckles on the back side of the moon. He's just a brilliant person, quick in perception and understanding. Wide-awake. Brightly alert. Sharp. Intelligent. Terry, oh tempting Terry, beautiful Terry. Milosh warned me to stay away from him. Roy told me to be careful.*

· · · · ·

Coolness is necessary. And just enough forgetfulness. But Roy danced as if his brain were asleep. The music, mustard yellow with no bass, followed him like a little fuzzy dog on a leash, a pooch mesmerized by Roy's somnolent stepping, his absent

turning, his swaying and slowly twirling. The yellow
sound-dog traced Roy's every move as Roy filled the
smallish room with forgotten graveyards, vandalized and
overgrown. Now and again Roy's lips moved, seeming
to say, "Permitted." No one interfered. No one else
stood up to dance.

· · · · ·

Two whitened panes of glass. And ninety
degrees away, two rectangles of moonlight frosting the
carpet. Nothing else was visible. Otherwise the room
was completely dark. Absolutely black.

From out of the darkness, Terry's head appeared
in one of the rectangles on the floor. His head lay on
the carpet looking up at the window and perhaps
through the glass at the moon itself.

· · · · ·

*Again, no where to go. Not floating away--bing, bing--
this time, just hanging limply in whatever light falls here. A
human with nothing to do. Clouds stampede across the window
that doesn't open, like buffalo out of the past. If something were
to actually--ha! ha!--come from the past to pass through the
present, where would it be going? Bing, bing. An unfamiliar
metal object materializes on the corner of the desk. It only lies
there, yet it seems to have volition. Maybe I think its promise of
power comes not from the object itself--meaning the base metal of
the object--but from the shine of its chrome plating. The light
changes. The clouds are all gone.*

• • • • •

Empty it was. The tables and stools were still there. The bed still waited in the corner. But the bed and tables had been stripped, and all signs of Willa and her work were gone. The studio could have been standing unused by humanity for a thousand years.

5

LIPORTWO

She--she being *f*DAN--sat very still, listening attentively to *m*ROY. Careful, she told herself, you don't want to interrupt him. Careful she was; yet she was also relaxed. Most-ly relaxed.

Sitting stiffly upright, not relaxed at all, his eyes down on his untouched plate, *m*ROY went on speaking in a husky voice as though the words were not his own, as though he were reading text boldly apparent in the textures of his food. "Having traded downriver the last slivers and bubbles of my heart-soul, I sat on the dirt floor of a dark cave talking to the cave's damp wall, drawing on the wall."

Indeed, *m*ROY's rough, dry voice sounded so little like his usual voice that *f*DAN kept sneaking peeks over his shoulder to catch sight of whatever was hiding behind him.

"But if you want me to render that drawing here and now for you," he said or read without change of pitch or key, "if you want me to describe my composition in mere words, the bewildering intricacy of its pictorial images must be greatly greatly reduced, reduced clear down to basic meanings." Air whooshed in through *m*ROY's mouth and nostrils to fill his lungs. That same breath flowed back out of him considerably slower and with brook-like undulations. "Although I must admit that much of the complexity of the drawing resulted from my using old, crumbly charcoal."

Wanting to say right back to *m*ROY that he

should then please go ahead and reduce but having not changed her mind about thinking that all-things would be much better if she didn't break his concentration, ʄDAN refrained from speaking a while longer. She sent her OK to mROY in the form of an encouraging nod of her head and shoulders.

It wasn't clear whether mROY noticed this signal of ʄDAN's. He didn't look up at her, and he seemed to continue in the same veering vein, talking, as previously, in a hoarse monotone to his plate. "And while numerous irregular patches of grey scattered about the wall couldn't and never will be positively identified, I will define them now as symbols for awareness. Awareness or awarenesses from outside the scheme being represented."

The rendering he promised? That came next. His description of what he had drawn on the wall of the hall outside his office deep in the night he worded thusly: "The sun and the moon don't work on the same clock. Their clocks may be related to each other, but midmorning for the sun might be midevening for the moon."

After an appropriate period of appreciative silence, total silence, had slithered on by, ʄDAN asked (out loud), "Other than the somewhat obvious lesson in astronomy, mROY, what were you trying to say with your drawing? Since 'midmorning for the sun' and 'midevening for the moon' would be meaningless concepts to the sun and the moon, you obviously were constructing your drawing from an outsider's point of view, say from the eyes of a human standing on the earth observing the heavens."

*m*ROY still didn't look up from his food. "Awareness or awarenesses from outside the scheme being represented." He hadn't taken even one bite from his plate.

"Yes," *f*DAN quickly replied. "I remember you saying that." Her foot jerked. She thought about checking her own food for messages. One stray finger of her left hand tapped three times on the table leg. Next it was her shoulder that did something unnecessary. Leaf by leaf *f*DAN began to fidget. She understood that *m*ROY might be feeling decidedly uncomfortable and perhaps even embarrassed talking to her about the events of the previous night; yet the exact, methodical cadence becoming more and more pronounced in his speech disturbed her. She wanted to help him, if she could; but she did not want to hear his confession. "Were you the one--or one of the ones," she haltingly asked, "who were on the outside looking in?"

"What?" *m*ROY's eyes got lost. And not just once. Several times on the short trip up from the pearled tabletop to *f*DAN's face, *m*ROY's eyes lost their way in the glaze. "What did you say?"

Just then something grabbed *f*DAN between her eyes and yanked her attention away from *m*ROY's perplexed face. Her awareness was hurled across the room to the brightly sunlit doors, where her eyes focused immediately on *m*TER standing outside one of the glass doors with his hand on the door as if he were about to pull it open and enter the filling center. He did not open the door but stood frozen in place, looking in through the glass. He stared in unblinkingly at *m*ROY. *f*DAN nearly panicked. She saw *m*TER peering in through her bathroom window again. She saw *m*TER discovering her up in her office with *m*ROY again. She saw *m*TER putting together another hasty plan to destroy what little remained of her self-confidence.

"Please, *f*DAN, what?" *m*ROY pleaded. "Please repeat your question."

If it does have a realm of its own, a realm outside the imagination, the future returned there. Rubbing her eyes, Dan climbed out of bed. *Another dream? Dreaming is a dream, of course.* She wasn't aware of it, but across the way, at that very same moment, Terry was getting out of bed, too. He stood up to yawn and stretch. He yawned and stretched and yawned and stretched until his knees gave out and he collapsed backward back onto his bed, where he fell at once into a dream. In this dream someone came to the edge of his fluffy bed and kneeled between his legs to examine the inside of his thighs. His dream of him. And while Terry is on the outside thinking he is dreaming, in another string of rowhouses not far away, Roy lies very quietly on his bed. Dan thinks about Roy and instantly can see him as clearly as she might if she were right there with him in his room. She has never been to Roy's house, yet she can see his room, see his bed, see him lying motionless with his arms and legs spread on a stark blue cotton sheet. *He's dead, isn't he? Dead and dumb. Dead and dumb and undressed. Blue naked alone. Dead. The scheme of things, the complexity that reveals the systematic design of nature. That's what this is all about! We are shaping ourselves into mortals.*

• • • • •

No people-hurting stick dangled from her waist. The woman wasn't wearing one of those cardboard costumes either. But the posture and the shoes she had down pat. She struck the door with a bam bam and a ram ram and a sam sam.

Gawking out her front window at the unknown person knocking at her door, Dan rubbed her cheek with the backs of her fingers. She waved to the woman and reached over to open the door.

"Security."

"Yes." Dan motioned for the woman to step inside. It was obvious the woman wanted to come in.

"Miss Butxn?"

"Yes."

"Dan Butxn?"

"Yes." Dan closed the door behind the thickly-built woman and bid her sit down.

Pushed into a dark and dingy two-piece suit, Dan's unexpected guest shook her head at the offered chair and turned and grimaced at Dan's bedroom door. The door was closed. "First Officer, Local Protection. Scotta is the name."

Dan all but said, "Great-a!" *No, I'd better keep my words ringed in tighter than that. This gal definitely does not look like she would take well to being teased about her name, even if it were only the second or third time in her entire life that anyone has had the courage to tease her about anything.*

First Officer Scotta spun on the heels of her telling shoes to confront Dan. "You were expecting me?"

"No-o-o. I don't think so, Scotta. Should I have been?"

"Not if you have been a good citizen."

"A good citizen, you say? Hmm. I don't think most people would look upon me as a good citizen. But certainly not a bad one either. Maybe a midcitizen."

Scotta cocked her head away just a smidgen so that she could skew her big eyes at Dan.

Dan tucked the tail of her black shirt into her pants and moseyed over to her couch to slip her sockless feet into a worn pair of purple thongs.

"Do you know why I am here, Miss Butxn?"

"I know not why you are here. Are you going to tell me?"

"Did you know Roy Kee?"

"*Did* I know him?"

"Are you home alone, Miss Butxn?

"Yes. There is no one else here."

"Mind if I open that door then?"

"Help yourself, First Officer Scotta."

The woman soft-stepped over to the bedroom door. She flung the door open and craned her neck to look every which way in the bedroom. "Maybe he was murdered." She didn't actually enter the bedroom, yet she seemed satisfied the room was empty. "We couldn't tell for sure. Not yet."

The shoes backed away from Dan's bedroom

door to carry the woman over to the kitchen door, not once allowing the woman to turn her back completely to Dan. *How can shoes take it upon themselves to act like that in someone else's home? Wrong assumptions made at an early age?*

· · · · ·

Certainly. By all means. Without fail. The following morning, soon after Dan arrived at her office--she hadn't even sat down yet--Roy ambled in through her open doorway. (Dan seldom closed the door while she was in that room.) The head of Dan Butxn did not explode at the sight of a quite healthy and unusually handsome Roy; her head merely whirled about on her shoulders, flapping its wings but never quite reaching take-off speed.

Roy breezed about the office, looking at everything but focusing on nothing, while Dan, frantically trying to stabilize herself, stared down unseeing at the piece of paper she had found fixed at eye level on the outside of her door just moments before. *Roy's doing what? Why's he flittering about my office like a butterfly? He's make-believing, that's what. He's pretending he's a ninny, a silly billy.*

Roy suddenly sobered and pointed with his forehead at the paper in Dan's hand. "I see you got the note, Dan."

Dan didn't look up from the paper. She could see now and again that it was a note. She read it.

"People don't
have a restart button.
The more a person learns
about life, the clearer it is
that everything is just a
continuation. Oh,
changes can be made.
Sure. But what do these
changes amount to? You
can kick your feet and
stoke with your arms and
maybe move over a
ripple or two. So I say,
'What?'"

What! What does that mean? From any direction
that Dan looked at the words, they made only limited
sense. They didn't explain anything at all, not really.
Nor did they lessen by one ounce Dan's profound
confusion about Roy's being there, about his standing in
her office big and fresh with life. "This is not your
handwriting, Roy." She glanced up timidly at him.

"Never said it was, Dan."

She waited. She was almost trembling.

He let his eyes bob freely about the office.

"So you don't know who stuck it on my door,
Roy?"

"Sure I know."

"Well? Are you going to tell me?"

"My sister. She came to see me. You met her.
She only came for a quick visit, and now she's gone

home."

Dan's head began to spin again. "I met her?"

Roy moved over a ripple or two closer to Dan. "She's chief rule enforcer in our home town, where she and I were born." He smiled like a trickster and tugged gently on a lock of Dan's hair.

Dan shivered violently. "Is she the woman who came to my house yesterday to tell me you had been murdered?"

"She was supposed to say that *maybe* I had been murdered."

"She did say *maybe*. But why…why did she want to scare the wadding out of me?"

Click. Dan hopped back away from Roy. "Why did *you* want to frighten me?"

Roy wiggled up close to her again. "To show you exactly what Terry is capable of."

• • • • •

What Dan should have worried about for the rest of that morning was not what she did worry about. She pondered and pondered what Roy had meant when he said that his sister is the chief rule enforcer. Is she the chief of the rule enforcers, as in *head protector of the laws*, or is she an enforcer of the chief rule, the chief rule being language itself and not the laws?

What certainly should have concerned Dan far more was the fact that Scotta had come to Dan's house to throw a fake murder in her face the very evening following the morning that Dan had had a vision, in the privacy of her bedroom, of Scotta's brother lying dead on his bed. Perhaps Dan was letting that matter cool down for a while in the back of her brain.

• • • • •

The sky--here, the sky does not signify unlimited space but stands for the restrictions, the tight confines of conceptualization--pressed down so brownly that Terry threw back his head to see if he had drifted up under the broad eaves of the recreation building. No, he was well clear of the roof overhang. And the air above him was a familiar pale blue, not dark brown.

The sky--this second sky does not signify space or the lack of it but stands like a canvas before a painter--should be green today, Terry decided. And the grass will be blue. And he himself will be orange. And Dan will be light purple, if and when she ever shows up.

Off to the left is the left. Off to the right is the right. Below Terry is nothing. The nothing is blue. Above him is his green wash. Out ahead of him, Dan grows gradually taller. Poop, poop, poop. Dan's reality pulses against Terry's eyeballs like the wind of memory. Pop, pop, pop. The throbs increase in strength and frequency as Terry's arms rise slowly in front of him. He reaches way up into the green wash to pull down *what?*

Dan, like most any woman--like most any man too, for that matter--tends to glance up at the heavens every so often for no reason whatsoever and resists looking sharply downward except when thinking fixedly or when proceeding warily across unknown terrain. Dan is still some distance from Terry when she looks up once again, at a cloud or something, and Terry sees her face come apart. Pieces of Dan's face fly away from her head. Triangular shards fill the sky and disappear. But Dan is not left faceless; no, now Terry sees her the way he has always wanted to see her. Suddenly Terry vows to never again remember how Dan looked to him while she was walking toward him that last time he ever saw her. He crumples to the ground, surprised that it is he who dies.

• • • • •

"What killed him?"

"The same ol' axe."

"And which axe would that be?"

"He just couldn't tolerate being alive any longer."

"That's the official explanation? The one you put on whatever forms there are?"

"No, Dan, the official explanation, the one that I put on the forms, is that he saw you coming and couldn't tolerate being alive any longer."

"Thank you kindly."

"You're welcome. Now get out of my office."

• • • • •

So she took herself down to the river Chuck. Dan had started calling the river "Chuck." Everyone else just called it "the river," which, without caps--or even with caps--is only a description of a long body of water, Dan believed, not a proper name. She gave the water a real name. Or sort of real. How did she come up with the name Chuck for a river? The name had come to her on her way to meet Terry that last time. Dan was walking along, thinking that the water needed a name, when a song blew by her barely heard, a song with a river in it, a river called Charles. The river was black. At least that's the way Dan saw the river in the song, black. *Black, deep, and real. Realer than this water I'm sitting beside. Realer than the water that comes out my faucet at home. In that song the river itself is a song. That's why it seems so real.*

Is Dan a song? She shakes her head no. Was Terry a song? Dan doesn't know. *Someone else will have to tell me that.* Someone else at some other time, for Dan is all alone, sitting cross-legged on the mud of the riverbank, drawing bird footprints on the surface of the earth with the tip of her fingernail.

No, wait. She's not alone. A crunch of grass followed by a whisper of weeds tells her someone is behind her. Not an animal, a human.

"I could just grab up this stack of clothes and run away. And then you'd be stuck out here till nightfall."

That's Milosh's voice. He must have followed me here.

Dan did not turn to look behind her. She said these words out over the river, loud enough that Milosh could hear: "Or you could take off your clothes, fair man, and join me."

"I just might. But first you have to tell me something, Dan." He stepped up beside her, swept the river with his eyes, then sat down on the mud. He had on tan pants (now undoubtedly browner about the butt) and a white shirt, semi see-through. "Are you experiencing the pleasures of mud? Or are you out here hiding away from people so that you can beat yourself up with sorrow?"

Dan pushed one finger deep into the sloppy dirt between them. "Which would you prefer?"

Milosh watched the finger pull up out of the mud. "I don't know. Just the truth, I guess."

Neither of them had looked yet at the other's face.

"And where would I find the truth today, Milosh? Here in the mud? Out there in my memory? In the joining of our genitals behind a bush?"

"You're not your most romantic self today, Guinevere. That's for sure."

Smirking bitterly, Dan leaned over to lay the side of her head on Milosh's shoulder.

Milosh shuddered. His voice quavered. "You've done this before!"

"Done what before? Let myself be followed when I thought I was alone?"

"Don't make me sorry I followed you, Dan."

"What then?"

"You have had someone in nice clothes come to sit beside you on the mud while you're naked."

Dan grabbed back her head from Milosh's shoulder and sat up. "What you just said." Still she avoided his eyes. "Was that a feeling or an understanding or cold knowledge about my past?"

"It was a feeling so strong it was almost a memory. But it's gone now." Milosh was gazing questioningly at Dan. "Did you feel it, too?"

Dan jerked her face clear away from him. "Perhaps. Can't say for sure."

"What did you say?" Milosh couldn't hear Dan with her head turned away like that.

Dan rolled her face back just far enough that she could see Milosh's lips out the corner of her eye. "We couldn't tell for sure. Not yet."

"Are you trying to mix me up on purpose?"

Dan's sidelong, nearly empty stare floated up three inches to Milosh's eyes. "Just an innocent game, Milo."

"If you say so, Dan."

They sat and talked and flopped around on the mud touching each other's genitals. They swam across Chuck and back, then played with each other some more while washing out Milosh's clothes. Milosh got dressed and bid Dan a fond goodbye. Dan sat back down on the mud. She whistled a brisk, staccato tune for Chuck, then sat quietly with her arms and legs crossed. When the sky above her started to get dark, Dan stood up and brushed the clingers off her tail. She limped over to her stack of clothes to get dressed. Under the top garment she found another smooth metal rod, light purple in color this time.

• • • • •

Jane. Mike. Margo. Diego.

Maybe we can get away with thinking, here, that *Jan* is or used to be a man's name and to make it into a woman's name a suffix was added. *Janette* or something like that. And then it was shortened and made more personal. *Janet* and then finally *Jane.* Tidy little package, don't you think?

Mike, Margo, Diego. $M+M$ and $o+o$. Symmetry, you know.

So if we bring *Jane* back into the fold, we have $e+e$ and $M+M$ and $o+o$.

Milosh is short and has brown hair. And the generation of *eMo* above may seem inconsequential.

• • • • •

Not even a cup of tea. She ran her eyes along the jagged outline of the sierra to the south. *No book-talk, no cup of tea. Just me.* It was the next morning, and Dan had hurried across the lane for a last look-around in Terry's rowhouse before someone came to clean out his things. She didn't have to break in or anything; Terry had made her a copy of his door key soon after they met. *When was that? How long ago did Terry and I meet? Ha! According to that screwy time schedule he tried to force on me, it would have been not long after my first birthday--less than a year ago.*

Dan was standing at the bedroom window in the early light staring out the glass when suddenly her consciousness reached, like a glowing tunnel, from ex-

---

82

Terry's bedroom to the rugged mountains far below. ("Far below" is used here as another way of saying "ever so many miles to the south.") Although Dan, in her corporeal body, had never been anywhere close to those mountains, she could feel and taste the hot and dusty air working up and down their forbidding slopes.

A glowing tunnel of consciousness? That's how Dan saw it. What else did she see? Streaming around the outside of this, her white conduit of consciousness, barely visible but screaming and making horrible faces in at her--the howlers. Nasty creatures. And out beyond the thin wrap of these scary but basically powerless figments lay the eternal nightjelly of nothingness.

Nothing to see, hear, feel. Nothing to remember. My heart is round. Round like a ball. Dan's blood once flowed in Terry's creeks, his blood in hers. *No longer.* A bit of homespun philosophy--"There are more curious things in life"--had come out the mouth of Milosh at the river the day before. Milosh had not meant to be unkind; he only wanted to help Dan in her time of trouble. But how could a tired old saw be of any help to Dan when it was quite obviously not true in this case? For what could be stranger than absolute loss?

So we have a tube of subtle light stretched between a recently vacated bedroom and a brown cluster of mountains. The outside of the tube is decorated with weird streamers, and the rest of the painting is black.

• • • • •

Dan spun away from the window to leave the
house, having forgotten all about looking around in the
rest of the rooms. The house didn't feel much like
Terry's home to her any more. But Dan stopped
immediately. Sola Resta stood in the bedroom doorway,
hat in hand. How long had Sola Resta been there?
How long had she been secretly watching Dan?
Needless to say, Dan had not heard a sound.

SR was standing up straight, not leaning against
the jamb. Her lips were their usual bright red. Her
mouth gradually turned up as if to smile. "Morning,
Dan."

"Morning, Sola. You had a key, too?" *Ginger oil.*
That's what Sola's approximation of a smile reminded
Dan of.

"Nope. Not me. Wouldn't have minded having
one though. For some reason, I could never get close
enough to Terry for him to take notice of me.
Especially this past year while he was all eyes for you.
You left the front door unlocked. I was walking up the
lane to your place and saw you come in here."

Dan had not forgotten she was leaving the
room. She hit her restart button and headed straight
toward the doorway, striding brusquely. "You were
coming to see me?"

"Right." Sola sniggered and stepped well out of
Dan's way. "And your next question is why. Why
would Sola Resta come to see Dan Butxn?" She

followed Dan out into the living room.

But Dan didn't stop there. Dan strode on out the front door and down the stone walkway and out to the middle of the lane. "Right." Dan stopped there. "And your next move is?"

Sola's gold shoes came to a halt next to the address post at the edge of the lane, a good ten shoe-lengths short of Dan's shoes. Glancing over Dan's shoulder at Dan's front door, Sola meekly gripped her black felt hat two-handedly behind her arse.

It should be stated here and now before a wrong color settles on the scene--if it hasn't already--that Sola Resta is anything but a meek or insecure person. *She is quite aggressive and acts downright mean to people at times. She can insult just about anyone before they even know a conversation has begun. What I want to know is what kind of nice game she is playing now with me.*

"How do you feel about me, Dan?"

Dan shook her head. She did not invite Sola to join her in her house. "I can see why you think Terry never took notice of you."

"I don't understand what you meant by that, but it sounded outright cruel. Remember, I am your nominal supervisor."

"I was not being cruel, Sola. I was merely saying that you are not viewing life the same way I am. And how could a supervisor be anything but nominal? They ceased to exist, except on their little badges, before you landed your first job."

"I must be all fuzzy-headed today, Dan. Can I or can I not take it that, according to you, I am not viewing life the way Terry did either?"

"I can't really say anything about how Terry saw things, you understand."

"Sure. I understand. In the little time since Terry left us, I have heard people describe Dan Butxn--skipping over the more caustic word choices--as impudent, imprudent, an unpleasant boor. Yes, I understand perfectly."

"That be a short list."

"Short? Short compared to the list you could give about me?" Sola coiled like a snake, smiled like an infant. "Is that what you meant? People say much worse things about me?"

"I wouldn't listen for one second if someone said something bad about my nominal supervisor."

Sola had to laugh. "You *are* being cruel. I can see it now. Dan Butxn does not like me."

Dan grinned like a infant's uncle. She stepped back one step and bowed low.

"Grin if you will. Grin if you will." Sola took herself over to one of the benches spaced along the lane and sat her body down.

Dan remained where she was. Stand pat, she instructed herself.

"You asked what my next move is, Dan. My next move is to draw this slip from my pocket and offer it to you."

Dan stared at the slip of paper in Sola's extended hand. Up or down, round and round, Dan couldn't figure what might be on the paper. She stepped over to Sola and took the slip. She read it. Dan

was being offered Terry's job. His office too. Just why
she should want his job and office, the paper didn't say.
One reason might be that she would then have a
different "nominal supervisor."

6

A SOFT CONTINUOUS ROAR

Rain? Realizing she is hearing a soft continuous roar, Dan leans her head to the side to look around Milosh and out the window. *Yes.* She nods her head. *Rain. No wind. Water rushes along the gutter, drops down the drain. Rain.* She shifts her head to look around the other side of Milosh and out the other window and spots two puffy raccoons scooting all eyes and ears across the flooded grass. *And it's not even dark yet.*

Milosh, noticing the change of expression on Dan's face, spins his head way around to see what she's looking at. He too sees the raccoons. "Look out there!" he calls to Dan without taking his eyes off the two normally nocturnal foragers. He doesn't miss a stroke.

"Hey, that felt great! Could you say that again?"

"Look out there!" pipes Milosh.

"Very nice," purrs Dan as she pets Milo's nappy butt in the shared tempo and beat of the moment.

"Look out there! Look out there! Look out there! Look out there!"

The raccoons, unaware that they've been sighted, sneak up to the house and raise their front feet onto the window ledge to look in through the tall glass. They peer from behind their black masks at the humans, Dan and Milosh.

Behold! The two humans see the four eyes above the window ledge. Smiling with their mouths wide open, they wave, Dan with both of her hands while Milosh can only use one of his. Dan and Milosh wave

wave wave enthusiastically. The humans don't stop what they were doing; even so, they're acting quite friendly to the raccoon couple.

Somewhere in the not far distance a big dog barks. The raccoons look back sharply over their left shoulders. Then, a quick three heartbeats later, the matched set of black and white heads swings back to stare in again through the window. Has the newly arrived duo rehearsed their actions and reactions so thoroughly that they move as one? *Hmmm.* Or has the couplet of wet witnesses tuned in on Milosh and Dan's syncopated dance? *If one or two or more of us find the rhythm…* The dog barks again, from closer this time. The bouffant pair simultaneously drop their front feet to the ground and run away, side by side.

"At least they weren't too busy just keeping up with the world to say howdy. Hey, sir?"

"Yes, I do agree. Hee, hee."

"Be that laughter, Milosh, derisive or senile? Or a foolish giggle?"

"A foolish giggle, Dan. That it was for sure. I'm gushing over. And I feel blessed for having had those two watch us."

He has to be covering my hand with the same naked hand that he waved at the raccoons, for his other hand is still tirelessly supporting him above me.

Coaxing her hand to slip and slide along his skin, Milosh moves Dan's hand from his slow-working hip up almost to his armpit, where he presses it tightly against his body in request that she leave it *right there* awhile. Sure, he probably would have missed a beat; but if he had looked up at the wall behind Dan's head just then, Milosh might have seen his first ghost.

• • • • •

If Dan were as curious as she believed herself to be about the origin and meaning of the three metal rods now residing in the black-lined box hidden in a cupboard in her kitchen, she would have asked Milosh about them. She had had any number of opportunities to ask him, but she never so much as mentioned the puzzle to him. Certainly he knew something. Hadn't he himself given her two of the three thingamajigs? Naturally Dan assumed that the rod concealed in her clothes at the river had been left there by Milosh. She had laid this third metal object in the middle recess of the box. She closed up the box, folded the paper back over, and stowed the mystery case in her cupboard. The box would hold two more of the palely colored rods. Who is Dan now? Dan is who now? Who is Terry? Where is Terry? Naturally Dan assumed that the woman concealed in her clothes at the river had been left there by Milosh.

• • • • •

Jill Surfred Atnoon. The nameplate stood proudly on the desk facing the chair that Dan had been directed to sit in and in which Dan was truly sitting. Jill S. Atnoon was--with no *if, and* or *but's*--a woman. With great posture and easygoing self-assurance she sat in her

armchair across the polished desk from Dan watching
Dan. Dan felt comfortable in Jill Atnoon's presence.
Dan would not have any problem working with/for her.
I could be wrong about that, Dan reminded herself.
For Jill had not opened her mouth yet, not even to greet
Dan. What would be the first word Jill said to Dan?

"*Dan*? Is that your name or a nickname?"

"That there is my name. Just *Dan*."

"B-u-t-x-n. How is that pronounced?"

"It varies."

"Give me a clue."

"Most people reduce it to *butt-zen*."

"And you don't have any problem with that,
Dan?"

"None. Names are relative, like everything
else."

"Relative?"

"'…meaningful only in relationship; not
absolute.'"

"That's from a dictionary?"

"From one or several dictionaries. I had to
review the various definitions of *relative* yesterday."

Jill sat silently contemplating Dan's face. Dan
was relaxed. Dan casually watched Jill's face.

"Do you know where your new office is located,
Dan?"

"Yes. I have been there before."

"Right. I remember hearing something about
that." Jill dropped her eyes but quickly raised them back
up to Dan's eyes, too quickly for Dan to read Jill's
reaction.

"You will operate pretty much as a self-contained unit here, Dan Butxn, as you did, I assume, in your previous assignment. Jobwise, we won't be seeing much of each other."

Dan inched forward on the chair. "And I have never seen you in the filling center."

"No. And you probably never will. I don't care for their food." Politely embarrassed by her manifesto, Jill gazed out the window between them.

Dan stood up, shifted her clothes on her body, and said, "OK. See ya around."

Jill rose from her chair and reached out her hand. "Please drop by for a chat anytime." She smiled golden sunlight.

Dan studied the goldy light for a moment, then gently shook Jill's hand and offered that Jill could do the same, please. Drop by for a chat, that is.

As Dan turned toward the door, Jill interlaced her fingers in front of her and said, "Fools we are."

Dan stopped, looked back at her. Jill's golden smile had turned silky silver. "Aye. And fools we will always be," returned Dan.

"From birth to death, from death to birth we act the fool, believing it is the best we can do at the moment."

Dan scratched Dan's head for effect. "Will that be the one rule of our working relationship, Jill?"

Jill grinned. "Goodbye, Dan."

· · · · ·

Press here.

They were warned it would cause them problems.

You don't knowingly do self-destructive things yourself?

· · · · ·

If I pay attention I don't need time.

Empty it was. The basic furniture was still there, but all signs of Terry and his work were gone. Everything of a personal nature had been removed, down to Terry's hand-woven wastepaper basket. Terry did not exist here anymore. The office, like Willa's studio, could have been standing unused for years.

Dan wasted a couple of minutes checking ex-Terry's machine. It had been cleaned, meaning "stripped bare," and refilled, meaning that whatever was on it before Terry died had been completely replaced with the stuff from the identical machine in Dan's ex-office. The transfer was complete: the new machine recognized Dan instantly.

About the only thing that's going to be at all different in this new office is the view out that window. Sitting in her new chair at her new desk, looking over her shoulder and out the window that opens, Dan thought she could see in the distance the glaze of Chuck. *Good.* In bad times she could stick her head outside the building and make believe she was smelling the water rolling on by.

Slowly Dan turned the chair, revolving the chair, surveying the minimally furnished room. Movers had been scheduled to collect Dan's personal effects from her ex-office and to have them here at her new office before she arrived this morning. But Dan's few belongings were not here waiting for her. They weren't here because Dan herself had carried them home (to her house) from her old office before she turned in her ex-key. She had other plans. Dan wanted to move her things into her new office herself, at nighttime, after everyone else had gone home or elsewhere. She had no special secrets; that wasn't the reason. For her, moving from one work or living space to another was a very private matter. *A primitive matter.*

Dan stopped her chair from turning. Out the open door she could see the door across the hall. *Tightly closed it is again…and it's still blue.* Dan wondered why it had occurred to her that the door's color had not changed. She stared at that blue door for some time before she drew her eyes back across the hall to examine her own door. *It's not red!* Dan hadn't been back to this office since the morning that she found ex-Terry's red door decorated with a violent black message. Terry never mentioned that vandalism to her (in the brief parcel of time allotted to him before he died), nor did he say anything about having his door replaced. *I really don't remember noticing the mint green color when I unlocked the door to come in here a while ago. How I missed it, I don't know.* The door looked so fresh it could have been installed just minutes before Dan arrived. Actually, it looked so fresh it could have been installed since she arrived. But surely she would have noticed that.

When Dan found herself searching the walls for fingerprints of *his*, she sprang from the chair so fiercely that she very nearly ended up as a pile on the floor. She slammed the green door closed behind her and hurtled headlong down the flights of concrete stairs. Milosh was standing in the lobby with his arms across his chest looking right at her when she exited the stairwell.

Dan slowed her pace, composed herself. She couldn't pretend she didn't see Milosh, for every step that she took took her directly toward him. And every step that she took compressed her body shorter and shorter until, when she reached Milosh, she had to look up to see the face of the not very tall man.

Out the side of her eye, Dan caught sight of Roy. *What is he doing in this building?* Roy, it seemed, was talking to someone. Dan turned her head to look at the two. Yes, she recognized the woman standing, talking with Roy. It was the woman who approached Dan one noon in the filling center to tell Dan that Terry would be gone for two days. *Diane…. That's the name Terry told me the next morning, the morning that he and I hugged and kissed and talked in his house…. Sort of tall, sort of skinny, dark skin and hair, lighter freckles. Yes, that's how Terry described her. And the description fits. But why did Terry not include her baby blue eyes? Maybe that isn't the natural color of lovely Diane's eyes. I probably wasn't paying very close attention, but I don't remember them looking like that in the filling center. Maybe she changes their color like she changes her socks. Milosh told me about a man who switches his eye colors every day. Or the light blue might be a misperception resulting from the hocus-pocus lighting here in the lobby.* The woman, Diane, had had the office across the hall from Terry; she was the person behind the blue door. And now, Dan assumed, this Diane had the office across the hall from her, from Dan. And *la mujer* was talking to Roy, Dan's neighbor in her old building.

Roy and Diane split company. He turned and exited the building while she hurried to reach an elevator before its door closed. Apparently neither of them had seen Dan. Probably they did see her.

Milosh saw her. He breathed on her. He pushed one fingertip against Dan's breastbone as if to topple her.

Dan mumbled something to let Milosh know she was aware he was there. "Hey shey pay ray."

"Sum cum rue," he replied, grinning like it was all a joke.

Dan hoped she would pass out fairly soon.

• • • • •

Minutes had passed with soft violin music as the only sound to be heard in the alcove. Jill smiled wistfully at her hand lying beside her plate. "Do you have a writing instrument with you?"

Dan took her pen from her pocket and handed it over the table to Jill.

"And a piece of paper?"

From her other shirt pocket Dan took a grocery purchase receipt.

Jill read the receipt, smiled with her lips pressed

together, and turned the strip of paper over. On the
back she wrote four short lines with excellent
penmanship. She laid the receipt and the pen on her
white linen napkin and pushed the napkin to Dan.

You have a Dollar
I have a Dime;
You have a Reader
I have a Rhyme.

"Do you like it?" asked Jill.

Dan returned the pen to her pocket. She had
not touched the receipt but had turned the napkin
slightly to read Jill's words. "Did you just make it up,
Jill?"

"No! Of course not. It's something I heard a
long time ago. When I was a child. The romantic music
brought it to the top of my pile of memories. It begged
to be let out into the air again. Do you like it?"

"What is a reader?"

"A book for instruction and practice in reading.
Have you never seen one, Dan?"

"I don't think so. Who uses them?"

"School children usually. Sometimes people
trying to learn a new language."

Jill had sent a message to Dan's machine inviting
Dan to join her for lunch in The Tower. Yes, this is the
same restaurant that Roy once asked Dan to lunch in.
No one at the other tables could see Atnoon and Butxn
in their alcove.

"Oh! You mean those little school books. I

don't remember them being called *readers*, Jill."

"That's what they were called where I went to school. What do you think they are called?

"Primers."

"Oh yes. I remember that name too, Dan. But that was only in the first couple of grades. After that they were called *readers*."

Dan turned sideways on her chair and laid her upper arm along the top of the chairback. She grinned strangely at Jill. "How far back in your life can you remember?"

Jill frowned down at the words on the receipt on the napkin on the table. Was she frowning because of Dan's peculiar grin or because she thought that Dan was trying to steer their conversation forever away from her question, "Do you like it?" Most likely the latter. Dan had twice already avoided answering the question. Dan waited serenely. Jill tilted her head back away from the lines she had written. She shrugged, then frowned again, then said with a strain, "I can remember back before I was born, while I was inside my mother."

"How can you remember events that occurred before you learned a language, milady?"

"I didn't say anything about events, Dan. What I remember about then I would be forced to label now as a womb involvement. I remember it clearly; I just can't talk about it. I don't see any events."

Dan lowered her chin but kept her eyes fully on Jill's face. "Why did you say '...I would be forced to label now...'?"

"The inadequacies of our language."

98

"How so?"

Jill wouldn't answer. Or Jill did not answer until Dan raised her chin back up. Then Jill pointed a glistening dinner knife at Dan's bared neck and said, "You seem convinced that we cannot be conscious of events if we don't know a language." Jill turned the knife aside. "Maybe that is so, Dan; maybe it is not so. But at this very moment, you and I both not only know a language; it is our primary communication medium, which is oh so unfortunate because the language that we share is defective." Did Jill hear herself sounding preachy? Her tone softened. "The inadequacies of our language, if not of all languages, are the source of most if not all of our problems with life."

The knife started fluttering in Jill's hand. Catching and reflecting the midday light streaming into the alcove through a small window, that knife's blade played the light back and forth across Dan's face.

Dan couldn't stop herself from blinking every time the light struck either of her eyes. Sensing that she had gotten all the explanation she was going to get for Jill's declaration of "the inadequacies of our language," Dan backed up a bit. "And before you were inside your mother, Jill?"

"Unlimited space, unlimited time, infinite light." Jill twisted the knife one more time to send its final flash into Dan's right eye. She laid the knife down, took a sip of her iced water, crushed a piece of ice between her back teeth. "Why are you asking me these questions, Dan Butxn?"

"The romantic music brought them to the top

of my pile of conundrums, where they begged to be let out into the air."

"You do have a touch of the rascal in you, lassie."

"It is all in good fun, Jill."

"Mebbe so. But me thinks me sees you covering up something, Dan. This something is mebbe what I would be forced to label now as an identity problem."

"You do have a touch of the--"

"Don't you dare say *shrew*!"

"--a touch of the sharpie in you, lassie."

"It is all in good fun, my dear Dan. I'm unbeatable at arm wrestling too."

• • • • •

"Now listen to what she says here," said Milosh to the hair on the back of Dan's head. "Listen to this, Dan, please. And I quote--"

Milosh opened his mouth to quote, but Dan spoke first. "Foam. Nothing but foam." Dan bent her head lower over her desk. "Froth, spume, scum."

Milosh immediately closed up the ancient chapbook and returned it to his pocket. Standing behind Dan, facing Dan's back and the back of Dan's chair with his hands clasped over his stomach, Milosh tried to smile. "Try to understand. You're in the sky; I'm walking the earth."

"And Terry's under the ground."

"How long are you going to sing that sad tune, Dan?"

"And what happened to Sweet Willamette?"

"Who?"

"Red-orange Willa."

"Do you mean that artist woman with orange hair?"

"Yes, Willa-of-the-Words."

"I don't know. I haven't seen her around for a while, Dan, but I have no reason to think that something happened to her." Milosh glanced at the window, glanced at the other window. "And Terry was cremated. People aren't often buried anymore."

"You went to his funeral, Milo?" Dan raised her face a bit but still did not turn her head to look back at Milosh. She scratched behind her ear.

"No, I didn't." Milo was watching Dan's scratching finger. "I don't really know if they have funerals any more. I've never been to one." He touched his own two middle fingers momentarily to his temples. "Did you go?"

"I never heard when or where it was supposed to be. I probably would not have gone anyway."

Milosh said he thought it was time he went back to work. Dan pulled on her nose and said OK, nothing more. The door opened behind Dan. The door closed. The door opened. Milosh stared in around the edge of the door at Dan's back. Dan didn't look up from her desk.

7

OLD GARDEN, YOUNG CAT.

Milosh called Willa an artist. What makes a person an artist or not?

Dan looked up a-r-t-i-s-t but did not like what she found. This irritated her so thoroughly that she spent the rest of the afternoon of her first day in her new office searching hundreds of sources for a definition she did like.

> From chaos he makes
> order, from order he makes
> chaos. He takes down the fence
> between the two and tromps
> around freely on both sides.

Dan liked that one. Although she rode the fence herself, leaning somewhat to the turning-order-into-chaos side, she liked the thought that not everyone was as limited as she. If she ever saw Willa again, she would examine the woman anew. She would. Dan would.

The absence of feminine pronouns in the passage quoted above, Dan attributed to the age of the writing. *For now. More on that later.*

She rose from her chair and was preparing to leave the office for the day when an unsolicited message appeared on the machine: "Unseen forces are often unaffected by the passage of time. Toil and sweat may influence these energies but usually not very much."

Only her eyes moved. Only her eyes showed emotion. Dan stood stock-still, staring darkly at her machine. What was she doing standing there with her eyes locked on the appliance on her desk? She was counting. *Twenty-two words, every letter of which is wearing the same mint green as this office's new door.* While all the letters of all the words were indeed the same green, *that* same green, the space, or, rather, the illusion of space behind the words was imbued with a vivid, uniform red. *And that's the plastic red of the previous door to this office, Terry's door.* Dan could not turn away and continue her leaving. Chills started shooting from her shoulders to her navel, from her navel to her shoulders. Having read the message, having counted the words, having noted the vexing color combination, she was rereading the two sentences, getting more upset by the second, when she was presented with something else to worry about, not by the machine but by her own brain. *Forever…a bomb…two buttons.* Whether taken together as one thought or taken separately as three, "forever…a bomb…two buttons" made no sense in particular to Dan. She cautioned herself, however. *I'd best remember that string of words. My mind wasn't just spinning out random concepts. "Forever…a bomb…two buttons" is somehow a clue to the meaning of the pair of green sentences someone has sent to me.* Suddenly Dan slapped her hip with her hand. *But isn't that just moonshine? "Forever…a bomb…two buttons" isn't a clue to anything; it's slapdash hooey concocted in desperation to cover the brand-new hole yawning at me: unseen forces unaffected by time and little influenced by toil and sweat.*

Dan refused to sit back down in her chair,

refused to make any attempt to discover the origin of the anonymous green-on-red message on her machine. *Any such endeavor by me would prove to be utterly futile.* She erased the message. She had better things to do, like getting out in the fresh air with the dogs and frogs and stiffly attired patrollers.

"Oh!" she gasped. As Dan Butxn stepped out into the hall and pulled her door closed behind her, she saw that the blue door across the way was unlatched. A thin line of light showed between the edge of the door and the jam. The door wasn't open, but neither was it closed. Should Dan push gently on the door? Should she knock first? Or should she just walk on down the hall to the door to the stairs and take her poor self outside the way she had planned?

Swoosh.

What was that? Dan found it a trifle difficult to switch her eyes away from the blue door. *Was it the elevator door opening?*

It was. Down the hall, on past the door to the stairs, at the very end of the hall, the elevator stood wide open and minimally occupied. *It's Milosh again, Milosh in the elevator.* If Dan hadn't stopped to talk to herself about the blue door, she would have been already down on the stairs. She would have been *not here* when the elevator door opened. She raised her hand to sign a hello.

Shoving his shoulder against the thick, complex edge to prevent the door from closing, Milosh called to her, "I'm heading home now. Want to walk along with me?"

Dan glanced again at the not-closed blue door. "Yes-s-s." Then she smiled back down the hall at Milosh in the elevator and said, truthfully, "I thought about stopping by your office to see if you were ready to go."

"Well, then come along." Delighted, Milosh waved for her to hurry up and join him.

A noise made Dan's head jerk around. The sudden sound had come from behind the blue door.

• • • • •

True, the writing that Dan found and embraced as a definition for the word *artist* did say, "From chaos he makes order, from order he makes chaos. He takes down the fence between the two and tromps around freely on both sides." But that writing went on to read, "The art experience, if we take away the artist's euphoria, is very similar to that of a mourner if we take away the grief: an eagle looks down from so high in the sky that the terrain below appears alien to him and he doesn't quite recognize anyone, not even his own kind…."

• • • • •

Blazing intensely red and orange, the sun sank lower and lower in the sky until its bottom edge just touched the vacillating horizon, where it stopped. The fireball came to a halt there, while it was still a complete circle, not to send Dan a fancy farewell but to afford her the opportunity to notice that she was not alone. Someone--no, two people were sitting on a bench alongside the walkway. If Dan hadn't stopped when the sun stopped, she would have walked directly in front of the two. *Roy? And that woman named Diane?* They looked like two mannequins glued together from shoulder to ankle with one hand each in the other's lap. They were watching her. They were watching Dan. Their eyes glowed like four little flashlights in the dusk.

Dan saw herself turning around to rush right back to Milosh's house. He *had* invited her to stay the night. She saw herself yelling and screaming and running around and round, before dashing blindly on by the bench. She saw herself slowly approaching the bench. Watching her hand reaching out and touching Roy's forehead, she felt her face smile. She sat her butt down beside his, her hip touching his, and sent a friendly hello to the woman pressed against Roy's other hip.

Poof! The sun disappeared.

The sensation of pressure persisting for a time after actual pressure has ceased has been named *aftertouch*, whereas wisdom or perception that comes after it can be of use is called *afterwit*. The similarity of these two *after*-words kept our Dan awake a good hour after she got home and went straight to bed.

· · · · ·

Roy Kee introduced Diane Potter and Dan Butxn, and Diane and Dan reached in front of Roy on the bench to shake hands. The skin of Diane's hand was soft; it had no calluses. The woman's grip was soft, too, yet not flabby or wincing. The dimness of the light made the color of her eyes indeterminable, but she had a pleasant voice, which Dan remembered from that noon some time ago in the filling center. By all signs available in the dark, Diane Potter was a gentlewoman.

Being a firm believer that one should always stop in the middle and take a deep breath before continuing with whatever activity one is engaged in, Milosh Veerwright wakes up in the middle of every night and sits up in bed. Dan has seen him do this. If she is there sharing his bed, peering up at him out one sleepy eye, Dan hears Milosh heave a long sigh before he slowly falls back on his bedding. But if Dan is at home alone in her own bed, as she is tonight, and if she wakes up at the right moment to catch sight of Milosh in his nonflesh, she only sees his chest silently rise and fall. And again, Milo slowly returns to his sheets.

Careful now. Toting a steaming cup of Terry's favorite blend of tea, Dan gingerly made her way across her living room to turn her padded chair around so that she could sit down on it and look out the front window at the empty house across the way while sipping the tea. *It's not empty!*

In the first full light of morning someone was inside the house opposite Dan's house, washing the front window. White, loose fitting coveralls covered this person's agile body. A white dustcap covered the hair. Light portrait-pink skin on the face and hands. A medium build that, inside the loose garment, could have been either male or female. The person waved. Dan waved. The person went on washing the window. Dan took her tea back into the kitchen.

• • • • •

Knock. Knock.

Dan had started keeping the door closed while she was in her office. "Yeah?"

"Can I come in?"

That's Roy's voice. Without looking back at the door, Dan sourly called, leaving an irregular crevice between the *D* and the *o*, "Do."

Roy spun into Dan's office like a whirlwind smelling of fresh sex. "I found something you'll be interested in." He marched right up behind Dan, grabbed hold of her chair, carefully rolled it back away from the desk a bit, then waltzed around in front of Dan to face her. He sat himself down again on her desktop. Different office, different desk, same desktop. But this time, instead of spreading his legs wide apart, Roy crossed them. He crossed one leg over the other and then raised both legs to plant the uncrossed foot on Dan's knee.

Dan did not, did not look to see if Roy's squirt had spotted his pants. "Having a nice lunch, dear?"

"Don't be that way, Dan. I'm your friend. Remember that."

"I will remember you said that."

Bouncing back from Dan's stony reply, Roy hauled his nose ridiculously high and batted and batted his eyes.

Dan, of course, could not see Roy's eyes, what with Roy sitting high on the desk with his nose grandly elevated and her sitting way down on the chair below. She could only see his flapping eyelashes. When Roy finally did gaze down at her, Dan, with great difficulty, managed to produce a weak smile for him, a smile that disappeared altogether from her face when Roy told her why he was there.

"I came upon something earlier today, quite by accident, in a memo that Terry wrote shortly before he died." Roy, slowly rotating the sole of his sandal on Dan's kneecap, watched her eyes while he spoke. "This memo is addressed to his next-up, Jill Atnoon. In it Terry said, 'Dan the woman is a highly sensitized creature. She only acts like an imbecile because she feels out of her place here. And/or out of her time....' Short and sweet, huh? Actually there was more, but it was mostly mud and didn't seem to have anything to do with you, Dan. All that I can infer from the part about you--and this is debatable!--is that Terry wanted to make his next-up aware of you, for some reason. And! This Jill Atnoon now hovers over you."

Dan curled her lips and spat something in the direction of the wastebasket. With her lips still twisted she hissed, "She's over Diane too."

Flustered. And downright displeased with Dan's corrosive diversion, Roy made a flat, apparently calm, three word reply, "She is, yes," which he followed with a wanton toss of his head and flip-flap of his hand.

Dan suddenly gripped Roy's ankle with her

strong right hand. Roy's eyes darted to the door. Dan didn't even think about looking back behind her at the door. Her wrap on Roy's ankle grew firm and firmer. Roy stopped breathing. Dan let go of him to lean way back in her chair, thereby freeing her knee from his foot and the weight of his legs.

She looked out the window, couldn't see Chuck. "Before he died, Terry was having problems holding on to the present, Roy. Certain possibilities--improbabilities that you and I would be embarrassed to entertain seriously--were becoming inordinately important to him."

Roy had slid forward unintentionally when Dan leaned back. His legs now hung separate from each other with his shoes nearly touching the floor. He loosened the bind in the crotch of his pants, as best he could. "What are you trying to say?"

"I've said it, Roy."

"That's it, Dan?"

"That's it. Except that I am probably dead wrong about what was happening in Terry's mind. It's enough said that he's dead."

Roy nodded his head in agreement but only in agreement with the fact that Terry was dead. Roy then closed his eyes partway, held his head perfectly still, and asked Dan (who was suffering the delusion that her own eyes were wide open), "Are you having problems with your sweet self-confidence, loveliest woman of my life?"

· · · · ·

The creek, I see, still flows right up against the backside of the building. Dan walked on around to the front of the concrete building and went inside. *People, I see, still sit at desks in small rooms with doors with tiny windows cut in them.* Dan took herself up the stairs to the next floor. *Nothing, I see, can be said about the second floor except that the wider spaced doors on this floor are no less windowless than before.* Everything seemed unchanged since the last time Dan was in the building, except that on the next level up, the top floor, the north studio was no longer unoccupied.

Half expecting, wholly hoping she would be greeted by Willa, Dan walked right in through the open door like she owned the place. A man working over by the big window glanced up at her. Seconds flew past like a flock of sparrows. "Hello, neighbor," said the man in a riveting, melodious voice.

Dan did not comprehend the man's use of *neighbor*, not fully, not right away anyway. But she did recognize him. To her memory she had seen him three times before. *The first time was in this very room.* The second time, he was standing at the front door of her home deep in the night. The third time was also at night, the night he walked into her bedroom to join her on her bed. *It's him! Willa's "greying undies." The bearer of the rod in the box. The man with underwater caves in his skin.* Willa had said, "See him in time." Dan was seeing him in time. Then, gradually, the whole scene paled before her eyes.

"You're turning frightfully pale," the man said.

He shuffled across the floor to stand close to Dan without touching her. "Do you want to lie down?"

Lie down? Dan's head wrenched to the right. A cotton spread now covered the bed still waiting in the east corner of the room. Beneath the spread, the hump of a pillow. Dan didn't want to, not now--she tried to swing her eyes back to the man's face--but she knew she was just about to swoon.

The man punched her hard on the shoulder. Dan's eyes turned to iron and steel as they came around fast to glare at him. Then Dan understood the purpose of the blow. She laughed and rubbed her shoulder. "Thanks. I was in need of that."

The man massaged his knuckles and mirrored her smile. "No thanks is needed," he said in that gorgeous male voice. "We are in this together, aren't we?"

Dan didn't comprehend that either, not fully, probably not ever.

• • • • •

He waited for her to speak. If she said anything, it was all to herself; so he went back to work. He was a painter. People do still paint. They still paint by hand with a brush or knife on canvas or board. With a long, lightly loaded brush, held as if weightless in his left pink hand, the painter stood and applied paint to a canvas stretched nearly as tall as he, never looking away from the surface he was working on, except to mix another color.

Meanwhile, Dan had not budged from the spot on the floor where she got herself slugged. She stood like a waxwork, watching the man across the room, trying to understand what he was doing and how he was doing it.

A name! Dan woke up to another problem. The man had not offered his name. *What am I to do? I cannot very well ask him the whereabouts of Willa or the what-fors of that metal gizmo in the black lined box that he gave me if he doesn't even want me to know his name.*

Dan had other questions too. *Does he know Milosh? And if he doesn't, how come Milosh had two more of those same phallic things to stealthily leave in my clothes? And by the way, when can I expect the next two rods, to complete the set?*

The man turned his head to look at her. No time had passed. The exact instant that Dan finished thinking that last, presumptuous question, the question about when would she be getting two more of the rods, the man turned his head to fix his dark eyes on her. He may have had pink skin and light brown hair, but his eyes were very dark. "Soon," he said reassuringly.

Dan quivered. She would not let herself shake. *Is this man going to take over where Terry left off with reading my thoughts?* "Soon?" she whimpered.

"I'll be reaching a quitting point here pretty quick. We can take a walk, if you would like to."

That...that is precisely what Terry might have said. That was what he always did. After pricking Dan's ears with a word or two that sounded every bit like a response to something Dan had just said inside herself, Terry had often gone on as if he had been talking about something else, something altogether different that made perfectly good sense.

The man stared at her with a concerned look on his face. "Why don't you sit down until I'm ready, Dan?"

He knows my name! Dan shook her head like a horse waving its mane and looked wildly for a chair. She sort of noticed that there was a stool immediately behind the man, right behind where he was standing. *Of course he knows my name. Hasn't he been to my house twice?*

"Why don't you come over here to sit, Dan; so that I can keep an eye on you." He hooked a chair with his foot and pulled the chair into position facing the canvas, not far from his empty stool.

His *soon* was certainly not what Dan would have called *soon* any other time. This time was different, though. She sat spellbound beside him for two hours watching him standing there painting. *At least two hours.* She had absolutely no idea what he was painting, what the image was supposed to represent, if anything; no, the thing that was getting to her was the *way* he was painting. She could see his hand thinking, deciding, making its strokes, while visions of otherness curled and furled about his head, while memory rode time everywhere, anywhere, no where.

He came to that quitting point, cleaned his brush and put it away. Finally, finished with the brushes and paints, he sat down on his stool. He turned on the stool and reached over to push up on Dan's lower jaw to close her mouth. "Few flies venture this high above the ground." His smile would have turned the vilest brawl into a gay soirée.

Dan jumped to her feet and hung her head over the man like a vulture. *Flies and a vulture?* She heard him laugh with delight at her impetuosity. "Tell me your name," she whispered eagerly down into his hair.

He looked surprised, truly surprised. He had started to stand up but now remained seated. "You don't already know it?"

"No. Please tell me."

He reached out as if to touch the front of Dan's shirt. His hand stopped just short of her shirt and returned to his lap. "There has never in history been a room so empty." His eyes remained on Dan's shirt.

"That is your name?" Dan flung her arms behind her back to clasp her hands tightly together.

"The room is so full of her, I feel I will suffocate." The man's head rolled back to aim its face up at Dan's face.

"Are we playing a guessing game?" Dan acted dumb in case hers was a dumb question.

The man's eyes were on her eyes. His eyes were in her eyes. His words were barely seen bubbles rising in the air. "We have been intimate, you and I."

Dan turned decidedly antsy. "Yes. But I still don't know your name."

"How can you wrap a man in your sweet flower and not know his name?"

"You came into my room in the wee hours of night."

"And you did not say one word," he softly answered.

"Neither did you."

He smiled. His hand started toward Dan again. "That is true. Neither did I." He reached up and touched the tip of Dan's nose with the tip of his finger.

His eyes inched away from her. He took a quick last look at his painting, then glanced on out the window. "As hard to believe as this may be, I've never been out to the river. Why don't we walk there? Maybe we will discover my name along the way."

• • • • •

"I call the river Chuck." Dan picked up a short stick to peel as they walked.

The as yet unnamed man promptly knocked the stick from her hand. Grinning roguishly, he said, "Leave the vegetable matter on the ground, please." He offered no explanation for his action or for his request.

Not knowing what to do with her hands, Dan mounded them on the top of her head. She squeezed her scalp to give the impression she was wiggling her ears. Her hands then slid away from each other to fall from her head drawing cascading ringlets in the air all the way down to her belt.

The man tugged on her shirt-sleeve. "Use my hand if you need something to play with." He tugged again. "You can introduce me to Chuck when we reach him."

"By what name will I introduce you?"

The man hadn't let go of Dan's shirt. He closed his eyes at her.

They had left the last of the mowed areas and were following a faint, winding trail through weeds. When the man opened his eyes, Dan closed her eyes at him.

Little by little she opened her eyes. In a forged dainty voice she said, "I don't know whether Chuck should be termed a *him*."

"I see running water as male, Dan, standing water as female."

Dan's voice returned to normal. No, her voice had a tad more bass than normal. "I guess that sounds OK to me." She pulled the man's hand from her sleeve and raised it to her mouth to kiss his palm. She nearly tripped from not paying attention to where she was going. "We will regard Chuck as a big male."

"Are we becoming intimate again, my female friend?"

"Only if you tell me your name."

He crushed her hand. But he crushed her hand so quickly and briefly that it didn't hurt her at all. It left her hand feeling like a warm peach. He did not let go of her hand. "How about...*Dot*?" he said.

Dan thought for a moment. She made her eyes all big and bulgy. "Dot and Dan?" She shook her head no.

"Tell me why not?"

"Let me quote you something that does not apply to every use of the word *dot* but does to yours." Dan hid the man's hand under her arm and said, "'A dot, sometimes referred to as a point or period, may be considered a condensed zero.'" She then pushed her mouth closer to his moving ear to confidentially inquire, "Do you want me to call you a zero? A nothing?"

"You made up that quotation, didn't you, Dan?"

"Sure. Probably."

"Why?"

"Because you threw me a false name that made fun of my name." Dan double-stepped and sailed her gaze off away from the man. "But I don't want to insult anyone who actually bears the name *Dot*. It's sort of a nice handle."

"Easy to spell too."

Stretching her neck to lift her head high, Dan exclaimed in a loud voice, "If it ain't relative it ain't real!"

Not-Dot wagged his head. "Was that another one you made up on the spot?"

"Yep. Nope. Probably. Probably not. Maybe. I don't remember."

"And why this time?"

"Because you--" Dan suddenly and totally stopped moving her mouth. For no apparent reason.

"Because I what?" The man craned his neck to see the eyes of the woman tottering along the dusty trail beside him.

What he saw frightened him. He immediately stopped Dan dead and stood facing her, pressing her arms firmly against her sides with his painter hands. "Speak to me, Dan."

"Light is not light," she mumbled like a zombie. "Our story is but a silver reflection."

He moved his head here and there to view her terrible eyes from various angles. "If you are teasing me," he threatened. He started a smile but prevented it from growing. "I will find it necessary to be very severe with you. And most malign."

Dan broke free and ran. The man shouted hey and chased after her. He could hear her laughing up ahead, but he didn't catch up with her until she was stopped and panting on the bank of Chuck. There was no sloping muddy beach here; the drop to the water, maybe six feet, was nearly vertical.

He hung his arm around her, resting his hand on her opposite hip, and hugged up close beside her. He, like she, gazed at the river. Two people stared at the powerful water. Both smiled contentedly.

Dan raised her hand, the one hanging between them. She raised it high out in front of them and swung it back over the man's head to wrap her arm around his back. Her voice was like velvet. "The big male out there says hi to you."

"Hiya, Chuck."

"I think he wants to know if you could paint his picture."

"I don't usually do portraits, Dan."

"Oh." Dan could see the fellow was not totally rejecting the idea; he was giving it some thought. To give him all the room he needed, Dan pretended to forget the matter.

"Maybe I could do a group picture. Of you and him. A family portrait."

"Oh!" Dan giggled with surprise and pleasure. "That's a marvelous idea."

She turned to face the man. She touched her

finger to the tip of his nose exactly the way he had touched her nose earlier in the studio. "And if you sign the canvas, then I'll know your name."

• • • • •

Taking the first letter of each word of that first sentence, "There has never in history been a room so empty," gives us Thnihbarse. And the first letters from the second sentence, "The room is so full of her I feel I will suffocate," yield Trisfohifiws. Thnihbarse Trisfohifiws? Now, that would be a pretty hopeless name to have to pack around. Let us then take a look at all the letters used one or more times in either one or both of the sentences, alphabetically listed: a, b, e, f, h, i, n, o, r, s, t, w. *Twelve letters. Right? With twelve letters we have possibly--*

"What are you doing there, Dan?"

Seated side by side on the very edge of the drop-off with their knees out beyond the edge so that their feet dangled freely above the water, the man asked Dan what she was doing and she came out of her reverie to lie to him.

"I was just making up some new sayings to have ready to shoot back at you."

"Oh, Dan Butxn!" He covered his mouth. "I will most humbly accept that as the truth if you wish, even though I know it is not."

"What was I doing then, smarty?"

"Burning up your brain trying to figure out who I am."

"Why don't you just tell me."

"Dot Sett."

Dan's face went absolutely blank for one, two seconds.

"Well," she blurted, "*Dot* is certainly not short for *Dorothy* or *Dorothea*."

"It's short for nothing. Remember?" Dot wagged his head. "A condensed zero, that's me."

Dan fell back on the dirt. She covered her face with her hands and bawled, "I cannot live with this shame!"

Dot fell back, too, and for just one moment they both lie motionless on their backs. ...*we lay silently on our backs looking up at the ceiling...*

Dot rolled over. He rolled over and up on top of Dan. Belly to belly they were.

"The two sentences you were trying so hard to figure the meanings of," said Dot as he parted Dan's hands, "cannot mean anything to you." He touched his tongue to her lips.

Shocked. Thoroughly jolted but instantly wary-wary-wary, Dan queried the mouth above hers, "Must I assume that Dot Sett and Dan Butxn are thinking of the same two sentences?"

Then she became confused. *Wasn't there another pair of sentences? Wasn't there another twosome of toughies?* Dan's memory flashed to her office, to that alarming message on her machine, the two green sentences. *Unseen forces.... Toil and sweat....*

"The empty room and the full room?"

"Those be the sentences, all right, Dot. How could you have possibly known I was trying to figure them out?"

"You are fairly transparent, Dan."

"Other people have said just the opposite about me."

"They probably meant what they said. The aspects that you show me, you might not show to them. And vice versa."

Dan slipped her hands up under the tail of Dot's shirt to caress the skin of his back. She softly sang, "My back is on the warm dirt, you are on me, the sun is on your warm back."

"Sun and soil sandwiching two happy people, huh?"

"My mind sinks into dreamland, Dot."

"Take me with you, Dan."

Dot and Dan.

Dan and Dot.

8

TEN MOONS RISING

The next day, at noon, he looked out the big glass of his studio and saw me sitting down at the picnic table on the grass across the creek from his building holding up sandwiches I had made for us, him and me. I had been loitering there for half an hour or so, waiting under his window for him to notice me. He gave me a giant, exaggerated nod and disappeared from the window.

...34...35...36. I had counted to only thirty-six when he strolled into sight around the corner of the building. Nope, he could not have strolled nice and easy like that and made it all the way down, out of, and around the building in just thirty-six seconds. I enjoyed the thought, true or not, that he had run like crazy to join me but didn't want me to know it. "Moochy moochy," he called to me when I waved high and wide at him. At the edge of the creek, he kicked off his shoes and rolled up his pant legs, underestimating the depth of the water by the thickness of the rolls.

The water runs deeper here where it pushes up against the building, but crossing the creek is not proving to be a problem for surefooted Dot Sett. And here he is. Here he comes now. He steps up out of the water onto the bank, turns all the way around, just once, and flits over the grass to the table to touch his talented hand to my hair. He says to me, "Moo moo."

Sitting on one of the two attached benches, leaning back against the edge of the wood table, Dan reached up for Dot's hand, to catch his hand and hold it against the side of her head for just a little while longer, above her ear. *And I say back to him,* "A good noon to you too."

Having wished Dot well, Dan then immediately asked him a personal question. "You might as well de-roll your pants, don't you think?"

Dot looked down to cursorily examine his wet legs and pants. "Yeah, you're probably right. But I think I'll leave them rolled up awhile anyway."

"Yeah yeah," agreed Dan, awarding Dot's bare legs a longer, more grateful glance. "I guess you might as well."

"Meow?" said he.

Dan relinquished Dot's hand to place her own hand over her heart. "Do you have time to dine with me, dashing wizard of the high castle?"

Dot quickly cupped his hands together behind his head. Smiling and nodding his head again and again, he silently moved back away from Dan another foot or so and slowly brought his hands forward from behind his head to show her their backs, the backs of his hands. He spread his fingers and pointed them at the sun above.

What was Dan supposed to see? *Ahh! He has painted his fingernails. No, he has painted just the moons of his fingernails. Bright red-orange. Red-orange? Why that color? Willa? Is he wanting me to ask him about Willa?*

So Dan did ask, rather bluntly. "Tell me where Willa is."

"Willamette Washingstone was a singular woman."

Dot had responded much too quickly for Dan's comfort, impelling her to shoot back pronto, "*Was* means what?"

Dot dropped his hands and swung them out of sight behind him. His smile vanished, too. "It means she's gone." He stumped around the table and sat down across from Dan on the other bench.

Dan spun around on her bench to face the table and Dot. "Gone forever?" *He's acting uneasy now. Did I upset him by asking him about Willa?* As Dan laid the sandwich she had made for Dot in front of him, she recalled the comment he had made the day before about sun and soil sandwiching two happy people.

Dot unwrapped the sandwich. "Yes, for all eternity." His dark eyes closed completely as he took his first small bite. The vertical sunlight paled his already lightly colored hair, making it appear greyish yellow.

"Why? What happened, Dot?"

Chewing the bite, he shook his head.

"Please," begged Dan.

Dot stared over his sandwich and over Dan's shoulder until she gave up.

Dan found her own sandwich, took a bite. She chewed and chewed her food and then took another bite.

Dot bit his upper lip. "Do you remember the day you told Willa about your name, Dan, how it was not short for *Danielle* but stood for *Dandelion* etc.?"

"She told you what I said?"

"No. Willa had a great respect for other

people's privacy. She wouldn't have repeated a single word to anyone."

"Whoa!" shouted Dan.

Startled by Dan's sudden outburst, rattled by her sudden interruption, Dot cried in a high voice, "What? What?"

"So that's it!" Dan swallowed the food in her mouth, chewed or not. "Something you said while we were sitting out by the river yesterday has been bothering me ever since. After you told me that your name is Dot Sett, I said that certainly *Dot* was not short for *Dorothy* or *Dorothea*. You said that *Dot* was short for nothing, and then you asked me if I remembered. Your voice had a certain ringing to it when you asked if I remembered. That ringing stuck in my head. I can see now that you weren't *just* paying me back by making me remember that cuckoo, inconsiderate quotation I had put together about dots being condensed zeros, their being nothing. No, you were referring all the way back to what I once said to Willa about my name, that *Dan* is not a shortening of *Danielle*. Weren't you?"

Dot grinned nervously, just barely nodding his head. "Is it going to be nearly twenty-four hours after I say something that you catch on?"

His puny grin turned upside down to make a frown. Scowling with his mouth partly open, not glooming at Dan but at some thought he had in mind, Dot dropped his eyes and attacked his sandwich, while Dan tried to fix in her mind (all) the ends and outs of what she and he had said to each other about their names.

"If Willa didn't tell you," said Dan, ready now to go on with the discussion that they were into before, "how do you know about '*Dandelion* etc.'?"

Dot made the necessary effort and visibly calmed himself. His facial expression relaxed. "I was awake enough to hear you guys' entire conversation."

"Oh." Dan didn't know whether to smile or frown after hearing that.

Dot didn't know whether to smile or frown after telling her that. He flicked food away from the corner of his mouth with one finger.

Dan's eyes caught again on the bright red-orange. "So what does my little spiel about my name have to do with Willa's fate?"

"Nothing, really. I asked if you remembered that day."

"We have firmly established that I do remember the day."

"It was your voice."

"My voice?"

"And what little I could see of you without actually opening my eyes."

"Hmm."

Dot's mouth twitched. Was he about to smile? Yes, a huge smile bloomed on his face. "I was quite taken with you, Dan. Yes, yes. So infatuated I was that I wended my way in the dark to your abode, that same night, bearing a gift. Remember?"

The skin of his cheek! Dan saw the true color of Dot's cheek. *Naw, it's gone now.* For one brief moment Dan had seen Dot's cheek, and it was the rose of the gift he just mentioned, the rod he had passed to her on her doorstep late at night.

Dan confessed, "I wasn't sure at the time that I wasn't dreaming."

"Is that why you didn't invite me in?"

"I was in shock, Dot."

Dot's eyes blinked. He narrowed his nostrils. "If I can believe that, then it was probably a good thing I didn't bother to knock the next time I came to visit you, the next night."

They both nodded their heads.

Dot was taking another bite of his sandwich when Dan asked again. "What about Willa?"

Dot just sat there. He chewed his food. He looked off into the distance. Dan waited again.

"Our time together, Willa's and mine, was over. We both knew it. I left her that same fateful day, the day you came to visit her, shortly after you left the studio."

What does that mean? How should I interpret "I left her..."? Dan fixed her gaze on Dot's left eyelash. "Where is she now?"

Dot would not return Dan's look. He peered high into the trees behind her. "I don't know anything about Willa's whereabouts. Nothing. Having known Willa, though, I would guess she is far away from here."

"But you're working in her studio, Dot."

"When I heard she had given up the studio, I petitioned for it. And got it. Then I worked a deal on the house across from yours."

"What is that thing in that box you gave me?"

Dot's eyes streaked from the trees down to Dan's face. He stared at her, at her whole face. Then he burst into laughter. He laughed out loud, shaking his head and tapping his wrists on the weathered tabletop.

He leaned across the table to caress Dan's chin. "Didn't you know what it was? And you still don't know?"

"Righto."

"I'm sorry I laughed at you, Dan. I truly did not know you didn't know. It's a token of sexual love. Men--and sometimes women--are giving them to their special someones as expressions of their hornyness. I bought a whole five-pack of them. The other four are up in the studio awaiting their turns--"

Dot cut short his description of "that thing in that box" to beam at Dan. "You are blushing, girl!"

"Yes, I feel totally ignorant, Dot."

"Naive too?"

"Yes, naive too."

Dot squirmed on his bench. "If I had one of those little metal babies with me right now, I would slip it under the table to you, wench. Can you hear me roaring for you?"

9

OCCASIONAL LIGHT

"So you say. So you say." Now Dan was *really* blushing. "Well, anyway, Dot, I'm glad to hear that Willa isn't pushing up daisies."

Dot immediately stopped sliding around on his bench like a maniac. In fact, he stopped moving altogether; all visible movement of his body ceased. Then his head jerked. And jerked again. Dot's head was soon lurching about like the last windblown leaf on a hibernating branch. He opened up what was left of his sandwich to see what ingredients it contained. His voice was cold as ice. "You didn't hear that from me, Dandelion Butxn."

What? Dan didn't know what to make of Dot's frigid retort. She watched him retrieve a crumb that had fallen to the table and pop it into his mouth. His head had stopped jerking. Dan's blush faded away. Clear, clear away. She felt cold. Very cold. She closed her mouth. *Is Willa alive and safe or not?* Struggling to return to their conversation, she stuttered, "Well...then...anyway, Dot."

"Well, then, anyway, Dan."

"I'm...I'm glad to hear you're coming along fine with your painting."

"Am I?"

"If you are."

"Thank you, stinko."

"What is it, Dot?"

"What is what?"

"The painting. The one you were working on yesterday."

"Are you asking my purpose in applying paint to this particular canvas?"

"Probably." The cold had spread all over Dan's body. *This chill feeling will seep and dilute until it all but disappears, yet a tiny replica of the feeling will be preserved somewhere forever.*

"Let me put it to you this way, Dan Dan: I am trying to capture in paint a light, a certain slanting light that only occasionally visits our earth."

Dan couldn't tell if Dot was being stern, serious, or sly. "Would I know this light, Dot?"

"This light never appears here more than once a season. In the summertime, it's usually early morning when I catch sight of it. In the fall, it sneaks down late one afternoon. Spring, it comes in the soft evening time. But in the winter--oh wonderful winter--the magic light slants across my world all day long. It still comes here only once, only one time all winter, just for that single day; yet the light lasts from sunup to sundown, maybe."

"So what's special about the light?"

"Standing in this light, I feel blessed. Yes, Dan, blessed. For I am temporarily gifted with the capacity to assess the influence of my imagination on my interpretation of everyday events. And that's no mean gift!"

Dan frowned down at her lunch. *Milosh told me he felt blessed having the two raccoons watch us. And now Dot is telling me that he feels blessed standing in some wonderful slanting light.* She pushed her fingernail into a crack on the tabletop. *Does Dot truly feel blessed in this light, or is that just the word he chose at the moment? Oh, I know, it doesn't matter. It makes no difference one way or the other right now. Blessedness is surely not what Dot's getting at here.* She glanced up innocently at the studio window. Dot's head didn't move, but his eyes snapped up to his window, too. Dan looked full at Dot's face. He gazed back sphinxlike at hers. Dan pointed her ten unpainted fingernails at the sun above. "Hark! Did I hear in the roll of this man's big words a little transmission meant for me?"

Dot flipped a seed from the crust of the bread at Dan's chest. "Your imagination's influence on how you see things could stand a bit of assessing, yes, indeed."

Dan reached across the table to unbutton a button on Dot's paint-spotted shirt. "There," she said.

"There?"

"Yep, there you go, Dot-your-*i*'s."

Dot squinted his eyes while looking down at his shirtfront. He looked up at Dan and puckered his lips, not to kiss or to be kissed but to deliver this threat: "Touch me again, you evil barbarian, and you will instantly perish."

Dan reached over and undid another of Dot's buttons. Before Dot could either take action against her or repeat his warning, she said cunningly, "If I am indeed a sick woman and don't know right from wrong or real from fake or truth from a lie, an artist like you should allow me to touch him anytime and anywhere that I need to."

Dot snorted. Then he laughed, a laugh that was

almost soundless. His eyes jumped about. "That's some kind of weird reasoning, even for a female of our species."

"My personality is undergoing a gradual disintegration, Dot."

"I think you're just full of honey, honey."

Dot took off his shirt and draped it over Dan's head so that it flowed down her back like a cape. Dan glanced all around to see if Gawkabit Howlsey, sometimes known as Lousy Chickentruck, had spotted them yet.

· · · · ·

Bravely bang it.

Bang! Dan Butxn is standing out in front of her house the next morning when Dot Sett looks out of his house and sees her waiting on the lane between their houses with her hands raised in supplication to his front window. Bang! Bang! Bang! Dan sees Dot grin, she sees him reach down, she sees him lift something. Bang! The big white card of Terry's! Bang! Dot's putting the card up in the window! Bang! How could he know about that card? Bang! He might have walked by here once while it was up in the window--bang!--but how does he know what it meant? Bang! Is he asking me to come there, to his house, into the house I have not been inside of since that burned-out day Sola Resta followed me in? Bang! Bang! Bang-g! I knock on Dot's door, he opens the door, I step inside, holding my breath.

133

"I found this thing in the coat closet." Dot guided Dan to the window and pointed at the card. "See what it says right there. Did you know about it, Dan?"

Dan was still holding her breath. She leaned closer to the card. *Capital letters, not very large, along one edge of the card. What do they say?* Dan had to exhale, which she did. STAND THIS IN THE FRONT WINDOW IF YOU WANT DAN BUTXN TO COME FOR A VISIT. Dan hurried to take in a new breath. Freshening the air in her lungs may have prevented her immediate departure, but in no other way did it provide the stability that Dan was experiencing a definite lack of.

"You're all of a sudden looking all woozy again, Dan. Do you want me to hit you again?"

"No."

"What does it mean?" Dot nodded at the card.

"It means that Terry knew he was going to die." Dan's voice broke twice in that one short sentence.

Dot absently raised his hand to cover one of his ears. Yesterday's hot color was gone from his fingernails. "Terry is the man who lived here before?"

"Yes."

"He died?"

"Yes, quite suddenly."

Dot chewed on this fact, this bit of the history of his new house. He lowered his hand from his ear. He rocked his head from side to side. "I think most people know when their time is nigh."

"This is different."

"How?"

"It's just different, Dot."

Dot's eyes tightened on Dan's face. "Do you remember what we were talking about yesterday, Dan?"

"My imagination's influence on how I see everyday events?"

"Right." Dot laid the palm of his hand on Dan's chest with the tip of his middle finger touching her throat. He pressed gently against her to force her to catch her balance. "Tell me how it is different, Dan."

• • • • •

See him in time. A command in time. Time in time.

Hunched in her office chair, her eyes riveted to her machine, Dan was not aware she had failed to close her door. Nor was she aware that Milosh stood in her doorway behind her watching her. Nor was Milosh aware that Diane Potter and Roy Kee stood in Diane's doorway watching him, Milosh.

Neither Milosh nor Dan noticed when Diane and Roy backed back into Diane's office and quietly closed the door. Dan didn't notice when Milosh reluctantly turned from her door and took himself back down the hall to the elevator. And when Dan climbed to her feet to reel like a *dronkaard* to the filling center for lunch, she didn't know that that was where Milosh had headed just moments before. And. When Dan was good and gone down the stairs, Diane and Roy tried again to leave Diane's office to go to the center, too. Hubba hubba/ding ding/ding.

· · · · ·

When Milosh caught sight of Dan back at the end of the line, he dropped back to ask her if she wanted him to help her select her food. "No," said Dan after not one second of deliberation. "I'm doing it myself nowadays. Gotta learn to feed myself sometime, huh." She hadn't even looked at Milosh. Milosh and his battered feelings did not resume his more advanced place in line. No, he stuck close to Dan, hoping she didn't mind his company. Across the room, a waxy redhead on his way out of the center held the door open for Diane and Roy. D&R sashayed in side by side, arm in arm, a pair. They stopped several times to exchange pleasantries with people they knew; still, when Diane and Roy joined the food line they were directly behind Dan and Milosh.

Diane and Milosh worked in the same building; hence she knew him somewhat, yes. And Roy had seen Milosh around, not often but a few times, most recently while Milosh stood in Dan's doorway. Yet neither Diane nor Roy spoke to Milosh. Or, for that matter, to Dan. Why not? Well, Dan was making it ever so clear that she didn't want to talk to anyone, and Milosh was clearly not wanting to talk to anyone but Dan.

"Terry disappeared one morning, reappeared the next, saying he didn't remember a thing. But during the night, that missing night, while he was gone wheresoever he went or was taken, I saw him on my ceiling. He was with someone. And the moment that I looked away from the ceiling, a man, none other than

Dot Sett, walked into my bedroom. What I want to know now more than ever is where is Willa."

Milosh slanted his body closer and still closer to Dan. "Are you talking to me, Dan?" he asked. "I can't hear you if you are. You're talking way too soft." Milosh stopped in the middle of what he was doing to take his customary deep breath. By the time he had finished the breath, Dan's head had started turning slowly, mechanically toward him.

When Dan's eyes finally reached Milosh's face, Dan's mouth opened. But just then a herd of wild horses ran by behind Milosh, and Dan's eyes followed the horses across the room and through the wall. Out of Dan's already opened mouth came a whispered quote. "'Unseen forces are often unaffected by the passage of time.'" If Dot had been there, he would have punched Dan solidly on her shoulder without asking her first.

"I still cannot hear you, Dan."

"Terry knew he was going to die."

"I heard that." Milosh grinned broadly at Dan, who was talking to him now, he thought. Maybe she was. Maybe Dan had been talking to Milosh all along. And maybe Milosh had heard more than he realized. He grinned. He frowned. "But I don't believe it. Terry died unexpectedly. Of natural causes."

Forever, a bomb, two buttons. Didn't I unbutton two buttons on Dot's shirt yesterday? And maybe Terry's death was the bomb. And "forever" might stand for Terry's and my relationship before the bomb. And didn't Milosh here warn me in chalk to stay away from Terry? And right after Terry died,

Milosh said that worse things have happened…or something like that. Wasn't I told on the day that Terry disappeared that he would be gone for a while, when Terry didn't even know that himself? Isn't the woman who told me that standing right behind me? "Diane!"

"And Roy," added Roy with an amusing and clever wrinkling of his chin. "I'm glad to see you are back with us, Dan."

Was she back? *A wisp of a tree I am, bent by a savage wind till I beat and scrape against the ground.*

"Obviously," continued Roy in his smart vein, "if you don't look at all like other people, they won't see you." Perhaps Roy heard the chaos banging about inside Dan. "Unless your appearance makes those other people either afraid or envious." He lowered his head to look up at a certain angle into Dan's eyes. "Or lonely. But then they're not really seeing *you* anyway. Are they?"

"What?" Dan's eyes rushed from face to face, skipping Roy's.

That didn't stop Roy. "What's it like for you, Dan, when you lay down by yourself and try to mentally picture people you have known--or still know but haven't seen for a while? Me, I fall into an incredible emptiness. Even if I didn't particularly like the person. There's not even any light. I don't even know for sure if I'm there myself. You could call it abject loneliness but *lonely* is too small a word. This is big! And it hurts desperately. The pain is beyond belief."

Dan was frightened, so frightened her heart was palpitating. Her eyes fixed slavishly on Roy's. "What on earth are you going on about?"

"Dan?"

"Roy?"

"Dan!"

"I hear you, Roy."

"That's a good girl."

"Yes…I can hear you now."

"Good."

"Thank you."

"You are welcome, Dan. Do you want me to pick out your food for you?"

Dan's eyes were clearer than they had been anytime that morning. (This was still the same morning--the very end of the same morning that began with Dan wallowing out of bed to hurry out to the lane in front of her house.) "Thanks again, Roy. But Milosh said he would do it for me." With that said, Dan's eyes instantly clouded back over. *As if it were a line of a song I would remember, Terry sang to me, "I might be gone when you get back."*

● ● ● ● ●

She wrapped the string of words, *Earth And Sky Battle For My Heart*, into a rough circle, gradually closing the circle until the end of *Heart* nearly touched the beginning of *Earth*. Then Dan curved a single, thin line around the outside of the writing, trying to form the line into a heart shape like the three she had once seen drawn in white chalk on a walkway. The drawing on her machine was blue, light blue like the shadow of the human realm. Dot had told her about the blue shadow. Dan examined her drawing, decided it was finished. Thinking that either a rain or the lawn sprinklers probably washed away those chalked hearts on the sidewalk, Dan started erasing her blue heart and didn't stop working with the small circular eraser until the drawing was completely gone. The door opened behind her. Someone stepped into Dan's office and said, "I hear that you and Dot are neighbors now."

Turning her head to see who was there, Dan replied before she fully comprehended whom she was talking to. "The best of neighbors."

"Do you have a minute or two to waste on the likes of me?"

"You had better believe I do! Grab that chair, Willa. Where have you been?"

"I just couldn't handle this whole place." Sweet Willamette plumped down heavily on Dan's extra chair. "I had to move on."

"But you are back now."

Willa nodded her red-orange hair slowly up and down, up and down, up and down. "I came back to see if Dot had changed his mind and would come with me."

"Oh." Dan was at a loss for words. She cleared her throat, twice. "Is he going with you?"

"You are a simple woman, Dan."

"Undoubtedly."

Willa wrinkled the rusty-black skin around her eyes. "You're the simplest, most complex woman I hope to ever meet. No, he's not going with me, Dan. He is staying here if you are staying here. If you leave, take a glance behind you. He *will* be following you. And I'm sure Dot Sett has never followed anyone more than five feet before in his life."

"Why do I suddenly feel sad, Willa?"

"Your heart is pure and you love the truth. That's why."

"Did you know Terry?"

"Not unless he's that guy you used to be seen with, Dan."

"That was him."

"You keep talking past-tense. Has he gone away, too?"

"Permanently, I'm told."

Willa shuddered her head. "Are we talking about death?"

"Exactly."

"The fellow I saw you with from time to time has died since I left, Dan, and you are bitter about it? Is that the picture?"

Dan started to reply but stopped. She reconsidered and said, "That was the picture. I think I am over it now."

"Right now?"

"Right, right now."

"Good for you, Dan. Bitterness is unbecoming on anybody."

"Does that *anybody* include you, Willa?"

"Includes me."

"Then you will be sticking around?"

"I'll consider it, Danakil. But chances are that I won't, no." With a slick and a slack and a jim jim rack,

Willa was gone.

Twenty minutes passed while Dan remained in her chair staring out into the hall through the open door, waiting for the woman to return. Eventually the focus of Dan's waiting changed. She started sort of expecting Terry to all of a sudden walk into her office. Alas, Dan never sees either of these people again. Willa and Terry. Not ever. Dan's waiting was not, however, for naught. Dot appeared in her doorway, his clothes splashed with color. He rolled his head in a horizontal figure eight. "This is a weird place! Nothing but windowless elevators opening onto narrow halls lined with nothing but doors. One would think he had just about reached the end of his life line."

"You missed her, Dot."

"Dot missed who, Dan?"

"Willa. She left a while ago. Didn't say where she was going."

"My pea brain whirls. It crashes about. It cannot understand the cruelty of your joke."

"No joke."

"No joke? I'm having double trouble believing that, Dandelion."

"Her fingerprints are on that chair right there."

"Yo! Let me take a look." Dot packed his sarcasm over to the chair, where he dropped to his knees to take a very close look.

"Don't be dumb, Dot."

"Dumb Dot. Dumb Dot. Dan's got a dumb dot."

Dan leapt up from her chair to kneel down

beside him. "See! Right there." She touched the arm of the chair.

Dot checked out Dan's face. Yes, she was smiling. Yes, she was kidding him now, he decided. But was she kidding him before? Or had Willa actually been there?

• • • • •

Dot gets a visit from Milosh. Dot was knocking about his studio, bumping and grumping, looking for that first point, when Milosh Veerwright tapped lightly on the door.

"Hello," said Milosh civilly. "You don't know me."

"You are quite right. I do not know you. Adiós, muchacho."

Milosh jerked his hand up in front of Dot before Dot could close the door.

Pretending that Milosh's raised hand held a mirror, Dot bent his knees--Milosh was shorter than he- -and primped and pushed at his hair. "Thanks ever so, deary. But now I really really really really must go."

"Dan Butxn."

"Nice name."

"I would like to talk to you about her."

"Oh, I see. Dan Butxn is not *your* name but the name of some female creature that you know." Dot stepped aside and bowed Milosh in.

Milosh meandered about the studio examining this and that. Dot sat down at his easel and forgot about his visitor.

An hour has flown by. Dot is still working at his easel, though he has not applied any paint as yet. And Milosh has sat himself down on a giant pillow and is looking out the expanse of untinted glass at the clear sky. The blue of the sky is the same blue that the all-people chose for their shadow.

10

DOT CALLS DAN

It was dark outside, very dark, unusually dark, darker than any dark either of them could remember. And as dark as it was outside the house, it was just as black dark in Dot's bedroom, once Terry's bedroom. The window shade had been raised all the way up to let in the night, and D&D stood in the sheer darkness leaning arm in arm against the windowsill, looking out at the one and only thing visible in the world, a faint jagged line far in the distance. The sierra to the south.

"I tried writing once."

This packet of rather simple sounds had issued from Dot's mouth. It was followed shortly by a not altogether dissimilar packet sent out into the blackness from Dan's mouth.

"Do tell. With what results?"

"I kept getting all hung up on names for parts of the body. Our bodies, Dan. Or names for our bodily experiences. I wanted to write about nonbody experiences, about nonbodily existence; but when I tried to describe even just a measly feeling in my heart--see! That's a good example right there. *Feeling* and *heart* are body words."

"So is *see*, Dot."

"That's what I'm talking about all right: bodies everywhere. With words, Dan…with words we can only point back at ourselves."

I shan't comment on that last statement of Dot's. Dan merely made a throat-clearing sound. *Not just yet.*

Certainly there is more to come. He won't be satisfied with what he just said. Certainly there was more to come from Dot; it was not, however, immediately forthcoming. *Dot's silence endures. It lives on. And on. As if it aspires to the most profound quiet, the cold silence beyond eternity.* Not wanting to wait way into the distant future to discover whether she would ever again hear a sound, Dan said, "Peep."

"I know, I know." Dot hurried to say, "I said 'with words we can only point back at *ourselves*.' And that, of course, is not what I wanted to say. What word could I use besides *ourselves*? Is there a word like *ourbodies*?"

"*Ourbodies*? No, I don't think so, not spelled as one word. Two words, yes; one word, no. Not that I've ever heard of, anyway," allowed Dan.

Did Dan have something more to say?

"I don't know about this either, Dot, but perhaps there is no actual need/use for words outside the material world, outside the world of bodies."

"Then what is that whole Fine Art of Writing about?" Dot turned his foot sideways to shove his big toe against the side of Dan's foot. Neither of them were wearing shoes or clothes. "And what about prayers and mantras?"

"You got me there." Did Dan really believe that? She faked a cough and a wheeze. "And there and there. So you decided to become a painter?"

Dot had to wrest his arm out from under Dan's arm before he could stand up straight and stop leaning against the windowsill. He forced Dan to stand up straight, too. And he made her move back just a bit so that he could blindly crowd his body between her body and the windowsill and still be facing out the window himself. Pushing his bare back and butt back firmly against Dan's nudity, Dot said, "Oh, I was a painter long before I ever attempted to write. I was born with seven different paintbrushes sticking out of my body."

Dan wrapped her arms one at a time about Dot's shoulders. "Sure you were."

"I was, I tell you. I was."

Just then Dan perceived something she had never observed before, something almost wonderful. While Dot himself was absolutely unseeable, his hair was not. In this deep darkness Dot's hair, quite possibly due to its light pigmentation, did not blend in completely with the night but absorbed the rich black of the room to show a faint otherworldly midnight-blue.

"All right, Dot, you convinced me. You *did* look like a porcupine when you were a baby. But maybe that's the problem. Maybe you were too well-grounded in painting before you first gave writing a chance."

"Or maybe, Dan. Maybe everyone has just one load to carry around life."

Dan's mouth advanced into the forest of Dot's unearthly hair. "One load for life, huh?" she asked. Deep in the forest, Dan's mouth moved slowly and purposely to the right. It stopped and waited when the side of Dan's nose recognized the feel of an ear. Softly Dan said to Dot's ear, which she herself could not see at all, "I seem to be confused, dearest. Does this one load weigh us down equally on both our material and immaterial sides? Or did you mean to imply that we pack around one load in the world of our bodies and another one in our incorporeal world? Or, a third possibility, do we carry the same burden first on one side and then on the other?"

"You had better watch your step, wise-ass." Dot rolled his eyes, privately of course. Then he wiggled his sleek fanny in the dark to make sure he still had every bit of Dan's attention. "But..."

Uh-oh! Dot's in trouble. Can he finish his sentence? There! I think he just gave up trying to complete it. Oh well, he got out the first word anyway. While I'm waiting, let me guess. He could be wanting to say something more about his one attempt at writing. Or he could be wanting to spit out a certain stinging, brittle, unfeeling, ridiculing opinion comparing his life as a painter to my life as a slob. Or--I rather think that this is it--he is utterly burning to deliver some deviant, erotic tidbit about bodies vs. nonbodies that would put me solidly on my place, so to speak; but he can't find the right words tonight because of this position he has taken on words, that they always and only point back to our bodies.

"But what? But what? What was I going to say, Dan? See, we can't even talk about what an immaterial load might consist of."

Aha! Yes, yes. It does seem he was indeed wanting to put me in my place, wanting to make me eat my facetious/fatuous questions. "Agreed, Dot. At least on one end, words are tied tight to the physical world. But what about paint? Isn't paint even more physical than words?"

"More physical but less restricted to rendering the physical."

Dan scratched her chin by rubbing it back and

forth on Dot's back. "I hesitate to believe that," she said.

"Why?"

"My reason for hesitating is way too woolly to describe. The only way I can articulate it at all is to say that neither painting nor writing enables a person to jump ahead of themselves more than one step at a time."

"Do you really think that is true, Dandelion?"

"Yes. Mostly I do, dot dot Dot."

"Then you don't need to ever waste your time learning to paint."

Dan winced.

And Dot felt it. He spun himself in Dan's arms to face her, even though he could not, properly speaking, see Dan. Grabbing two big handfuls of Dan's back and pulling, Dot squashed Dan's chest against his.

"Yelp!" That was Dot yelping, not Dan. "You won't believe this either, my cat Dan. But while I cannot see anything here around us clearly enough to make out what it is, nothing in this room, not one single thing, not even you and me, I *can* see the mountains way out there behind me perfectly reflected on your eyeballs."

Thinking maybe she should examine the ceiling, Dan flopped her head way back. The ceiling was, of course, invisible. *Or missing.*

"You looked away! Dan! Don't be mean now. Please look at them again. Pretty please."

She did.

"Thankayou, Dan."

Another long silence ensued.

Then Dot said--gushed, "Yes, I was right. There is something extra extraordinary about seeing your eyes seeing those mountains. Most unusual. Have you been there? Have you ever been up on them? I hear there are nearly no trees up there. A couple of weird old men in caves perhaps, but next to no trees. You're not a weird young lover headed for a cave in your old age, are you? Now that would surely be a waste of your time. -- Don't pretend you're not here! I can feel your tuffy trying to grab hold of my ding-a-ring. And ghosts don't have hair down there. Or at least not any kind of hair that could verticalize my ding-a-ring. And this stiff, wiry stuff that I now have in my hand is without question doing exactly that."

"My darling Dot. That is not my tuffy you have in your hand."

"It is dark in here, yes. Truly dark. But it is never so dark that I don't know when I have got a tuffy in my hand."

"You might be wrong this time."

"Shall we give it a test, Dan? A taste test?"

"Surely not *we* but *ye.*"

"That's fine with me. I'll be back up in a few minutes. Bye for now."

Why can't I see the sky out the window? If not the moon, at least stars. I can see the mountains; so there has to be light out there. Light? The light of the mountains...is it out there or in here?

"Argue not. I have proven beyond a doubt that that was and is your tuffy."

"Welcome back, Dot Sett. I made a mistake, you say? OK, I admit the possibility. Yet I would request another test, a *we* test this time."

· · · · ·

Lying facedown on the damp grass with her nose mashed against the earth one noontime under a warm sun with a hint of rain in the near future, DB heard a fast-stepping dog stride by. *That same tall, female dog?* The dog came right back, whined, licked Dan's cheek. Without raising her nose from the grass or even opening her eyes, Dan responded brilliantly, "Hi." The dog barked, tried to smile, ran off in her original direction. Not two minutes later, Dan's cheek got another licking. This time, Dan opened her eyes and turned her head to see whose tongue it was. *It's Milosh-- no, it's Dot--no, it's not anyone!* Laughing at herself, Dan rolled over onto her back to have the sun shining on her face. She saw the sun up there, saw a bird flying overhead. *Is that bluebird looking at me?* That is not all she saw. Standing rigidly upright like a thick, sullen post at Dan's feet, frowning down at Dan's grass-creased nose, was Sola Resta. Standing close behind Sola Resta, like a second glum post, was Roy Kee.

"Hi low," joked Dan, lolling on her back as if she had made up her mind to lounge away the remainder of her days on this magic bed of grass. The inside of her nose popped back to its regular shape.

Sola said nothing. Her dark frown drew down to an even blacker scowl.

"Hi low," breathed Roy, just faintly echoing Dan's greeting.

The fact that Sola wasn't smiling did not strike Dan as out of place, but the lack of a smile on Roy's face was noteworthy. Sola Resta was no longer Dan's supervisor; but, as far as Dan knew, Sola was still Roy's supervisor.

Dan gazed at them, they glowered at Dan. Roy didn't exactly glower, yet he still would not smile. Dan looked straight up in the sky. It occurred to her that she could leave this earth forever by simply following her vision up, up and away. She could feel her muscles getting ready for the ascent. Only a thought, just one thought prevented her rising: her departure might leave a long, lonely, empty, deep, dark hole in someone's life. Who that someone might be she didn't concern herself with; instead, she calmly remembered the giant piece torn out of her heart/mind by someone's leaving.

"Mind if we join you, Dan?"

Lying faceup on the damp grass between Roy and Sola. A little past noon. Warm sun. A hint of coming rain. The dog wandered back by but didn't get too close to the pack of humans.

• • • • •

When their lunch break was over, Roy told Sola Resta that he wanted to go up with Dan to see what she had been working on and that he would see her, Sola, back in their building in a short while. As Dan unlocked her door, Roy said thanks and ducked into the office across the hall.

Dan continued on into her office and was closing the door behind her when she noticed something was waiting for her on her machine. A picture. She stopped, stiffened, stood immobile with her hand still clenching the doorknob. Her breathing slowed way down. A hyperrealistic picture of a sheet of tan paper floating on the lucid blue-green water of a shallow pond. Below the paper, a large golden fish, clearly visible. Below the fish, the pebbly bottom. Dan let go of the closed door and stepped up closer to the machine to read what was written on the floating sheet of paper. Afore the paper in the picture got wet, someone had printed near the top of the sheet with an oil pencil: "Abc Def." And under that, also printed in roundish letters: "Howdy cowdy sowdy!" The third line read: "Dan doesn't know she doesn't belong here." The next and last line seemed to be a signature, for it was written in cursive. "Ab absurdo." Or maybe it was not cursive but an approximation of italics, sometimes used for foreign words and phrases.

Dan sat down on her chair and actually made an attempt, weak as it was, to find out who had sent the picture, quickly convincing herself again, however, that she didn't have whatever it takes to trace a graphic to its source if an adept sender did not want to be known.

Three soft knocks came from the plastic door behind Dan. Dan's shoulders didn't move even the slightest bit as her head rotated farther around a circle than seemed possible for a grown woman's body. Her wide, staring eyes watched the door open a crack. Roy stuck just his head into the office. Dan's head rotated back, back to stare at her machine. The picture was gone. Dan's head rotated back, back to stare at Roy's head.

Roy fluttered his eyelids at her and said, "Having a bad afternoon, baby?"

"I wouldn't say *bad*." Dan sounded, especially when she said the word *bad*, as if she had a dozen waterworn pebbles slopping around in her mouth.

"What would you say then?"

"I'm thinking, Roy."

"No rush."

"I seem to be splitting."

Roy waited. "Is that all you have to say, baby girl?"

Dan got up from her chair to stagger over to Roy's head. "That pretty much sums it up, yes."

Below Roy's head, a hand and part of an arm reached into the office. "Let me rub your chin, sweetlips."

Dan dropped to her knees before the cracked door.

Yellow light! A soft, clear light appeared before her eyes. It seemed to float in an unknown space just inches from her face. This yellow light faded and was replaced by a purple light. The purple light shrank and disappeared, too; and then there came a green light. *Dandelion? Dan? Danakil?*

Releasing Dan's chin to grab her gently by the hair, Roy whispered kindly to Dan, "I have to go now. But if you get yourself into a real box, do hurry on over to my office."

Click, the door closed. Click clack, Dan stood up. Possessing not even the beginnings of an idea as to what she should do next, she took one and a half steps backward and remained standing there not far from the door for an indeterminate period (of time). Yellow, purple, green. Was she splitting? Or was she wholly changing? Or was she *becoming* just what she had always been? Dot came to her rescue. Dan saw him walk in right through the door without opening it first.

"Those aren't mountains reflecting from your eyeballs, Dan. Not this time. Oh! It looks to be a bodacious man! Where is he? I'd like to stare at him, too."

"It's you, Dot."

"Oh, Dan!" Dot coyly bent his knees and touched his hand to his cheek. "You say the most wonderful things."

He helped her lock up, then walked her down the flights of stairs and out into the (nearly) infinite air of evening. Neither of them liked the elevators.

• • • • •

Sitting on a bench a few minutes later, breathing nervously, trying to put on pleasant faces…

Dot pulled something from his pocket and pushed it under Dan's arm. He waited, watching Dan. He didn't say anything, didn't offer her any help. Dan too remained silent. Dot could see she was in a fix.

Actually Dan was in a little fix inside of a larger

fix. Or she was until the bench beneath her told her
that even one glimpse of herself inside of larger and
larger dilemmas *ad infinitum* would permanently paralyze
her. Dan's mind concentrated on the little fix, which
was centered on the object under her arm, another of
the metal rods. This rod, just the fourth one Dan had
ever seen, was green, barely. *Only one more of these things
will fit in that box. No, the lined box is from Dot; and if he
gives me the remaining three of the five rods that he said were in
the box when he bought it, then I will have to find some different
place to store the two rods from Milosh.*

   Dan closed her eyes and leaned her shoulder
against Dot's shoulder. She opened her eyes and looked
down again at the rod sticking out from under her arm.
Dot grinned, Dan didn't. Folded around the green
metal reminder was a sheet of glossy paper. Dan took
both the rod and the paper from under her arm. *Dot has
never said that he intends to eventually give the whole set to me.*
The paper was a page cut from a magazine. *Two columns
of short paragraphs...on both sides...with one of the paragraphs
circled in india ink.*

     DOT SETT: Four new
   abstract paintings in wildly
   frivolous yellows, startlingly
   personal greens, deliciously lurid
   purples. Having apparently
   abandoned his heavy reds that
   invariably contoured down to
   soft pinks and the stony blue-
   blacks that unavoidably melted

to earthy greyed browns, he now
invites the viewer to swoop back
into the vivid, sometimes garish
paintings, although one is
tempted to linger on the surface,
where the viewer can almost
taste Dot Sett's vision of light.

"A questionable writing style, don't you think,
Dot?"

"Of course, Dot's Dan. It's supposed to be less
than good writing. That is supposed to make it
grabby...punchy...interesting."

"It sort of does that, I guess."

"You're not pleased, Dan?"

"Oh, yes! I am. Certainly." She twirled the rod.
She closed her hand around it. "The smooth metal of
love--or it was lust, wasn't it, not love. No, it was
hornyness."

"I said 'a token of sexual love.' But either lust or
hornyness is close enough."

"You said *hornyness* too. But I won't hold you to
any single word. --And this page!" Dan waved the
magazine page above her head. She was still not light
enough emotionally to be truly joking. She was, in fact,
a bit grim. "It is great and all that. Yet something
bothers me about it."

"What?"

"I was deeply immersed in yellow/purple/green
when you voodooed into my office a while ago. And
right here it says that you are now working with those

very colors. Why? What? How?"

Dot studied Dan's face, studied the side of her serious face as she stared down at the page, which she had laid on her leg. No, Dot realized Dan was looking at their feet, their shoes.

"Think, Dan," said Dot unambiguously. "Paint is very powerful. You have been to my studio, where you couldn't help but see my paintings...these paintings, the ones written about. Your brain simply fixed on the colors."

I am thinking. I am considering his explanation. Thinking, thinking, thinking I see another explanation. The yellow light, the purple light, the green light I saw while kneeling before Roy might not have been colors from Dot's paintings--they might be my colors. In fact, Dot might have seen my colors early on and used them in his paintings. If so, is he aware of it? Has he painted Willa's colors? Was she the heavy reds and soft pinks and the stony blue-blacks that unavoidably melted to earthy greyed browns? "Are you sure of that, Dot? Is that what happened?"

"Nothing is for sure, Dan. You have to take your chances, mate. Life is one risk after another. And I didn't voodoo into your office. I knocked, called your name, opened the door, walked in, closed the door and said your name again. Your eyeballs were as big as your fists."

"So *that* is why you could see yourself on my eyes in a well lit room." Dan meant that as a question.

"Naw-w-w." Dot curled his upper lip up into a camel's grin. He threatened to kiss Dan with his mouth like that. His lip returned to normal when he said, "I couldn't actually see my reflection. I made that up to jolt you, Dan, to get you to look at me as if I were a human being, a friendly human being and not some kinky monster come to brazenly abduct you."

"Was I really looking at you like that?"

"You bet! For a number of heartthrobs there I felt absolutely guilty for every crazy hurt you had ever suffered. But then you recognized me, and your eyes got all soft and squishy. Then I felt wonderful."

Dan grinned at last. "Like a man in love, you say?"

"Did I say that? No. Yes. No. Yes. No. Yes. No. Yes. No. Yes. No." He had nodded or shook his head appropriately with each and every answer.

"Yes." Dan completed Dot's row of answers. She smiled at him.

"No." Dot extended his row of answers. He protruded his lips.

"Is this a come-hither?" Dan pointed her nose at Dot's mouth.

"No, ma'am, it is not. And if you don't unhand me right this instant, I swear I'll call out for assistance!"

The implicated hand jerked away from Dot's leg to jam itself between Dan's legs. But while that hand hid out of sight, Dan's other hand rose in the air. This high hand swooped down to silently insert the green metal rod between Dot's pant-covered thighs, not far from his crotch. Dot sighed. Dan mimicked his sigh. Dot sighed again. *Is that littlebird looking at me?*

-11-

THE MISSING MIND OF WOMAN

One rainy day, comfortably ensconced inside and out of the wet, a three-color cat, sitting between the curtain and the glass of an upstairs window, pressed its forehead against the glass to look down the outside of the house but couldn't quite see the woman standing, facing out her open back door, yelling, probably at someone behind her inside the house, "If you get your jelly shaking with pleasure, then you will understand!" If cats have foreheads. Whatever the woman was yelling about, her words cut through the rain like a razor, slicing over the common area and into Dot's kitchen through an open window.

Dot was sitting in his kitchen. He heard the incoming words. He heard them clearly. He couldn't have heard them any plainer if he had been waiting for them. He smiled. Perched on his yah-yah (chair) with one shin propped against the edge of the kitchen table and one curved finger pushed through the handle of a black-and-white striped ceramic cup, he proceeded to nod his head and say out loud as if he were instructing a whole roomful of people, though he sat all by himself at the table, "Seeing into a meaning can have as strong a pull as nostalgia, and connecting perfectly with a meaning can be nearly devastating. Why?" He answered his *why*. "Meaning. Meaning could well be, just might be an alternate form of light."

Then Dot Sett sang. Looking out that open window over his sink, gazing at the now closed door where the woman had stood hollering just a few moments before, Dot melodized, "If I get my jelly shaking, if I get my jelly to shake shaking with pleasure, will I see to the heart of the heart of hearts, to the very core of cores? Will I see through the very door of doors to the great inner essential nature? Will I then understand?" He closed his little song with an irreverent nasal honk-honk.

Dot drank deep from that striped cup. Clunking the heavy cup down on the table, addressing first his big coldbox and then a nearby cupboard, he began another lecture. His feet? Both of his feet were now planted flat on the floor. "To be insensitive? To steel the will? Again? This year of this decade? Is it again better to represent oneself as cagey and unillusioned? I myself would prefer to think that we--" He quit his sermon so abruptly because something touched him on the top of his head, scaring the living stickings out of him. It was someone's hand.

"You left your front door standing open," this someone said with a hint of giggle. "And the card was up in the window."

"Do come in, oh silent-as-a-shadow-walking woman, née Dan Butxn. Do come in please and clean up the mess you caused under my chair."

Dan hid her mouth behind her hand. "She softly say this, 'Bo Rinka, you looked durn silly.'"

Dot sprang to his feet and wheeled around to face Dan. "She say this so softly because she be afraid Bo Rinka'd rub herself's nose in it?"

"She" didn't reply, couldn't reply. Dan had been

caught with nary a quick comeback. She closed one eye, opened it, closed her other eye, opened it. Nothing came to her. Zilch. So she hopped up onto the seat of Dot's chair. Why? To stand tall and tower over him with her fists pressed together knuckles-to-knuckles before her chest. She tightly compressed her lips, then opened her hands, spreading her fingers as wide as she could get them to go. Raising her arms up and out like a vexed eagle, she bared her shining teeth in a ludicrous grin.

Dot rushed around behind the chair to grab the chair's back and shake Dan down from her craggy heights. But swifter than swift, Dan swung a leg around him, mounting Dot as if he were a bull, a bull she was going to ride right down into the ground. Dot spun about and ran out of the kitchen with Dan screaming hi-yo from his back and ducking timely to fit through the doorway.

On out the front door (which Dan had left open, too, since she didn't know why Dot had left it open) Dot ran. He ran down the lane in the rain, ran clear around the cluster of houses and back into his house and into his bedroom, where he dove for the bed without stopping his feet from running, turning himself in the air as he flew so that he and Dan landed on their sides on the soft.

Dan yelled, "We will get your bedspread all wet!"

Dot heard her warning, grasped its implication, and changed his plan in an instant. He quickly grabbed Dan while they were still bouncing and pulled her after him as he rolled on off the bed onto the floor. Again, they landed on their sides; but this time they landed facing each other.

Dan immediately caught Dot's head and held it immobile between her hands to whisper to his eyes, "Meaning. Understanding. Insensitivity. And now frivolousness."

It took Dot a couple of seconds to realize what Dan had said. And then he shrieked. Dot yanked Dan's hands away from his head and got all over her, all over her verbally and all over her physically, demanding to know just how long she had been standing behind him. He called her a grey villain. Dan laughed and wiggled around beneath him.

Dot persuaded Dan to hold still by pinning her wrists firmly to the floor with his hands and then rapidly stretching out his full length on top of her body and arching his back so that nearly all of his weight rested on nothing but her stomach. His dripping wet hair dropped drops on her face.

Dan raised Dot's whole body an inch or two by merely tightening her stomach muscles, his whole body save his hands. She then told him how long she had been standing behind him. "I heard the woman's voice come in the window."

Dot pressed his lips tightly together so that his true emotions didn't show on his face. Was he copying Dan's compressing of her lips? No, his lip pose was different. "And I looked durn silly to you?"

"No! I didn't mean the whole time, Dot. I meant just for a moment, right after I touched your head." Dan wisely didn't smirk at him. "Until you zoomed around and saw it was me behind you."

Dan relaxed her stomach muscles, and Dot sort of sank down. He didn't spread out over her like heated butter; he sank somewhat but neither relaxed his body nor let go of her. Dan figured she had better come up with something fast. *Before he finds a knife.* So she glued her eyes to the ceiling and matter-of-factly described an actual event, if pictures streaking through the brain can be called events. "You know, for just an instant there in that tinky bit of time between when you spotted me and when I spoke to you, the look on your face made me think of gold melting in a flash without using up or giving off heat."

"So now I'm not only soaked to the bone, I'm a cold, metallic bastard." Dot tightened his grips on her wrists.

Wasn't it you who packed me outside in the rain, Mr. Sett? "Whoops! Why didn't I grasp aforehand that you would interpret my inoffensive observation that way, kind sir? I am a fool surely."

"How else could I interpret it, Butxn?"

Dan cringed at the rough tone of his voice. "Gold changing from a solid to a liquid in an instant, Dot, without consuming or producing the natural heat that comes and goes with all such changes? I don't see that as cold, I see it as divine. As consciousness changing from one state to another miraculously."

"Whew! So now I'm miraculous!" Dot whipped his head about, wrapping his wet hair across his face as if to conceal something. "You don't have to turn on the girlish charm to convince me to park my whistle in your garage." He did, however, loosen his holds on Dan a little.

"I wasn't trying to charm you, Dotsy. I was trying to show you something, something I had seen, to find out if you had ever had that experience yourself."

"Yes, I have. But not really, not exactly the same. --And I refuse to believe you weren't trying to get me in you, Dan! Our friend in my pants betrays your intention."

"You can't always trust friends. Friends have minds of their own, you know."

"You know! You know! That's all you are saying to me, spy. Spy in my house, spy in my house, I've got a spooky spy in my house."

"I have much to learn from you, Dot."

"You didn't say that!"

"I have never said it to anyone before. Even so, I said it. Yes, Dan did."

Dot rose to his knees to stand on his knees straddling Dan's legs. He locked his hands behind his neck and said to his left armpit, "I would like to believe her." Rotating his head, he then said in a whisper to his right pit, "However, I just can't. She is a woman wanting to be a full-time god, and she knows full well that I don't have what she needs for that gig."

"Why did you say *gig*, Dot?"

"I meant gig like in a one-night stand. In the long run gods don't have much going for them. They're all attitude/context. It's like they only play a single engagement."

"Where did all this *god* stuff come from, anyway?"

"From you, Dan. I've been watching you."

"So I've noticed."

Dot lowered his hands to his hips and slipped back into his lecturer's voice. "I have seen you occasionally turn one eye toward the earthbounders and their feeble pursuits. Yes, on occasion. But otherwise, Dan, you are either standing atop your little tower gazing at the heavens or you are up there in one heaven or another, up there swimming in bliss in those outer realms--where we wee folk certainly can't go--frolicking about as if you belonged there."

It doesn't matter, I guess, that I'm the wee one lying on the floor with him hovering over me. "You consider yourself tied to the earth?"

"That is why I paint, Dan. Paint is earth."

"And what should I do, Dot?"

"You should realize, my beautiful willow tree, that this cloud love of yours is a large part of why you have so much trouble with daily life."

"I seldom even notice clouds."

"A figure of speech, Dan."

• • • • •

Dan thought for a longish moment before she replied. "If I were to cut off my hand and you cut off your hand, and we stuck the two stumps end to end and your blood flowed into me and mine into you, would we be earthbound people or outer-realm people?"

Dot gaped down round-eyed at Dan's face, his mouth slowly opening, then quickly closing. He stood up and rushed to the bathroom.

Dan didn't move. *Did I shock him or hurt his feelings or insult his intelligence or what?* She lay there on the floor beside Dot's bed not moving a muscle.

Ahh! Dan heard Dot's wet clothes coming off and dropping to the tile floor of the bathroom. She piled one fist on top of her other fist under the back of her head to raise her head so that she could see his body gleaming in there in the white washroom. He's the first human to land on this planet, Dan imagined. *No, make that the first one to return to this world after all humans had migrated elsewhere.* Dan roared like a lion at the man in the bathroom, though lions maybe don't roar while they're lying like lions on their backs. But they might.

The door slammed closed.

The door opened, and Dot marched out of the bathroom on his toes, naked as a newborn. "I am slipping into slurs," he sang, "slipping into slurs. Oh, won't you join me, won't you please join me, slipping into slurs?"

The word *slur* has a number of meanings, but only one popped into Dan's head: *Two or more tones of different pitch smoothly connected in succession so that they form one syllable.* Dan stood up to dance with Dot and with their newly freed mutual friend.

· · · · ·

Were you wading and
wading and wading through the
illusory world of the senses when
you stopped to rest on a rotting
log in a primeval bog? Yes, yes,
yes. You guessed it, didn't you?
It's not a gooey log in a smelly
bog--that's your chair. Your
assigned chair in your assigned
office in your assigned building
in your assigned cluster. Good
morning, fellow workers. One
ton of maya.

This was not the first time Dan had spotted and
read an unexpected greeting on her machine before she
was all the way into her office. She seriously considered
turning right around and leaving. No, she only shook
her head and went ahead and closed the door. She laid
down the bag she had carried with her from home and
positioned herself, standing behind her chair, to reread
the three score and ten words before she erased them.
She decided it was not a personal message. *This hello will
be waiting for a great many people when they arrive at work this
morning. It can even be read as friendly.* That thought led to
another: *But what does friendship amount to in this gale of
cosmic illusion? Good question. Judging from the epistle I just
deleted, even the pranksters of the world are worrying over this
enigma.* That thought led to another: *Ah, the phenomenal*

world. Moving my hand from my face to a more distant object…so simple an action. Dan sat down to look out the window. She could not make out Chuck in the early haze. She remembered gazing for long spells into Terry's eyes. What had she seen in there? When she looks at Dot's eyes, what does she see? At Willa's eyes? *Voices come from people's mouths. Smells come from their skin and hair. So many ways to recognize people. So many clues to what people are. Yet expressive words coming from a person's gifted mouth are often incomprehensible. Or an ugly person will wax handsome in a matter of seconds. And vice versa. Contrary to what some/most people apparently believe, if I pay very close attention, movement, like my moving my hand away from my face, doesn't always add up, doesn't always make complete sense. And if that is so for my own hand, what meaning, if any, can I safely attribute to someone else's movements?* Dan snickered when a ridiculous statement that she had recently overheard jumped up out of her memory: "It's enough to make me kiss my machine."

Having thus started her day on one foot only, Dan Butxn went to work. *I would never kiss a machine.* She went to work but didn't get to work. Someone tapped on her door and let themselves in before Dan could ask who is it. Her visitor, Jill Surfred Atnoon, quietly sat down behind Dan on the other chair and waited for Dan to turn around to see who is it. Jill was wearing a mask. She had on a Sola Resta mask.

Very droll. Very very very sly. Dan watched Jill. *The wag isn't moving, isn't making a sound.* Dan listened intently but didn't hear one peep or pop out of Jill. Through the eyeholes in the mask, Jill looked long into

Dan's eyes.

Dan didn't know whether to laugh or to surrender to Jill's deep gaze. She wanted to do both. This was the first time she had seen Jill, her present nominal supervisor, except in passing, since their lunch date that first day Dan came to work in this building. Dan still felt comfortable in Jill's presence. "Where did you get that?" Dan waved at the mask.

The mask answered, "Are you referring to the woman sitting behind me?"

Dan chuckled and waved again. Yet the woman behind the mask remained behind the mask.

"I just thought I would drop by to see how you are doing in your new building," the mask reported. "Along my way here *she* started following me."

Grinning like a wise old moon, Dan wrinkled her brow and wondered out loud, "Should I talk now as if I were speaking to Sola Resta or to her follower, Jill Atnoon?"

"Oh! So that is who it is back there. Jill Atnoon."

"I think so, yes."

Jill took off the mask. "Boo."

"Boo back to you, Jill."

Jill held up the mask. "Nice, huh?" She laid it down next to the bag that Dan had brought from home. "I borrowed it from Sola. I've got one of my own, too. My own face, that is. A guy named Clifton Means is making them. You have to make an appointment with him and then let him put this skunky stuff all over your face. But it only takes a few minutes. And it's painless."

"It's quite realistic, looks just like Sola, red lips and all."

"Want me to make an appointment for you, Dan?"

"Nope."

"Just plain *nope?*

"Just plain nope."

"Let me guess, Dan. You think that having a likeness made of your face is vain, don't you?"

"Vain? No, vanity hadn't occurred to me, Jill. I just don't know what I would want one for. I've got a mirror over my bathroom sink."

"So do I, Dan. So do I. And I do wish I had brought that mirror with me this morning. It would have come in very handy a short while ago, when you turned around and saw the apparition behind you. You were quick, Dan, but for one second there your face was the perfect picture of confusion. Just perfect."

Just call me "Bo Rinka." Or maybe I'd be "Doe Rinda" instead. "Perhaps I will repay you someday, J.S. Atnoon."

"Is that a threat or a promise?"

"Not a threat. I enjoyed your masquerade." Dan tilted her head and scratched the side of her nose with one hooked finger. "I can't make it a promise either, I'm afraid. I am not terribly skilled at pretense."

"Ow! Now she's getting into name-calling!"

"No, I'm not. Not at all. It's just that *I* have always been the fool that others play games with. Not me with them. I have walked up behind someone without their knowing it, once or twice; but I simply didn't know what to say or do next."

"I think you're grossly understating your role, Dan. That's what I think. And you are doing it because you are sneaky."

"Now who's calling names? Me? Sneaky?"

"You have never dropped by for a chat."

Dan looked confused again, until she remembered. "Yes. Right. I said I would, didn't I. We exchanged invitations in your office my first morning here."

"Fools we are."

Dan's jaw dropped. The clarity of the memory brought forth by Jill's three words gave Dan a real start. Jill had said those words to her before. It was in Jill's office that same first morning. And Dan remembered just as clearly her own reply. "Aye. And fools we will always be." Dan remembered the whole scene perfectly, as if her visit to Jill's office had been but minutes before.

Together, in unison, in Dan's office they repeated, "From birth to death, from death to birth we act the fool, believing it's the best we can do at the moment."

"Will that be the one rule of our working relationship, Jill?"

Jill grinned. "Goodbye, Dan."

"And before you were inside your mother, Jill?"

"Unlimited space, unlimited time, infinite light."

．．．．．

Jill closed the door softly behind her as she left Dan's office.

Dan wondered what that was all about. Why had Jill come? Just to play a trick on Dan? Dan shuffled the cards in her brain time and again, over and over again until the right card came up on top. *Lunch.* Did Jill want Dan to meet her for lunch again? *Maybe. Well, it's worth a try. The only way to find out, to ever know, is to go there and find out. Right?*

Dan entered the same restaurant at the same time of day and had the same person receive her inside the door with the same greeting: "Welcome to The Tower. Would you like...."

When Dan approached the table in the alcove, Jill looked up at her as if surprised to see her. "Didn't I smell sandwiches in that bag in your office, Dan?"

"Just one sandwich. But big enough to be two."

"Have you already eaten it? Or are you going to sit down with me?"

"May I join you?"

"Yes, you may. And you don't have to make believe that you just happened by. Remember, you said yourself that you are not particularly skilled at pretense."

"I won't pretend, Jill, if you don't." Dan sat down across the table from her. "Your reason for not saying anything while you were in my office about our having lunch together today didn't have anything to do with your smelling the food in my bag. No, your stopping by was another little game/test. Wasn't it? I was supposed to grasp out of the blue your purpose in coming to see me."

"And you did. Congratulations, Dan."

"It wasn't all that easy."

"Worthwhile things are seldom easy."

Dan's eyes searched the tabletop. "You sounded a bit old-fashioned there, Jill."

"Just a bit old-fashioned, I am. Just enough to keep my head screwed on straight, as the old-fashioned saying goes."

Jill reached across the table to lay her hand on Dan's hand. "If you are looking for a menu, don't. I've already ordered for you. I ordered the same as you had last time."

"Your confidence in me is amazing."

"Not really. I told the waiter to not start preparing our food until you showed up."

"Good thinking." Dan undid her napkin and laid it in her lap. "I'm glad *you* can remember what I ate the last time I was here."

She awakens, sits up, looks around, up and down, side to side. "No violin today, Jill?"

"The young woman's finger is broken."

"Really?" Dan had trouble believing that.

"I heard that someone broke it for her."

"A competitor?"

"A lover."

"Again, that sounds a bit old-fashioned, Jill."

"Jealousy has not yet been totally wiped out."

"Is that a fact?"

"No, that's a guess, Dan."

A waiter brought Dan a glass of water and asked, "Can I get you anything else to drink, madam?"

"No. Thank you," said Dan. "Did this woman tell you I would want water?"

"That she did, madam. Is there a problem?"

"No. No problem at all. Thank you much."

Saying that he would be back shortly with their food, the waiter left the alcove.

"We both had only iced water to drink last time, Dan."

Dan shook her head but smiled. "Why are we...doing everything the same?"

"There are fewer decisions to make that way. Fewer distractions. We can get to the point sooner."

"Oh." Squinting up at the ceiling, Dan said, "So there is a point to get to. Besides food."

Jill placed one hand, just one of her hands, flat on the very back of her head--her own head. She leaned back in her chair and probably crossed her legs under the table. "How blunt would you like it, Dan Butxn?"

"Just straight out."

"Would you consider moving in with me? Into my house, not my office."

"Nope."

"Just plain *nope*, Dan?"

"Just plain nope."

"Can I move in with you then?"

"I live alone, Jill. I wouldn't be able to function any other way."

"Have you ever tried living with someone else?"

"No, I haven't. But I know my limits. At least

some of my limits."

The food arrived. Jill was cool for a while. Dan was nervous for a while. But eventually, as they ate, they worked their way around the deadspot and found themselves joking and playing with each other again.

DRAG FACT, DROP TRUTH

Rose, cream, purple, green. Top to bottom, that's how they were dressed, the both of them. Rose colored caps, creamy snap-on shirts, soft shapeless purple pants, green shoes. Dan had picked out the colors. Behind them, streaming from their left to their right, flexing his muscles and shining in the sun, flowed Chuck.

The first time ever that Chuck met Dot, Chuck immediately asked Dan to ask Dot to paint his picture, or so Dan told Dot at the time anyway. Dot agreed to do a painting not of just Chuck but of Chuck and Dan together. And before Dan&Dot had reached mowed grass on their hike back from the river that day, Dan had talked Dot into including himself in the portrait. In his conversation with Dan beside the river, Dot had called the painting "a family portrait"; and that's what he called it ever after. In the finished picture Dan and Dot, gaily attired as described in the paragraph above, stand side-by-side, arm-in-arm on the bank, with Chuck smiling big from right behind them. With lots of puffy clouds in the distance.

The first time ever that Dot met Chuck, Dot told Dan, "I don't usually do portraits." In truth, Dot had had exactly no experience at portraiture. He had never even done a still life. Before he undertook the group picture--which he himself called "a family portrait" but which he formally titled "Dan & Chuck & Myself"--Dot had never suffered any interest whatsoever in painting people or people's things or people's places. Or so he told Dan anyway. By the time Dot had finished painting the agreed-upon portrait, however, all that had changed. Now he was considering doing nothing but pictures of humans in settings of their choice. It was a radical idea for him. He said he was having dreams about it. His dreams were not about the people or the places in which they chose to be painted but about the paintings themselves: the pigments and mediums, the stretcher bars and canvases. In Dot's dreams these familiar ingredients came together to produce more than just portraits of people; the materials bonded and ripened into bona fide beings--real people, flesh and bone walking about, making decisions, saying things, talking to each other.

Where to hang the family portrait was a problem. The painting could not be left standing out on an easel by the river, for a number of obvious reasons. And if it were hung in Dan's office, Chuck may or may not have been able to see it through the window, the office and river being quite some distance from each other. Dan could hang it on her living room wall so that Dot could see it from his house; but then there would be no way for Chuck to ever see it. *No, that's not so. There is a way.* Hanging the painting between them like a banner in a parade, Dan and Dot could march from Dan's living room to the river, packing a picnic lunch with them, once or twice a month or whenever the urge hit them. So it was decided.

· · · · ·

"Do I know what you are thinking about?"

"Do I know what you are thinking I am thinking about?"

"Not cats?"

"Not big or not little cats?"

"Not big."

"Not real big?"

"Not more that knee high to you or me."

"Ah. Not medium to not large then."

"OK. Not medium to not large then."

"No. I am not thinking about not cats. Not of any size."

"Not dogs?"

"No."

"Not raccoons?"

"I could be thinking about raccoons. Yes, I will say that I am thinking about raccoons, even though I can't really remember what they look like, Dan. I haven't seen one in years."

Dot and Dan had had numerous exchanges like the one barely begun above. Usually the long dialogues unraveled from some invisible fabric while they were enjoying sexual intercourse (with each other) or while they were bathing together in Dot's oversized shower/tub. But this chat was uncoiling in Dot's studio. It was a sunny morning. Dot was working at his easel, and Dan was sitting a comfortable distance away, looking past Dot and out the window at the blue sky. It was Dan's turn to speak. She was opening her mouth to do so when two knocks sounded from the door.

K-knock. K-knock.

Dan glanced at Dot. Dot hadn't looked away from his work. Dan returned her eyes to the sky. She was opening her mouth again.

K-knock. K-knock.

"Two knocks twice, Dot. Does that mean that whoever is out there is in a hurry or that they are known to one or both of us?"

"Two knocks twice could mean either, Dan. Could you answer the door?"

Dan saw herself spring up from her sitting position to leap like a giant frog halfway to the door. She saw herself wondering if her getting up to go to the door looked anything like that to Dot. He would only have been able to see her out the corner of his eye, if he saw her at all. Even so, Dan said in her head to the door just before she pulled it open, *Dot sees everything.*

A man dressed in light grey flannel tipped his hatless head to Dan. "Is Dot Sett here, please?"

Dan turned sideways in the doorway so that the man could see on by. "Yes, I think that is he over there." Dan pointed at Dot, who was grinning at them.

"Could you give this to him?" The man in grey offered Dan a long, narrow box.

A dizzyingly blue paperboard box with a pebbly finish. "Certainly." Dan took the box. *It's so light it could contain all of time and all of space.* The box had a wide, deeper blue ribbon tied round it.

"Thank you." The man nodded once more to Dan, then spun smartly about and left.

Dan closed the door, whistled at the box, and swung her body around to face Dot. "There must be an old, worn-out bottle of glue or something in here," she said after taking a deep sniff of the box. "It smells terrible."

"Bring it here, Dan. And keep your wisecracking lip to yourself."

"Must I, dear?"

"Bring it here!"

"Or you will what?"

Eye to eye. Smile to smile. Grin to grin.

Dan gave in and took the box to Dot. She laid it ever so gracefully on his lap, then spun smartly about and left the studio.

• • • • •

"Dabble, dabble, dabble." The man smirked like a conceited child. "Boon bong babble."

The woman didn't bother to look up at him. Boredom boomed on the horizon of her voice. "If you insist."

"Don't just dismiss me, dear. Relate!" The man's eyes shifted, enlarged, protruded until they looked--to at least one observer at a nearby table--like the eyes of a huge winged scavenging beast circling way up above but dropping lower and lower in the sky. "You are all talk and no bluff today."

The woman glanced up from her food but not at the man's bizarre eyes. "Don't get me started, Bill. I'm liable to flop all over the place."

"Yeah, and I'm going to--"

Bing! Dan's diamond-like attention snapped. Roy had grabbed her arm to snatch her back from the conversation at the next table.

"Don't listen to them, Dan. It gets real messy with them sometimes."

Bing! Dan's eyes whizzed away from that other table but not to stop on Roy. Dan's eyes zipped on by Roy to focus three feet above the floor, ten feet out from their table.

Roy did not miss the sudden jump of Dan's eyes to another world. "What are you seeing?" he asked, wanting both lively interest and nagging concern to be heard in his voice.

Some seconds passed before Dan reported back. "Lines. Ragged brown lines. Strips of earthy brown, all more or less parallel, all more or less horizontal."

"Do they block your vision of the filling center?"

"No, Roy, everything around me looks quite normal. The strips of brown are in another kind of seeing."

"The kind of seeing one does in a dream, Dan?"

"Sort of. Maybe it is like in a dream. If this whole room were blacked out, like a bedroom at night, the lines might be a dream."

"Do these lines/strips have actuality?"

"If you are asking if they have personality, I would say they do. Yes."

Roy laughed gleefully. "How could you possibly equate *personality* with *actuality*? That's daft, Dan! You're weird."

"It is only by developing a personality that anything makes itself known to the greater world." Dan's eyes drifted back to Roy's. "And being known to the world is *actuality*, isn't it? *That* is how I hooked the two together."

"Good answer." Roy bobbed his head in approval. "I'm impressed. What's happening with the lines now?"

"They disappeared when you laughed. Your personality outweighed theirs."

"Great! Thank you." He tapped his fist on Dan's arm. "I will take that as a compliment."

"It was intended to be one."

"Are you and Milosh avoiding each other?"

"Wherever did you get that idea, Roy?"

"From no where. I don't know what I was asking. Please forget about the question."

"Will do," said Dan.

Milosh was sitting with others at a table across the room. Dan watched him for the best part of a minute before she returned to her food.

Glancing up from her plate at Roy, noticing that even though he was smiling he looked unhappy, Dan asked him, "Where is your Diane? You two have lunch together nearly every day."

"My Diane is eating with her boss today."

"Jill Atnoon?"

"The very one," snidely came back Roy. "Her name fits nicely, doesn't it? Jill at noon."

"Is this their first time?"

"Their first time to what, Dan?"

183

"To have lunch together."

"As far as I know, yes."

"And why are you bristling, Roy?"

"And why are you asking, Dan?"

"And why would you think?"

"And why haven't you mentioned Terry lately?"

"Wasn't it Milosh's well-being that concerned you but a minute ago?"

"Can't you see that I'm crying, you lout?"

"That would be *loutess*," corrected Dan.

Roy was telling the truth: his eyes were damp, and a small tear worked its way down his cheek. Tears, other than her own, scared Dan, nearly threw her into a panic. She could never figure out what she was supposed to do about them. She clamped both her hands on the edge and hung on to the table. "I can see now that you are crying. Do you wish to continue with that activity, or do you want me to try to do something that might help you stop it?"

Laughing and sobbing and rolling his hands, Roy tilted his head at Dan. "You are unbelievable as a person, poopsie. You ought to be locked up. Not to protect society, to protect and preserve you. You are a darling."

Dan had never seen Roy act like this. *Why is he weeping? His biggest problem at the moment looks to be his own selfishness.* Neither crying in public nor openly displaying such a high level of self-interest fit any of Dan's images of Roy. It seems Jill Atnoon was right when she said that jealousy has not yet been totally wiped out.

．．．．．

Jill.

Jill pulled the slip of paper out from under Dan's pen to see what Dan had doodled. Dan had found the waste piece of white on the tiny tea table at the end of Jill's couch while Jill was back in her kitchen.

Jill.

Jill smiled with her mouth tightly closed, as she was in the habit of doing. "You said you were just doodling, Dan. These are not doodles. Not what I would call doodles." On the paper were words, sentences. Jill read what Dan had written. "It's kind of cute for you, isn't it?" she asked without looking away from the paper. She reread the words to herself as she sat down on the next couch cushion to Dan's left.

> Tears. What are they?
> Where do they come from?
> How do they work so quickly
> and powerfully, so penetratingly,
> so movingly? And then they are
> gone, as if they were never here.

"Cute?" questioned Dan, wanting Jill to define what she had meant by the word. Dan offered a synonym: "Shallow?"

Jill trapped the piece of paper between the palm of her flat hand and her thigh bone. "Not necessarily."

Dan tried again. "Corny?"

Jill raised her hand from her thigh--forsaking the paper on her leg--to stretch that arm along the top back of the couch so that her hand was resting right behind Dan's head. "Maybe. Maybe not."

"Unmercifully mawkish?"

Jill tittered at Dan's choice of words. "*Cute* covers enough territory all by itself, Dan."

"It doesn't seem any cuter to me than that rhyme you once wrote on a grocery receipt of mine."

"Touché!" cracked Jill. "Point made and accepted."

Touché? She had us fencing? Then I shall put away my foil and take off my protective mask. Dan made several miniature moves with her hands and head, then said, "I am whispering to you that I accept your acceptance."

Jill laid the side of her head on her arm--the arm she had extended along the couch behind Dan's head-- as if her arm were a soft, cuddly pillow. She all but shut her eyes. In a lower, more private voice she said, "Now that we are known to each other as gentle idiots with froth about our mouths, Dan, how best should we proceed?"

"Proceed with what, Lady Atnoon?"

"Oh! Oh!" Jill's eyes opened wide as her head rose from her arm. She shivered with pleasure. "Lady Atnoon. That has such a nice sound. You can call me that any time you want."

"Maybe it will catch on, and everyone will address her ladyship so."

"You are teasing me, Dan Butxn. Remember that I bite."

"It truly seems that we *are* proceeding." Dan twirled a long phantom mustache. "Whether we are proceeding by the best possible path, I am sure I could not say."

"You once called me *milady*, didn't you?"

"Did I?" Dan raised her eyebrows higher than they had ever been.

"You must see me as either noble or fashionable. Or both."

"Must I?"

"Be careful there, Dan."

"Should I?"

Stopping herself before she riposted too quickly, Jill paused to think, to reconsider. She dragged her arm down from the back of the couch, set the butt of that hand on her thigh, then snapped the edge of the piece of paper with her finger to propel the paper away from her. The paper sailed out into the room and sank harmlessly to the floor. "Did the last two words you said have an underlying meaning intended to titillate me?"

"The layers and layers of underlying meanings reach clear down to the unbelievable, incorrigible heat at the center of the earth, Lady Atnoon."

"There! You did it again, Dan. You made me tremble all over. Your saying my name that way sets my whole body to trembling, from my head to my toes."

"Are you quick to tremble?"

Jill starts to laugh, starts to answer me but hesitates. Something smells not quite right to her about my question?

Jill's doorbell chimed.

No, it wasn't the man in grey bearing another long, dazzling box. Neither was it Diane come to visit Jill, not knowing that Dan would be there. And, no, it was not Roy on a hateful, fateful errand. It wasn't Gawkabit Howlsey in her official capacity nor Roy's sister Scotta, chief rule enforcer for their home town, helping out her brother again. It was no one. Not anyone, not even a solicitous missionary or two without a god to sell. No one stood waiting on Jill's step when she opened the door.

"An atmospheric phenomenon. Undoubtedly," said Dan when Jill closed the door and looked back at the couch with a puzzled look on her face.

Jill backtracked to her cushion beside Dan. Dan smiled at her. Jill liked Dan's smile and forgot about the problem at the door. "Yes," she promptly replied to Dan's query as to whether she, Jill, would like Dan to take off her, Jill's, clothes.

Just the thought of the couch touching her soft, warm skin. The mere idea of the satiny cloth pressing directly against her clear flesh.

"Now that you have me undressed, Dan, you are supposed to do something other than just kneel before me on the floor staring at my body like an infant gawking at her mother's nipple."

Dan chuckled and stood up. "Is that the way I looked to you?"

"Oh, I don't know. Probably I was just making it up." Jill let her head fall to one side. She leaned forward slightly on the couch and gazed up at Dan's face. "But we could, if you want to."

"We could what?"

"We could pretend that my whole body is your mother's nipple, Dan."

"That might be difficult for me and less than rewarding for you, Jill, since I have neither memories of nor images/fantasies about suckling at a mother's breast. But if you do," suggested Dan as she tugged off her own pants and underpants, "we could pretend that this small part of my body right here is *your* mother's nipple."

Jill nodded and eagerly cupped that part of Dan's body with her hand. "You don't like women's breasts?"

"No, no, no! I did not say or imply that, Lady Atnoon. Certainly not. We were talking about a mother/child relationship, which I have little if any experience at."

"Whatever!" Jill drew Dan closer.

But before Jill went any further, she peeked up at Dan's eyes to offer another idea. "How about: I will be a thirsty traveler if you will be a rocky cliff with an ancient vent from which dribbles the purest mountain water."

"That's from some old poem?"

"I think so, Dan."

"We could do that, Jilly. OK. We could do that. For a while. Then--"

"Stop yakking. Do we have an agreement or not?"

"Tis agreed, mysterious traveler. I'm a rock wall."

• • • • •

Back up. Sit down. Look around. How did you get here? Clean body, clean teeth, clean hair and mind. Clothed and shod. Ready for the world. You're ready in all respects except one: You don't know where you are. Go look in that mirror over there. Do you recognize yourself? Is that the you you remember being? Look first at the forehead, then let your eyes gradually drop and settle on the eyes in the mirror. Is that you? Is there anyone in there?

• • • • •

"Our name, Timothy Dorsey, may remind some of you of two names from out of the distant past. We had been performing together, calling ourselves Timothy Dorsey for nearly a year before we woke up to the fact that we had unconsciously blended those two names into one. But we are four, four musicians with one name, one music, and no further identity. We are one."

Indeed, the four of them did play as if they were one. Timothy Dorsey generated such a tight sound that their music flowed from one color to the next quite imperceptibly. Theirs was a journey without scenery, a voyage without direction. This smooth sonic excursion produced in the listener, initially anyway, an agreeable impression of being lulled and caressed by the air itself. Dan's second impression was of slight nausea. She didn't say anything about it and acted as if she were enjoying the performance.

She didn't fool Dot. He gripped her wrist. "We can go now, Dan." Dot got up from his chair, drawing Dan up with him. Taking her in tow, he hauled her, tripping and stumbling, down the row of big shoes and long legs to the aisle.

When they reached the main aisle, Dot unceremoniously dropped Dan's arm and headed himself up the aisle toward the exit, taking long, swift steps. But then something made him glance back. He saw that Dan wasn't following him. In fact the smiling Dan had stopped dead in her tracks, having taken but one step up the aisle. Dot stopped, spun around, strode right back down to her. The still smiling Dan neither cooperated with Dot nor resisted his effort when he arranged himself behind her to shove brusquely against her back. And once Dot got Dan to moving this time, he didn't let go of her; he kept a secure grip on her with both his hands as he pushed her on up the aisle toward the exit.

Holding her fisted arms straight down and tight to her sides like a cheap toy killer doll, Dan grinned and winked a conspiratorial goodbye to everyone who squinted up at them. "Amour," she explained to the guard at the last door.

Out of the club, The Epiphany of the Puffed Up, and into the brisk, moonless night Dot pushed Dan. Not far from the club's entrance, he let go of her and stopped himself so all-at-once that he could have hit a wall. His hands then drooped to his sides.

With no one applying force against her back,

Dan stopped, too. She turned round and round in the lamplight with her arms raised to the stars. "The night is full of desires!"

Dot paid little attention to Dan's rapture. His lips quivered sporadically even after he had started speaking. "You did not like the music, I take it." His eyes were mostly downcast.

"For a minute it was all right. Until I got lost in its nothingness."

"That's the point. You are supposed to get lost."

"I understood that, Dot. But then it started making me sort of sick to my stomach."

"I could tell that from looking at you," said Dot with a grimace.

Dot's deformation of his face maybe went unnoticed in the less than perfect light. Dan acted as if she had not *heard* him, either. She hopped up and down a couple of times on one foot, energetically, her arms swinging randomly. "Well, what should we do next?" She crossed her arms over her chest to scratch both sides of her ribcage. Overflowing with pep, she stuffed her hands up into her armpits.

"What am I saying!" Dan immediately set her hands free. "There's no need for me to ask what we should do next. Righto, Dotto?" She gestured broadly. "Certainly not! What needs to be asked is not *what* we should do but *where* we should do it. Your place? Mine? The studio? Or...!" Dan grinned too widely as she glanced around, superficially searching what little could be seen beyond the area lit by the pole lamps. "As dark as it is out there tonight, we just might be able to find us a secluded grassy spot behind some vegetation."

Dot stared unflinchingly at Dan. "I am finding your manner increasingly distasteful." His stare turned out to be a glare. "I think you are going to have to get down on your knees and weep and beg and beseech and plead and whine and grovel before I ever lay down anywhere with you."

Had Dan really not seen this coming? Yes or no, she was not prepared for Dot's statement/attitude and therefore wasn't up to responding other than stupidly. "Are you kidding me, Dot?"

"No! I'm not!" Dot ran eight unyielding fingers up the back of his head through his hair. "I might have thought when I started that list that I was stretching the truth a bit, but in no way was I kidding." When he wasn't actually speaking, he was clenching his teeth tightly together.

"When you started that list, you say?" Dan pushed her fingers up into her hair more or less the way Dot had. "That was then. What do you think now?"

Dot repeated one of Dan's words quite loudly. "Think!" And again. "Think, you say!" He wiped his nose on the back of his hand. "I don't *think*, I *know*!" He slapped Dan's arm to knock her mocking hand away from her head. "I wasn't stretching the truth, not at all, not one bit. What I said about my not lying down with you is exactly, is perfectly the way I am feeling."

Dan laughed hollowly and lowered her other hand from her hair, too. "Do you know why you are feeling this way, Dot?"

"Yes."

"Why?" Dan was watching Dot's temperature rise. *He is getting quite hot.*

"I am not going to tell you why, Dan Butxn."

Did either of them notice the wetting of his eyes?

"Why not?"

"Because talking about it with you would only embarrass me even further."

"Embarrass? Which way do you have that word pointed, Dot? Are you saying that you don't approve of the way you yourself are feeling?"

"Yes! That's right. I don't like my reactions. But I do feel justified in having them."

"Reactions? I may not be understanding you very well. Are they reactions to the way I've acted since the music began?"

"No, Dan. To the way you've acted for the past couple of centuries." Dot's words were sharp with rebuke and anger and conceivably a little cruel satire too.

Dan shook her head. Dot just stood there, fuming.

Dan shrugged gravely and silently started walking. When Dot didn't come along, too, Dan stopped walking but did not look behind her. Looking only straight ahead of her, she walked backward, retracing her steps, coming to a halt beside Dot. Still, he just stood there.

Dan stepped around in front of Dot to face him. "I could beg and weep and such, Dot. But it would not be for real."

"Then that is not good enough."

"Then we will have to do it standing up."

Dot slugged her. He had aimed for Dan's chin, but his fist struck her on the collarbone. Crack!

• • • • •

She expected something to be waiting for her on her machine the next morning, something like "You have observed the classic symptoms, haven't you? And who has shown them to you? It's been all males, hasn't it? Only men. So far. Ha-ha! So far." *Nix.* Nothing was waiting on her machine. *Scratch.* No ghastly ultimatums were found scribbled on the outside of her office door. *Squat.* Nothing was turned upside down inside the room. Everything was exactly as she had left it. *But maybe that's the message. "It's you. You get to make the choices. You control your life. It's all what you make it, girlie. It's all up to you." Yep, people have been repeating dribble like that forever, haven't they. But for how long do they believe it? A day and a night and maybe one more day? People can hold their breath for only so long. Sooner or later they find themselves dancing with the Other.*

• • • • •

"Take, for example, an old grey cone that finally falls from its tree, Milosh, not here but somewhere where cones and trees get big and old, old as in ancient. And if this cone crashes to the earth just a couple of feet from where I'm standing, exploding into a million pieces, where is the reality? For me, which is the event? The being of the cone in the tree for a long time? Its brief plunge downward? The instantaneous explosion? Or the being of the pieces on the ground for a long time?"

"Can't all of those things be the one event to remember, Dan?"

"I don't think so, Milo. Memory, with a capital *M*, will focus on one aspect or another and thereby define that as the event."

"Then you don't have a problem and, hence, your question is not reasonable, Dan. All you have to do is wait for your memory to tell you what is real."

Dan smiled tentatively. The smile soon blossomed into a toothy grin. "A very good answer. That's a very good answer."

"It was an accident."

"How can an answer like that be an accident?"

"It just popped into my head, Dan. Pop!"

Milosh Veerwright and Dan Butxn had not come into the filling center together. A casual observer might have said that it was only by chance they sat down at the same table at the same time. A second observer, one paying closer attention to the scene-- anyone peering in deeper than the dance of stick figures on the outermost surface of life would have found it exceedingly difficult to see chance functioning as the governing force.

"Pop!" repeated Dan with a not quite sardonic twist of her head.

Milosh glanced around the room. "So where is Terry--I mean Dot?"

Milosh's *faux pas* jerked Dan's head back to the table. She had been glancing around at people, too. She stared at Milosh's face, below his eyes, above his mouth.

"Please try to excuse me, Dan. I really didn't mean to mention him."

"Would that be Terry or Dot you didn't mean to mention?"

Milosh quickly nodded his head. "Terry."

Then Milosh shook his head. Was Dan's question changing shape in his mind? He nodded again, with moderate certainty. "Yeah, I meant to say his name. Dot's name. I did not mean to mention Terry."

"I don't know where Dot is. But you needn't bother to look around here for him. He has never been in this building and is not likely to ever enter it. Most likely he is up in his studio or out on the lawn somewhere there close by eating his lunch."

"Oh."

"May I ask, Milosh, why you asked where Dot is?"

"Of course you can ask. It wouldn't be right to not let you ask."

"But you don't have an answer? Is that it?"

"It's not that I don't have an answer..." Milosh wanted to look at something other than Dan's face, but he didn't find a danged thing. "It's just that I don't have any special reason. I just thought I would ask."

"The question just popped into your head?"

"Don't be mean to me, Dan. I meant no harm."

They hadn't forgotten about their food. Both of them had been taking bites every so often. They finished eating at the same time and bussed their dishes. "If you are heading back to our building, Dan, can I walk along with you?"

But what about Willa? My not observing the classic symptoms during my last meetings with her does not mean that Willamette Washingstone wasn't jealous, too. No sirree bob. While bravely telling me with beautiful composure that bitterness is unbecoming on anybody, she could well have been totally blasted and bitter about Dot leaving her.

Willa had called Dan a simple woman.

-13-

ROOM BREAKS

He's not moving out of my way. She had plainly asked him if she could come in. *Is he aware he has parted his lips to show his teeth like a dangerous dog?*

Dot stood flatfooted with his knees locked and his feet wide apart in the studio doorway, defiantly not stepping back to let Dan in. His fingers tapped the same tense, monotonous tune on both of his hipbones. His face drew up even tighter, and he let out a low, mean, affrontive snarl. "If you allow me the space I need!" And after he had swallowed up half the air of the doorway with one huge breath, he delivered a second, nastier if shorter snarl. "Now and forevermore!"

What? Dan pressed her palms to her temples. *I can see that Dot is very upset; I can understand that he might reply violently, pitilessly to my harmless question; but what he actually said hits me as upside-down--no, not upside-down, reversed.* Yes, reversed. Dot had said just the opposite of what Dan would have expected him to say if Dan had permitted herself to expect anything. *So what should I say back to him?* Should she play along? Dan had not seen Dot since their altercation outside the club. "What kind of space?" she asked in a pinched voice. She lowered her hands from her temples but quickly clasped them behind her waist. "And how much are you going to need?"

"The kind of space where a person can do something!" Dot's sentence fragments grew fiercer and louder and more daunting the longer that Dan stood there facing him. "Anything at all! Anything that seems appropriate to him! Without the shadow of someone else weighing him down!"

Without the shadow of someone else weighing him down? How can two people who are standing close together not cast shadows on one another? Dan squeezed her butt muscles together. This produced a fleeting vision of Dot's penis. "What if this person and the someone-else are in physical proximity?" Dot appeared to Dan to be even hotter than he had been when he hit her out in front of The Epiphany of the Puffed Up.

"Yes!" he railed. "Even then!" And he grew still hotter. "Even if they have their arms around each other!"

Dan aimed a conciliatory smile at Dot's burning eyes, but the fire in those eyes only flamed higher. Dan immediately shifted her smile to Dot's ear. "It seems to me, Dot, that for the someone-else to never cast a shadow on this person, the someone-else would have to be either dead or without a soul or would have to be content to be totally ignored, which implies an ignoring in return, or at least a looking upon the person not wanting to be shadowed as if that person were far, far away." Somewhere in there Dan had lost track of which of the two, the person not shadowing or the person not wanting to be shadowed, was supposed to be her and which one Dot.

Slowly. Wrapping. His hand around the doorknob, Dot answered one scary word at a time. "Not…all…shadows…weigh…people…down!"

Dan watched the muscles tightening in Dot's arm. Twisting her own arm behind her back, twisting it till it ached, she made a show of coolly scratching the back of her head with her other hand. *Seems he's squeezing that knob pretty darny hard.*

Dot refused to glance down at his arm to see what Dan was looking at.

Dan did not respond.

Dot continued with what he was saying. He spoke somewhat softer, but the softening of his voice did not make his voice any less emphatic or one bit less hair-raising. "Some shadows are neutral! Some, in fact, have lift!"

Dan allowed her eyes to float slowly up Dot's body from his forearm. There was no fear now in her eyes, not a trace. "*Lifting Shadows* sounds like the name of a romantic outdoorsy song from yesteryear."

"Are you skirting the subject?"

"Of course not, Dot. I only wanted to not miss sharing a musical experience with you."

That was the wrong thing for Dan to say. Very calmly Dot instructed her, "You are going to find trouble if you keep looking for it." He slammed the door against her nose. And he closed and locked the door when she stepped back in pain.

In that pain Dan saw her office machine. The machine was displaying a title page:

The Transmigration of Souls
by Harpsichordo Deald.

· · · · ·

Dandelion did her dishes. She washed and dried them herself, by hand. She waxed the kitchen floor, washed the bedclothes, dusted everything in the house, then sat down on the couch under the family portrait to look out her front window at the window across the way, Dot's front window. No big white card stood in that window. No lights were on in Dot's house, and Dan had not seen him coming or going all evening.

Dan did not get up from the couch. She did not go on about her life. She remained there, hour after hour, not moving, not budging one inch. All night long she sat as still as death on the couch, staring out her window at the other window. Early the following morning, she stood up like a zombie and left the room. She took a shower, got dressed and walked in a daze to work. There was a message on her machine. This time there really was a message waiting for her, a *message* message, an official request that she contact Security regarding the death of Dot Sett.

Bing!

· · · · ·

Bing!

She petitioned for Willa's studio. When asked why she wanted a space like that when she already had a perfectly workable office, Dan replied that she was also an artist and that this moment, right now, was as good a time as any to let that be known. The clerk, a bored but active fellow, did not know Dan or Dot or Willa or that their lives had intermingled. He searched the records for a minute or so, then said that Dan would have to pay for the studio herself, since the space was not necessary for her salaried job. And could she afford the extra cost? Dan answered yes, she had no expensive habits and could easily deal with the extra cost of the studio.

Her petition cleared all the hurdles in less than two days. Her copy-to-keep of her original application even had a green OK from Security *stamped* on it.

Key in hand, Dan entered the building in an exceptional clarity of mind. Climbing the stairs, she remembered exactly how the studio had looked to her the time she went up to see Willa after Willa had given up the studio and left the area. *Empty. Except for the tables and stools and the bed in the corner. A thousand years could have passed since anybody had been in the room.* Not so. Not this time. All signs of Dot and his work were right where he had left them. The smells were there, too; they were everywhere. The room looked and smelled and felt just as if Dot Sett were sitting at his easel painting. The effect was overwhelming. Dan had to sit down before she fell down. *Dot's stool.* Sitting on Dot's stool, she could see Dot's easel. On the easel stood his last canvas, unfinished forever. Dan figured the painting was--would have been another in his most recent series, portraits of people in settings they chose themselves. This painting was not of someone's face, however; it showed the back of a naked man, from about his knees to well above his head. The all orange man seemed to be looking up at something, perhaps at the broad eaves of the dark brown building nearby. In the distance: a green sky, blue grass, a light purple woman walking toward the man. Although the woman is faceless because she is still too far away to be clearly seen, it might well be that she is smiling. Painters prefer to have sinks in their workspaces, for obvious reasons. A reason that might not be so obvious is that art severely distorts time and space and memory, and when the artist's sense of reality and/or possibilities gets all messed up beyond her or his endurance, often that painter will have to puke. Dan did her first throwing up in the sink.

· · · · ·

That is the last stroke. That's the next to last stroke. There is the second to last, and there's the third. That's the fourth to last stroke; that's the fifth, and that the sixth.

Having sat behind Dot for endless hours watching him paint, Dan felt confident that she could identify the last brush strokes he had made on his last, unfinished painting. *But! Are the last seven brush strokes equivalent to the last seven words said or to the last seven sentences said? And said by whom? The woman in the painting? The orange man? Or by the painter himself? Then again, maybe the strokes and the paint have absolutely nothing to do with words.* Didn't Dot talk to Dan once about his unsuccessful attempt to write? *Besides, these are his last strokes, not his final or concluding strokes.*

Dan wrote with a pencil on the edge of the

canvas, along the stretcher bar: "The number seven. Seven times seven. The word forty-nine. Not spoken aloud. Heard internally." She added her initials and the date of Dot Sett's death, then filed away the painting in the tall cabinet attached to the wall near the studio's bed.

Seven days passed. Sleep, eat, work, paint. That is all Dan did the first week she had the studio, spending as many hours painting as she spent on the other three activities combined. At the end of a week she had to make some admissions to herself. *Painting is more difficult than it looks from the outside. It takes more than talent, much more; and it cannot in any way be described with words. Self-confidence, attention, avoiding the right-wrong trap, searching below the surface, primal understanding, beauty, synthesis, practice, mastery, stamina, relevance--the standard art-words/art-ideas. Though they are often repeated, they don't work. When it comes down to actually applying the paint, the words have no meaning/ the ideas fall flat. Phflat! Rules don't work either. Any kind of rules. On and on like that to no avail. A ton of motivation is insufficient. According to Dot, painting is simple: the hand applies the paint while the mind watches. "That is all there is to it," he once said.*

More important than all the admissions to herself was Dan's grasping how she might go about restructuring herself--her expectations, her attitude, her approach--to fit the reality of the discipline.

More important even than that was Dan's grasping, finally and totally, that she had never been Koben Gissing Quintus, the painter portrayed in that play Terry had taken her to see. This knowledge-without-words came to Dan in the middle of the night, during a long painting session, while she was adrift in a sustained period of under-thinking, a state in which "the mind watches." Had Dan ever been Wilkan Xeniat, the playwright? No, probably not him either, judging solely from the view of life presented in Xeniat's play about Quintus.

Neither was she Dot Sett. Nor Willa Washingstone. Nor Terry. She was no one but herself, a small pale purple spot of color in a vast nonphysical universe. She had no friends, no relatives, no groups to join, no home to return to, no town to be from, no country to feel good or bad about, no world to be rooted to. She was Dan Butxn, the dreamer who rose from the sand and rocks to see the wind, a human with no where to go.

A WHITE TWIRLING SCINCOID SHAPE

"Tell me, am I sad or am I glad? Am I morose or filled with bliss?" Sounding more pompous than perplexed, the speaker, our own Dandelion Butxn, her face wooden with humorlessness, paused to take a sip of her water and then to dutifully return her water glass to its ring on the table. She let go of the glass. She stared at the glass. She raised her hand above her head in a gesture frequently used either to draw attention to oneself or to interrupt someone else, or both. "But tell me first, is there any measurable difference anywise between these four states of mind?"

Milosh Veerwright licked his lips. He licked his top lip, licked his bottom lip as he leaned back his head to look unwaveringly (at nothing) well above Dan's head. "First." He said that one word, then waited. He waited composedly, as if he had intended the word to be heard as a complete and meaningful sentence packed with elaborate innuendoes. Then his loyal nose pulled his bold face upright, and he held his head positively erect. "Sad, glad, morose, and blissful are four distinct moods, Dan." He grinned at Dan, he didn't, he grinned again. "So, yes, they are very different; there are any number of measurable differences between them." Milosh's eyes swung deep into one corner of their sockets and stayed there while he said another one word sentence. "Next." His eyes then swayed like empty tree swings over to the opposite corner of their sockets, where they remained for only a second before returning to their center positions to examine Dan's face, which still would be classified by most passersby as expressionless, even though Dan's face and eyes had lost some small amount of their stiffness. "Backing up to your initial question, Dan, it is difficult to say, yet I would say that you look more glad than sad. But only just slightly more glad than sad." Milosh helpfully nodded his head at Dan across the table. "And while you're not morose--this is in answer to your second question--you sure don't appear to be full of bliss." He helpfully shook his head at her. "And..."

Dan didn't smile, didn't frown. *Am I indifferent to what's being said here, even though I began this conversation myself?* "And what, Milosh?"

"You certainly sounded pontifical, Dan."

"When?"

"When you up and said, like a bolt from heaven, 'Tell me, am I sad or am I glad? Am I morose or filled with bliss?'"

Milosh's imitation of the way Dan had said those two sentences startled Dan. But Dan asked anyway, as if she hadn't recognized herself in Milosh's performance, which she had, "Did I really sound over inflated, rather than, say, slapstickish?"

"Slapstickish?"

"Well, you know, Milosh." *No, I am not indifferent. Or mostly not. On the other hand, am I particularly interested? No. To some extent, no. But I must say yes too. Up under my new mask, yes, I am interested in what Milosh thinks. A little bit.*

"Over inflated, Dan." Milosh openly sighed.

"Yes. Really. Unduly overly inflated."

Milosh's head then rolled to the side till it crumpled his earlobe on the point of his shoulder. "And you sound only a little less so right now," he told Dan.

I am seeing Milosh's words turned sideways coming out of his sideways mouth. "That's how I sound, Milo?"

"That's how you sound." With a smack of his lips, Milosh raised his head from his shoulder.

"Do I?

"You do, Dan."

"In that case I do certainly need to critically analyze my sense of my importance." *Kidding aside, do I?*

"Oh, you are plenty important, Dan, especially to me. But people don't enjoy other people sounding self-important."

"And I do?" *Haven't we just about worn out this subject?*

"You did."

"I *did?*"

"Yes, you *did.*"

Escalating another small bite of food to his mouth, Milosh abruptly cocked his eyes the way someone might if they had just been hit by a sharp pain in their back. "I think you're spending too much time alone up in your hideout, Dan." The quake in Milosh's voice when he labeled Dan's studio a hideout should not be heard as an indication that he was losing his budding intellectual self-assurance. "You work all day and you paint all night."

It dawned on Dan that she had never said even

one word to Milosh about the metal rods he gave her. The two smooth monads from him still lay side by side between the two tokens of sexual love from Dot, in the box from Dot in a cupboard in Dan's kitchen. *What should I do with those things? Start a dead file and an alive file? If I don't do that and I do leave all four rods in that box, a more logical arrangement for them would be for me to move both of the dead ones to the right end and move the two live ones to the left end, with the single unused slot left empty between the two sets of two.* "Painting is not 'time alone,' Milosh." *How does he know I paint all night?* "It is more like a period of ultracommunication."

Milosh laid down his fork and wiped his hands on the napkin in his lap. "Communication with whom or what?"

Dan stared at the back of someone's head, a woman at another table. "I guess that depends on what the painter defines as her or his field of interest."

"And you, Dan? What is your definition?"

Dan didn't like the question. But she thought about it awhile and decided she would answer. She didn't know what she would answer until she heard her own words. Her words were edged by her petty irritation. "I have no idea, Milosh. The nonphysical universe, I guess. I am yet to define myself."

"The nonphysical universe is a big big subject."

This time Dan responded immediately. "Yes. It is. And it's as wide open to exploration today as it has ever been."

"Which probably means that in the long run, Dan, exploring it is a waste of time."

"Breathing is a waste of time, Milo."

"Hi!" Milosh dropped his chin to his chest and gazed through his eyebrows at Dan. "I read those very words on one of the bulletin boards this morning."

"So did I. And I've seen the same saying in records two hundred years old," claimed Dan in a jagged voice. "I wasn't trying to sound original." She used her hand to knead the back of her neck.

"But you are serious about this new painting interest of yours. Right?"

"Oh, I think so." Dan deposited a major forkful of food in her mouth. *So he still considers my involvement with painting to be something new.* "I am somewhat bothered"--*stopping mid sentence to finish my chewing*--"by the fact that I was not drawn to art earlier. I ask myself if painting will prove to be a whim that will up and disappear when I reach a certain level of proficiency."

"Is your need to paint tied to your memories of Dot?"

"No! Sorry!" Dan all of a sudden sounded more than a little testy. "If you can, try looking back to the other end of my relationship with him, the beginning. You might see there, as I do, that a newfound desire to try my hand at art was the very energy that drew Dot into my life. My desire to paint made Dot materialize as if out of nothing."

"I was under the impression at that time that you were desiring me, Dan."

"That is a whole different subject."

"Different from what?"

"From art."

"Aren't we talking about Dot?"

"No, I think you got lost, Milosh." Dan faked an expansive grin. It was a bad fake. "We were talking about my *new* interest in painting."

"Right. I did lose my way there."

Dan's eyes suddenly opened wider. Her head raised higher. *Something has changed!* She glanced all around the immediate area. Not spotting anything unusual, she looked/stared at Milosh, forcing him to avert his eyes. *Milo looks taller.* This was the first lunch period in quite some time that Dan and Milosh shared a table. *Is that what's different? Could he have put on some weight in his butt so that he sits taller on his chair now? No, when I followed him in here not many minutes ago, his rear looked as firmly packed as ever. No new padding pounds there. Oops! Desire! Desire strikes again!* This variety of desire, this sudden and unexpected sexual desire, Dan had thoroughly familiarized herself with long before art ever touched her shores. Checking out the situation down in her lap, checking with a hidden hand that is, Dan smiled. Milosh smiled, too. *Why did Milo start smiling? He has no way of knowing what I'm smiling a real smile about.* Dan nearly giggled out loud. *Not unless he has a secret supertuned sense of smell.* Dan Butxn had never stopped lunching regularly in the filling center, not even during that gone period when Dot Sett was refusing her every invitation to join her there. *Jill never eats here, either. But Milosh does. Roy does. I do. A whole lot of people do. Diane does. And it hasn't killed them. --Say! Speaking of Roy Kee and Diane Potter.*

"Dan." Roy walked right up to Dan to stand

with his hand on her shoulder and with the changeable region below his navel pressed firmly against her arm, providing Dan with another good reason or three for not standing up to offer him a chair.

"Yes, Roy?"

"Diane has something she wants to talk to you about."

"Something she wants to talk to me about? Or something you want her to talk to me about?"

"Both," said Diane. She strode around Dan and Roy to the next side of the table. She pulled out the chair that was waiting there. "May I?"

"Yes," said Milosh on her left.

"Of course," said Dan on her right.

Roy took the remaining chair, across from Diane. He signaled to her with his hand, a tiny wave. "OK. Why don't you start."

Diane--a bit tall and a bit skinny with light blue eyes that, once you get used to their strangeness, contrast beautifully with her dark skin and pale freckles--inclined her head to Milosh and said, "It won't hurt our feelings if you need to leave."

Milosh raised and lowered his chest in a sigh, not an evanescent or secluded sigh but a sigh fully open to examination by the public, his second such sigh while sitting with Dan this time at this table. "Would it be all right if I stay?"

"I wish you would, Milosh." Diane could turn charming at the right moment.

Milosh reached out his hand and tapped her on the back of her hand. "Then I will."

Diane thanked him.

"This will sound peculiar to you two, for sure," she said apologetically, with a nod to Dan and a deeper nod to Milosh. "And it may strike you as egotistical, although I certainly hope it doesn't."

"Dan's a big girl now," said Roy reassuringly. And impatiently. "I'm sure Milosh has known a few people with problems, too."

"I sincerely believed that people are reasonable. All people." Diane had started her story. "No matter how unlike mine a person's philosophy was, I always saw that person as reasonable." She stared down at her hand, the one that Milosh had touched, while Milosh's hands sank to his lap. "I believed that everyone," Diane said, "not only can but does see, consider, decide, and act reasonably. Obviously," she added with a flash of humor, "to maintain such a belief I had to accept every possible style of reasoning."

She looked up at Dan, at Dan's eyes. Dan returned her look. Diane's voice dropped, and she spoke at just above a whisper. Even so, everyone at the table could clearly hear her every word. "Whenever I by chance ventured into a weird, dangerous scene, where violence was brewing and lives were hanging by threads, etc., the danger promptly dissolved." Diane straightened her back and lifted her head. She looked yet into Dan's eyes. "The ugly, mean, cruel thugs became merely aggressive game-players, just women and men, just people like everyone else."

Dan wiped her front teeth with her tongue. "But now?" she asked, peering into Diane's eyes.

"Something has changed?"

Diane knotted her hands together on the table. "My energy level is dropping, dropping too low too fast. And with my energy output steadily diminishing, I fear that my effect on people will soon undergo a drastic change, if this change hasn't already begun. I fear that weird scenes will no longer warp to fit my needs, that they will no longer turn soft and fun and sexy the second I appear. I am afraid violence won't immediately dissolve in the water of my presence."

Milosh had fixed his eyes on his hands in his lap. Dan pressed the side of her index finger against the tip of her nose.

"And she blames the lowering of her energy on me," said Roy. "Knowing me is putting her in jeopardy, she thinks."

Dan coughed. "You were right, Diane. It strikes me as--it struck me as egotistical." Dan crossed her arms over her chest. "I assume, however, that it sounded that way to me only because of the manner in which you presented it. If you had described the same problem differently, my initial reaction might have been something else."

"You're being kind, Dan?"

"Perhaps. But not necessarily, Diane."

Milosh's eyes jerked up from his lap when Dan said his name. "Yes, Dan?"

"Did you feel all funny and sexy the moment Diane 'appeared'?"

Milosh repositioned himself on his chair, wiggling his firm butt back and forth as if he were polishing the seat. "I did feel like that, yes--I did feel a change in that direction. But, truthfully, I was already feeling sexy from being here with you."

Roy shot his eyes to the ceiling--for effect, not to look at something up there. "Looks to me like everyone at this table is just plain horny."

He lowered his eyes from the ceiling and leaned a bit toward Milosh to smilingly scrutinize him. "I myself don't experience the effect that Diane says she has on everyone else, including perfect strangers." Rolling his face and shoulders away from Milosh and toward Dan, Roy reached out his arm to lay the palm of his hand fondly against the side of Dan's neck. "But I do feel something of that sort every time I get close to this one here."

Roy's trying to make trouble, thought Dan and Diane and Milosh.

When Roy lifted his hand from Dan's neck, Dan promptly fell forward to plant her elbows on the table. "Please allow me to continue with what I was saying a minute ago." She looked in turn at each of the three waiting faces. "I have further considered my impressions."

Addressing Diane, Dan said, "You say that there was an immediate calming of the troubled waters whenever you stepped into certain risky scenes. And you seemed to be saying to me, here, today, that this *calming* was an effect of your personal energy on the world-at-large. If you had presented this *calming* to me as a tendency of yours to quickly reinterpret what's going on whenever you're confronted with a potentially dangerous situation--in other words, if you had treated this whatever-it-is as something that the world did to you, instead of something that you did to the world, I think I would have soon got some kind of hold on your problem. As it is now, I don't know if I can allow myself even to hope to understand."

"That sounds like rejection, Dan. Just a minute or two ago you were assuming that my manner--and nothing but my manner--had negatively influenced your ability to sympathize with me. Now, after Milosh told you that he himself felt what I described, and had felt it before I described it, you don't even want to understand."

"It's not true that I don't want to understand, Diane. But if you meant for me to hear what you said as literally true and not as merely a colorful way of describing something that is hard to talk about..."

"I did. I was being entirely literal."

"Then I can't even hope to understand. Hero complexes are outside my sphere."

Milosh nearly choked. "Oh! Shame on you, Dan!"

Dan's face hardened even harder than the wood of humorlessness. She fell back against the back of her chair as Milosh glared scornfully over the table at her. Her arms hung straight down from her shoulders.

Squinting dark daggers at Dan, Milosh demanded that she recall the conversation they were having shortly before Diane and Roy came over to their table. "You said then that you want to explore the nonphysical universe. Isn't what Diane just described a part of that universe? There was no need for you to reduce her ordeal to delusion so quickly. No need whatsoever!"

Roy disagreed, but before he could say his first word Milosh spoke again, scolding Dan in the most intense voice she had ever heard come from his mouth. "And remember how you said that your desire made a man materialize out of thin air!"

Roy tried again. "Yes, Milosh, there was a need--"

Milosh wasn't finished with Dan; pealing his words right over the top of Roy's, he said vehemently, "And you told me that an artist has to find his or her own definition! Didn't you, Dan? It's not just artists-- every woman, man, and pig in the sky defines him- or herself. Let Diane define herself!"

Well, that ended that conversation. Roy and Diane watched Milosh and Dan finish eating their food. From that day on, Dan followed Dot's example: she left the filling center that noon and never again as much as pushed open a door into the place.

• • • • •

"Now, regarding the death of Dot Sett, I must tell you that--"

Dan's head lurched up from her pillow. *Who?* She pushed herself up on one arm. *Who said that?* She sat up. She sat bolt upright on her bed and anxiously scoured the dark room with her eyes.

Her hurried hunt ended on a chair pushed

against the wall. Something black and massive hung over the back of the chair--*my shirt from yesterday?*--but, no, not one villain sat on the seat smiling sadistically at her. *No one.* No one but Dan was anywhere in the room. *Not a shadowy soul.* Dan was as alone as one can get. *Terry used to talk about shadowy souls.*

"The only alchemy here is realism."

This time Dan didn't have to wonder who had spoken. This time she recognized the voice and knew where it was coming from. She had spent several hours that afternoon reading old news files, and for an hour or so she had had the machine-read turned on. The voice in the night was the default voice on her machine at work. The voice was stuck in her head.

Getting up. Getting out of bed, getting minimally dressed to wander outside to shuffle across the dark, silent lane to sit in the dim on Dot's front step. As Dan leaned back against the front door of the house, a thump came from behind her, from inside the house. *That's...That's not in my head! Dot's alive!* Dan jumped to her feet and high-stepped once, twice over some luminous flowering plants to look in the front window. The curtain was drawn. *That's not normal!* She rushed back to the door and pressed her ear against the wood. Not one sound came from the other side of the door, nary a sound for the next half hour. Fortunately, Dan spotted Gawkabit Howlsey strolling up the lane playing peekaboo with an invisible baby before Howlsey spotted Dan pushed against the door of an unoccupied house in the middle of the night. *That thump must have been a thermal pop.* By the time Dan got back to her bedroom, Dot was already in bed and asleep. Dan carefully didn't wake him as she crawled in behind him. But she cried so voluminously that he dissolved in the wet spot.

· · · · ·

Black sheep, white sheep, blue sheep, green sheep, pink. A two hundred year old bleat passed from sheep to sheep until it reached the here-and-now. "Baa!"

"Am I in your way, sir? Or madam, as the case may be." Dan had left her house early one morning and headed due south, traveling straight as an arrow's flight until the sierra grew wide and gradually wider on the horizon and she had to choose one peak from the many and direct her strides toward it. The peak that she picked is the roughest looking mountain of the bunch, the big brown pyramid of rugged rock more or less at the center of the range of mountains. She had reached the sierra--the mountains weren't all nicely lined up the way they looked from a distance--and was climbing the rocky brown pyramid when she encountered a pinkish grey sheep. The lone sheep was standing blocking the path. The rest of the flock had hurried away the moment that Dan appeared. Yes, there was a path, probably primarily an animal path. Had there not been a path, Dan would have had an extremely hard and slow time finding her way over and around and between the colossal boulders that fairly covered the steep slope.

The pink sheep spun away from Dan and

scurried up the path. "Lead on, James!" Dan followed along behind. She wasn't as fast on her feet as the sheep, not at this altitude; so the woolly had to stop every so often to let her catch up.

They hadn't reached the pointy top of the pyramid but were getting fairly close to it when the path crossed a solitary patch of bare earth. It was a flattish--meaning of gentler slope--meager piece of ground with no rocks (to speak of) much bigger than Dan's fist lying about. Near the upper edge of this clearing stood a picket fence outlining a not very large rectangle of ground. Many, if not most, of the fence's pickets were either broken or missing. The pickets and posts may have been painted white at one time. Inside the fence was a little graveyard, six or seven old piles of stone. Two of the graves had faded wooden markers; the rest were unmarked, except one, a fresher pile of rocks with a newer marker. Cut into that marker were these words: "Been waiting for ya, Lady D."

D for Death, or D for Dan?

No loving flowers lay on any of the graves. The air and the stony earth were so very dry that a bouquet of flowers would have lasted not five minutes on a grave, if by some trick the bouquet had made the trip up the hill without shriveling to dust. *So what does the flock of sheep eat?*

Dan spotted something up under a huge, singular rock above the graveyard. It looked to be a canteen. She went up there to investigate. The pink sheep had disappeared. It was a canteen all right, shaded day and night by the rock. Stuffed between the bottle and its holey cloth cover was a folded piece of paper, brittle and yellowed till it was nearly the brown of the rock it hid beneath.

Carefully opening up the paper.

Scribbled in second-grade block letters: "Help yourself to the water, stranger. But leave the hardware right here."

Stale and tepid the water was. Packed with minerals through and through. It was genuine water though.

Not at all curious about what she might see looking on south from the very summit of the peak, Dan just scaled the rock that protected the canteen and sat herself down on the rock's highest point. Crossing her legs, she looked way out over the graveyard at the thin silver line that was Chuck. Dan stared at Chuck till the sun went down and the light faded. Dan had brought along a light jacket; otherwise she was dressed just as she would have been any other day. She had no food or water, other than what water was left in the canteen below, and no blanket. But the moon rose as a lean crescent with its horns turned up; the stars shone bright; and the breeze blowing uphill at her was nice and warm, until somewhere around midnight, at which time the refrigeration unit kicked in. Dan shuddered and shook for an hour until her body adapted. She didn't change either her posture or her place on the rock all night long.

Sitting facing north as she was, the sun came up on her right. A blackhawk came swooping around the mountain. The bird changed course abruptly and lifted its tail to show Dan an asshole.

"Thank you, madam. Or sir, as the case may be."

Enough! She had had plenty of this woman-on-the-mountain stuff. Dan went home.

• • • • •

The day had descended on past twilight to the hushed last minutes of dusk. Worn out from her long walk and the two days without sleep, Dan dug out her keys and unlocked the front door of her house. *Glad to be back home?* She was stepping in through the doorway when she barely caught sight of the dark figure of someone slinking from her bedroom to the kitchen. As quietly as she could, Dan closed the door behind her. But just then she heard the back door close. She rushed straight across her house to a window that looks out the back. And saw no one out there in the gloaming. Quick, she said. Through the kitchen she skipped and on out the back door, rapidly looking this way and that, distinguishing no sign of life on the common area behind her house. No hint, no scent. No hint of *human* life, that is. The trees and flowers, of course, were busily closing up shop for the day, so to speak; and a few flying guys were romping in the air above Dan's back door. But no two-armed, two-legged being was seen running off into what little glow remained of the day. Was it a real person that Dan had seen skulking in her house, or was it someone/something that Dan's need had forced up into existence? What should she think about the kitchen door being unlocked? She turned on every light in the house and looked and saw nothing out of place and then searched more carefully and found not one single piece of evidence that anyone had been in her house since she left it the morning before.

· · · · ·

"Never say never," said the machine.

Dan closed the door, set down her things, and went over to see why her machine was talking without being told to. Dan very rarely allowed it to talk; she related to the machine as a visual tool, only turning on the voice when she was tired of reading long dreary text herself.

Dan spent four or five or ten minutes systematically examining the machine. Still, at the close of her examination she had no idea why or how the machine had greeted her with that tired three-worder as she came in her office door. She could no more explain the machine's behavior this morning than she could explain the fleeing figure in her house the night before. Would she have to be prepared for an unpleasant surprise every time she entered a room from now on?

"SOFT FLOWERY VOICE, probably masculine, no suggestiveness."

Voice selection number five sounded like the least objectionable alternative to the preset voice. The preset voice, the machine's default voice, was acutely getting on Dan's nerves.

No! A better thought! Yes! Disconnect the sound altogether. She was not thinking she should turn off the sound, which is easy enough to do; she was thinking she should *disconnect* the sound, which takes a bit more time. She got right to work.

She accomplished the disconnection by opening up the cabinet and completely removing the speakers. She gathered up those speakers and the remote speakers from about the room and packed them all down the hall to the big garbage can. Dan was aware that the trash in the can was routinely inspected. Someone would discover the speakers for sure. But she didn't care. She just wanted the machine permanently mute.

Glorious music would no longer fill her office and sweep her away. She knew that. She was sad.

15

VERY EDGES HAVE NO THICKNESS

The sun is fine and real and basic, she said, but I love the night. She stopped her already slow walking and sat down on the lane to concentrate on feeling the night. Finding no way to actually feel it, the night itself, not the air around her, etc., she wondered if the night is a man, a man for her to love but a lover who cannot be touched because he has no center, like the sun is the center of the day, a man like one of the characters in that early play by Wilkan Xeniat: *Beautiful Pieces Have No Quotable Parts*, the man who thought he was always wrong, wrong about everything, while everyone around him saw him as strikingly beautiful. Or is the night the mind of a woman? Holding that thought for a moment, Dan could see the warm daytime as a dreaming man and the cool night as a wide-eyed hunting woman.

She cups her hands behind her head the way Dot used to do and lies back on her back on the pavement. She looks up at the stars. Where is she? *Stretched out on my back on a public walkway under the night sky.* Yes, there she is. Yet she's not there, not just, not only there. She is someplace else at the same time, somewhere far away from her studio and house and office. Looking up at the stars, she is also looking down on a parched land. As real and present as the walkway beneath her back is the desert below her bosom. *Far below my bosom!* She's flying, soaring over sand and rocks and dark, secret bushes. *It's nighttime here too.* She rolls to her left and dives down to skim along just above the bottom of a dry gorge. Suddenly she swoops way up, higher and higher, up over the edge of a tall cliff to moonlit rock plates and scattered gnarled conifers. *Questions are a waste of eternal time.*

Tall Dog came trotting up the lane. The dog stopped beside Dan and looked down at Dan's face, which was looking up at her face. The dog stretched out her dog-body close beside Dan's woman-body and laid her chin on her paws. *Is she a desert bat, too? Flying silent in the night?*

A great slow ache crept from Dan's toes toward her brain. *The planet will pull me from the sky. I will fold my wings and enter the earth.*

16

SMOKE AND RAT

Asleep in her chair, having come directly to the
office from her studio several hours early, between four-
thirty and five o'clock, for no particular reason, except
maybe to avoid seeing/meeting people, Dan is dreaming
that she is sitting right where she is in fact sitting, facing
her machine. But in the dream she is awake facing her
machine, which has somehow recovered its ability to
speak and is demanding in a minacious tone that Dan
answer one impossible question after another. The
machine is using the default voice that Dan found so
perturbing and is simultaneously flaunting the
unsolvable problems on its display, spelling them out in
bold red text laid over a rising cloud of blue smoke.
She, Dan, isn't faring well in this dream; she hasn't been
holding her own against her machine, not at all. But she
perks up at the machine's next question: "What exactly
is death?" Dan smiles in her sleep, for she knows the
answer. Dreaming that she is speaking crisply and
confidently, she says back to the machine that she has
considered the issue long and hard and she feels that
death is to life what night is to day, in that a life or a day
will always have a center, while death and night don't
ever have one; so, if lives and days are spent pointing at
their centers, death, like the night, must be a continual
not-pointing.

Dan didn't open her eyes right away. She wasn't
completely awake yet. She listened. *No daytime noises
leaking in from outside the building.* She wondered at this

and listened again. *No morning wind whistling against the skin of our bronze and blue pyramid.* Nor could she hear voices (or sounds of any kind from the other occupants of the building) filtering into the room through the walls, floor or ceiling. Fully awake now, though her eyes were still completely closed, Dan tried to focus her hearing on the giant motors that work around the clock to keep the tall structure habitable. She listened. *Not a hum.* No, she did not then give up her search for sound. She honed her already focused hearing, sharpening it as finely as she thought possible (for her), hoping to maybe hear the slow groans of the building itself. She listened. Did she hear the native sounds of the complex, multi-storied construction? Did she hear low cries crawling along the steel framework that surrounded her? No. *Nothing.* It was dead quiet in her office. *The silence in here is unnerving!* The first emotion that Dan could put a name to that morning was dread.

She opened her eyes. Dread for her own welfare? No, that's not it, she assured herself while staring at her machine's blank display. *Then what?* When she tried to get up from her chair, she found out what. There was a body lying on the floor right behind the chair. Waking up in a too quiet room, trying to get up from her chair, turning a bit to look behind her to see why the chair would not move, Dan discovered a red word floating between her mind's eye and someone's body on the floor. The crimson word was *suitability.* Try as she might, Dan could not replace *suitability* with a word more fitting to the situation she had just found herself in. And if she could not produce one picayunish word to replace one other word, how was she going to create a whole golden sentence that would frame the first event of the day and make it hold still in her head? She carefully got up from her chair without moving the chair. The body was a man. It was no one she knew, nobody she had ever seen before. *Suitability and effect on others, yet more dear, more distant.* That was not the golden sentence that Dan needed; but as those words came to her and she said them in her head, the red word faded from her vision.

Dan thought she had pushed her chair back against the body during her first attempt to stand up. Not so. One of the chair's rollers had stopped on a shoe fallen from the man's foot. Dan shoved the chair off to one side and out of the way. *Is he dead?* She kneeled beside his head. No, his eyes were closed but she discerned his soft breathing. He was lying on his side, half curled up. Dan touched the man's arm. He opened one eye and looked at her. He looked up at her face. He smiled to himself. The smile flitted away as his mouth formed a word. No audible sound was produced by his mouth; so Dan had to guess at the word. She thought he had said, "What?"

"Don't you think I ought to be the one asking that question?" said Dan from the gravel bottom of her voice.

The man smiled again. He smiled at her this time. But he said nothing.

Dan secretly glanced at her door. The office door was closed and looked to be locked, as she remembered leaving it after she came in.

He's going to stand up now! Dan jumped to her feet to help him.

The man had no problem at all getting up from the floor. There appeared to be nothing physically wrong with him. Dan pulled the spare chair over to him. The man looked at the chair but did not sit down. He slipped his bare foot gracefully into the loose shoe, then stepped over to the window, the one that opens, opened it and pushed his head out into the outside air. *Can he smell Chuck?* Once or twice Dan had thought that she smelled the river from the window.

What's that word? Dan bit the tip of her tongue. *Pretty.* The man was the prettiest person she had ever laid her eyes on. At least that's what Dan's memory told her right at that moment. Remembrances of appearances are not to be trusted, she decided and recited to herself. *He has an interesting derrière too. Linen slacks, sandals, short-sleeved print shirt. He could be as light as his clothes.*

The man turned around to face Dan but leaned back against the window jamb so that the very back of his head was outside the room. *Outside of the building.* "The name is Sprat," he said in a clear, stirring voice brimming with essential qualities. "Not like those little herrings called sprats. Like *spunky* and *rat* pressed together but leaving the slightest pause between the *p* and the *r.* Sp-rat."

"Sprat."

"That's it, Dan."

Dan's eyes blinked. "Oh! You already know my name?"

"Isn't that your name there?" The man pointed at the nameplate Jill Surfred Atnoon had given to Dan Butxn.

"It might be."

"If you don't know for sure, who does?"

"I'm working on that, Sprat."

"Ha! You figured it out: my name is easy to rhyme with."

Dan noticed she was rapidly adapting to the man's intricate voice. *Or is he adapting his voice to my sloppy hearing?* "Were you asleep there on the floor?"

"Not really asleep. Sort of. But you were asleep, Dan. I counted your long slow breaths until they turned into ocean waves and then into ballet dancers. Do you mind if I go ahead and call you Dan?"

"No…"

Dan scratched along her jawbone. Staring at the man's exposed throat, staring without quitting, she asked in a slightly higher than normal voice, "What besides *Dan* would you call me?"

"I don't understand."

"Would you prefer to address me as Dandelion? Or Danakil?"

The man waved his fingertips at his own chest. "You're trying to figure out who I am, aren't you?"

"Did you know Dot Sett?"

"Not personally."

"Do you know Willamette Washingstone?"

"Yes. Personally."

"Is she the reason you are here?"

"I think we are moving much too fast for this

early in the morning, Dan Butxn." The man took just one step away from the window and toward Dan. Dan had not looked away from the man's throat for some time now. The man watched Dan watching his throat as he asked, "How's about we find us some breakfast?"

"How'd you get in here?"

"I walked in behind you."

"Huh?"

"Deep in a daze you were, Dan."

The man wagged his head to loosen his hair. Dan seemed deep in another daze; so he explained. "I was waiting in the dark in the stairwell outside Willa's studio--Willa's/Dot's/Dan's studio--when you came out the door looking like a bird from another planet. Willa's eyes get all big and weird like that, too, after she's worked all night. I assumed you were Dan Butxn; you fit the description; so I followed you to this building and then up all those stairs. You unlocked that door over there and stepped in here and I followed you in and you turned back to lock the door. You sat down and promptly went to sleep. I checked the nameplate on your desk, then lay down behind you and waited. And listened to you breathe."

Dan stared yet at Sprat's throat. She did nothing else. She didn't move. She stared at him. Hear the shrill hum of her whirling brain.

"I'm still thinking about breakfast." Sprat waved his hand at Dan's eyes. "Am I going to have to carry you?"

The colorful idea of a lightweight man throwing a full-sized woman over his shoulder and packing her down flights of stairs in search of food woke Dan up. Dan stepped forward to stand exactly in front of the man. She laid one hand lightly on each of his shoulders and moved her face toward his face till their noses were within a hand's breadth of touching each other. Her eyes fixed on his eyes. "Did you come here meaning to do me harm?"

Sprat grinned like crazy. "Do you deserve to be harmed?"

These muscles…in his shoulders are quite firm. He's a solid person, like a rock. Like hickory. Dan let go of Sprat's shoulders to push her hands, fingertips first, deep into his armpits. His grin flickered. She ran her open hands down the sides of his chest to his waist. *Nothing. Just the short-sleeved shirt. Not even any underwear.*

"You can do that again if you want to, Dan."

Dan's hands slid around the small of the man's back until they met and overlapped over his backbone. The hands pushed Sprat toward Dan. He resisted. She backed off.

When Dan had taken back her hands, Sprat said, "Whew! What I've heard about you is nothing but true, Dan Butxn. You send out energy like a powerhouse. But silent energy. Unexpected, unsuspected power. You can play at my house any time you want."

"Where is your house?"

"No sooner do I compliment you than you get tricky. Is that nice?"

"I merely asked where you live. Is that *getting tricky?* If so, I need to inquire what kind of game we are playing."

"Breakfast."

"OK."

Sprat padded along beside Dan like a panther, descending the stairs in sandals as quietly as if he were barefoot. Dan had to keep glancing sidelong to check whether he had disappeared into the sidewall. *Yes, I am nervous.* Was Dan enjoying the strain? She couldn't tell for sure, but she thought that she was, yes. The pure physicalness of his existing beside her outweighed the unknown factor, the danger, for now.

Milosh was standing in the lobby with his hands in his back pockets looking right at them when they exited the stairwell. Diane was standing beside him but was looking the other way. *Diane and Milosh? Hmm.*

Sprat came unexpectedly to a standstill. Dan quickly stopped and was turning to face Sprat when Sprat waved his hand in a grand sweep at the big room. "This is why I'm here."

Dan saw only a big white question mark. *What is he gesturing at?* Then she focused on the walls and saw the paintings. *Ka-ka-boom!* The lobby had sprouted paintings. She almost recognized them. But not quite. No, she had never seen any of these paintings before.

"They're all from private collections. I hung this show last night, after everyone had left the building. Then I wandered over to your studio to wait for you."

They were hanging here when I came in this morning?

Neither the frowning Dan nor the smiling Sprat spoke for maybe half a minute.

"Sprat?"

"Yes? I'm right here."

"Did Willa ask you to put up these paintings?"

"That she did, Dan."

"Why here? Why in this building? Dot didn't even like this building."

"Willa wanted to surprise you. You! And she wanted me to be with you when you first saw the show."

Jumping her eyes from painting to painting, Dan shook her head. She felt severely confused and didn't know what to reply. She moved her lips without saying a word. She glanced at Sprat's pretty face just as he was distorting it into an eerie grin.

"Willa's going to love my description of how you took her surprise, Dan."

Dan felt severely confused and anxious. Dread had been the first emotion she clearly recognized after she woke up in her chair. *Dread for my own welfare?* She could no longer tell herself, no, that's not it. "Who are you?" Dan's voice trembled.

"A spunky rat had Willa Washingstone sit on his lap. I not only hang art; I kill or damage people for fun. As well as for profit. For Willa? I couldn't charge her a penny, now could I?"

Dan's head started shaking again. She stumbled and strode over to a painting. She examined it, shook her head some more, sidestepped to another painting, and to another. They were real: the strokes were right, the pigment mixes were right, and Dot had signed them all.

When Dan had examined every single painting, she returned to Sprat. She caught up his hand and

lightly but sincerely shook it. "Nice show, Spunky Rat."
She kissed him on the cheek. His hand was cool, his
cheek was warm.

Sprat's head dangled to the side. "You're not
still deathly afraid I'm here to hurt you?"

"Right."

What exactly did that mean, that "right"? If Dan
had meant it to say that she was no longer afraid of
Sprat, then it was simply not the truth, no matter how
easy it was for her to say.

What a silly look of doubt on Sprat's face.

Dan had no idea herself what she was saying
with her unpremeditated "right" answer, but she
avoided reflecting on it, telling herself she didn't have
the time right then to think her feelings through.
"Impressive it is, Sprat. And not just the display of
paintings--the whole jarring surprise you and Willa
engineered for me."

Sprat was minutely observing Dan's face and
eyes and didn't reply.

Dan turned away from him. She gazed off at
the farthest painting, which was also the largest painting.
*Deep reds that bleed to pinks and hard blackish blues that grey to
browns.* Dan snapped her fingers three times in rapid
succession. "Is my seeing the paintings the sole reason
for our coming downstairs, Sprat? Or do you still want
breakfast?"

"No, mademoiselle, it's not, because,
yes, mademoiselle, I do, two plates full."

• • • • •

What is he doing here with me anyway? Dan tried
hard to look more relaxed. *Nothing about him adds up. No
intelligible pattern of any kind is forming in my head. He still…
He still… He gives me the royal shakes is what he does!*

Sprat did something in his lap. "Well, can we or
can we not, Dan?"

"If you want to, we can go up there as soon as
we're through eating. That would be fine with me,
Sprat. But you can't have it both ways: either we go up
to my studio to see my paintings or you give me a head
start and then come up to Dot's studio to see the
paintings he left behind." Dan was talking to Sprat's
forehead, for Sprat was still looking down at something
in his lap. "His or mine," told Dan. "Not both, not in
the same place at the same time."

"I understand," said Sprat frankly.

*So what is he doing under the table? And how is he
going to pay for this meal?* Sprat carried no bag slung over
his shoulder, packed no pouch on his thin belt; and his
clothes had no pockets. Yet, over Dan's objections, he
had insisted he would pay for both of their breakfasts if
she would only lead him to a "nice" restaurant.

"Have you ever eaten here before, Dan Dan?"

Dan hesitated before answering. Sprat had
doubled her name. Dot had called her that once, too.
"Twice."

Sprat glanced up only briefly from his lap. "Did
you pick up the tab either time?"

"No, Sprat."

"So both times it wasn't really your idea to come here."

"That is correct."

"And this is the third time."

"That is correct." Dan worked the inside of her cheek with her tongue. *OK. What is he really wanting to know?*

"This place is maybe too deluxe for your tastes, Dan Butxn?"

Dan blew a harsh blast of air out her nose. Sprat's linty probing had irritated her. Her reply had a haughty flavor. "My story is not already complete. I'm not just putting in my time here."

Sprat's face came up, and his eyes zoomed in on Dan's eyes. Sprat's gaze was rock steady, with not the faintest suggestion of insecurity. He raised his shoulders till they nearly covered his ears. "Great! Great! But what does that mean?" He seemed thoroughly pleased with Dan's arrogant response. "No! Don't tell me! Please let me guess." Sprat's shoulders fell from his ears as he raised his hands from his lap to lay them one on either side of his plate, palms down flat on the cloth.

They're empty! His hands are empty!

Sprat watched Dan gaping at his hands. He then raised the two of his hands just three or four inches and immediately slapped them back down on the tabletop. The entire table shook. Nothing spilled, however. "You used *story* as another way of saying…what?" He cocked his head and rolled his eyes as if giving the puzzle a mighty struggle. "It's your ability to believe--no, to not believe--to not believe in people anymore--no, to believe--to believe you've never believed in human beings…since you were little…since you were a child…since you were a baby…since you were born--if you were born and haven't just always been here, Madam Foreverness."

"Gasp." Dan pressed one of her hands to her brow. "That was totally marvelous, completely perplexing, way beyond my feeble attempt at indistinctness."

"Thank you, Dan."

Sprat looked quite amused when he saw Dan twirling a finger in her right ear much too intensely.

"What's your last name?" Dan glared at the finger she had used on her ear. "And don't tell me something like Foreverness or Nowness."

"Got me no last name. Got me just one tag. Sprat. That's it. That's all there is. All there ever was, too."

"Do you wear underpants?"

"Certainly, Dan."

"Not an undershirt."

"No. Right. Correct. Not a undershirt. Not today. Sometimes. Not today."

"Do you paint yourself?"

Sprat smirked. "No, I never use makeup, Dan."

"That's not what I meant. I wasn't talking about makeup. Paint!"

"I know, bonehead. No, I don't paint. People like Dot paint. His paintings make it all right--or almost all right--that we puny earthites cannot know anything indubitably. We can never be certain of anything. His paintings say that that's the way it is and that's the way it ought to be."

Dan didn't know if she agreed with Sprat's interpretation of Dot's paintings, but she was not in any mood to discuss the matter. "Dot once told me that I need not ever waste my time learning to paint."

"But you did."

"*Did* what?" demanded a somewhat surly Dan. "Did learn or did waste my time?"

Suddenly Sprat's hands sprang straight up from the tablecloth with both his thumbs reaching for the ceiling and both his index fingers aimed point-blank at Dan's eyes. "Dan did learn! Dan did learn!"

Bang! Bang! Dan did shiver.

Sprat did guffaw.

Dan quickly crooked her eyes away from the table. She was blushing and was thankful she hadn't wet her pants or something. Sprat had really startled her. She rubbed her nose-mouth-chin with the palm of her hand. In a narrow voice she said, "Perhaps I am starting to learn, Sprat. Maybe. But already I've had to change the way I look at many things."

Sprat subdued his devilish look. "Can you give me a quick example?"

To her own surprise, yes, Dan could. "Paint is silent the same way that knowledge is silent."

The waiter approached the table. Sprat immediately erased all expression from his face. He picked up his fork and selected some food from his plate. "I'll think about that, Dan."

The waiter couldn't help staring at Sprat. Dan watched the waiter. The immaculately dressed fellow all but shed a tear of happiness/gratitude at being allowed to come so near to Sprat. The waiter did not collapse in ecstasy, and he managed to refill their water glasses before he backed away from the table and out of sight around the corner. Sprat had not looked at him even once.

"Apparently he didn't live much like he painted. Dot that is. His paintings and his life had little in common. Don't you think so, Dan? You knew him."

"Sprat is a cat."

Sprat grinned. His eyes sparkled. "I beg your pardon."

Dan decided it would be opportunely appropriate that she now produce a grin herself. A minimal grin appeared on her face. "Your name *does* provoke rhymes."

"Yes. And not all of them are so simpleminded."

"Simpleminded is it!" Dan cast her eyes about the alcove pretending she was pretending she was offended. "Well, as names go, even if it is your one and only one, *Sprat* is not an overly complex word. It may be dual, the way you pronounce it; still, it's fairly straightforward, which leads most directly to simpleminded rhyming constructions."

"It's true that *Sprat* is not particularly labyrinthine. But neither is *Dan*. If Sprat is a cat, Dan is a can."

Dan made a face that looked somewhat like she

was smiling with her mouth open. Slowly she waved her hands in surrender. "Tell me about Willa. How is she doing?"

"Willa asked me to please not tell Dan Butxn where Willa Washingstone is. And I should please not divulge anything to D. Butxn about WW's life."

"How about her health?"

"Her health is good."

"How did she take Dot's death?"

"That is on the no-no list. I cannot answer."

Dan nodded and shook, nodded and shook, nodded and shook her head, just like Dot had, on a bench, one evening, after she had asked him if he was in love with her. Dan then sang in a low, gentle tone (crooning), "Where are you staying, Sprat? Or is that on the no-no list, too?"

"I am not going to have sex with you, Dan."

"Not here at the table?"

Sprat showed his teeth. He was not truly grinning any more than Dan was truly grinning. He tore off a small piece of biscuit, rolled it into a tight ball and flipped it with his finger at her. "Not ever."

"Could you say that real, real, real loud, Sprat, so that I don't forget?"

Sprat raised something dark and inhuman from his lap. *Finally*. He raised it just above the edge of the table and pointed it at Dan. *Finally*. He shot her dead for trying to steal another of Willa's lovers? No, the dusky object was not an implement of destruction. It was the wallet that Sprat kept strapped to his leg above his ankle when he was wearing long pants. He asked

Dan to excuse him. Dan settled back in her chair for the wait, foolishly thinking that Sprat would be gone for only a couple of minutes. Sprat left the table and the restaurant, paying their bill on his way out, to never return.

• • • • •

The next morning, the morning following the morning of Dan's first and last breakfast in The Tower, a statue appeared in the lobby of her office building. People had already started gathering around the statue when Dan arrived at work after a rough night alone. There, in the middle of the large lobby space, surrounded by Dot's paintings and fashioned from some new material that looked and felt both warm and cool, stood a life-sized Sprat, his phosphorescent green flesh wired with divinity. His body looked to Dan just exactly the way she had pictured it under his clothes, except for the unnatural green flesh, of course. "It has the light and color and scale of dreams," she overhead a woman say. A man in the woman's party said incredulously, "Your dreams look like that?" A second woman said, "I wish *my* dreams looked like that." The other man in the group: "I wish *I* looked like that. Not the color, the body." The first woman: "You know, I think I saw this guy around here yesterday or the day before. A real looker!"

That night and the next three nights, Dan hid in the lobby, waiting for Sprat to come to retrieve his likeness. The fifth night she spent in her studio. Next morning, the statue and the paintings were gone. Dan was the first one in the building that morning. On the floor where the statue had stood lay a flower. *The strongest, hottest, most florid red imaginable. No, more red than any red our milquetoast imagination has ever conjured up. The red of the real world!* Dan knew the flower was meant for her, but she wouldn't touch it. *Anguish of soul.* She tried to have no opinions, no hopes; but she held on tightly to the fact--*the fact!*--that she had seen him, had talked to him, had touched his arm, his shoulders, his torso, his hand, his cheek. *Green & red explosions.* Asleep or not, lying on the floor behind her chair, he had come to harm her.

17

EVENTUALLY THE DAY WILL COME

She cranked her head left and right in the dark. "What's that sound?" Peering up at the blackness, grinning tightly at the blackness, she whispered, "Is it rain?" She couldn't see the sky for the big tree branching out overhead, and she couldn't see the tree for the dark. "It is!" she cried with a thrill of joy in her voice. "I'm hearing the very first drops on the canopy of leaves up there." She drew in a long, slow breath through her widespread nose. "Heavendrops. Sounding just like people walking way off in the distance."

"That's a special way to put it," said the man sitting beside her in the night. "Are you feeling special this evening?"

She didn't answer immediately. But after a while, after she had taken in another deep breath, she said, "If experiencing the loveliness of the world is 'feeling special,' yes, I feel special." She had not spoken directly at the man, she was still peering intently upward.

He said to her, "I thought you would be feeling just the opposite."

She responded a tad quicker this time. "Why in the world would you think something like that?"

Roy Kee cocked his head at the sound of innocence in Dan Butxn's voice. "Why would I think something like that, you ask. Let me name you some why's, Dan. First, you were trying so hard to avoid me, bud-of-mine, that I nearly had to out-and-out force myself on you. But I--"

Dan cut Roy off right in the middle of what he was saying, stopping him cold with a sudden, imperious "no, not so" gesture, a jerky little movement of her hand that Roy might not have distinguished in the weak light if he hadn't roosted so touchingly close to her on the bench.

Having quieted Roy, Dan did not then speak herself. Nor did she return her hand to her lap. She held the hand out, palm up, to catch some raindrops. No drops landed on her hand. *Not many of them are making it through the leaves yet*, she told herself, talking inside her head instead of speaking out to Roy. No, she had not forgotten already that he was sitting beside her. Or mostly *no* and mostly *not*. Neither was she simply ignoring Roy. Not simply ignoring him. She could hear the rainfall quite clearly now but still could not see the drops, not even out beyond the spread of the tree. *Countless raindrops are falling to the grass unseen by my feeble eyes. An owl could see the drops. Many creatures could.*

Dan and Roy had sat together on this bench at least once before. *This is the bench on which Roy introduced me to Diane Potter.* But this time it was Dan who was sitting on the bench first and Roy had approached her and sat down beside her with his hip contacting hers. *And the sun is well gone; it's not just now setting like it was on that evening in the past; so it's much darker tonight. And the dark is even deeper because we have this cloud cover. Diane? Diane is who-knows-where with who-knows-who.*

Roy sat in the dimness silently waiting for Dan to say something. Too long became too too long, and

Roy brashly proceeded in a brassy voice telling Dan
what he had been telling her when she interrupted him
with that hand gesture. "But I don't feel too bad,
because from what I hear Dan Butxn has been avoiding
everyone. Cluck." He didn't say the word *cluck*; he had
clucked his tongue from the top of his mouth. "While I
don't feel personally affronted by her lack of hospitality,
I do feel sad. Sad for her. She lives alone, works alone.
And chances are she doesn't get much playtime to speak
of. How's a girl like that going to keep up a good
humor?" Roy's voice changed then from slowly-failing
brass to razor-sharp silver. "How's she going to feel
special?"

Thinking she was not paying nearly enough
attention to Roy to understand what he had meant by
what he just said, Dan was surprised to hear herself say
back to him, as if she were arguing with him, "Feeling
special does not always mean that one feels that way
relative to other people. A person can feel that she or
he is special, at this time on this certain piece of ground,
even if she or he hasn't seen another person for twenty
years."

"Are you quite sure of that?" taunted Roy.

"No," snapped Dan. "Of course not." She
looked away from Roy (farther away) and muttered, "I
have no way to test the idea." She made that brute little
movement of her hand again, as if to cut him off this
time before he had even started to speak.

At the sight of Dan's mean hand, Roy pitched
his head to the side away from her and clamped his
mouth closed. The bench sat without conversation

again. Dan and Roy. The two, who couldn't be called a couple, remained mute this time a good three minutes longer than their previous long silence.

Roy said hey and Dan slowly turned her head to gaze at the puny light reflecting from his face and he said oh never mind and stood up to kiss her goodbye on the forehead. He shambled away toward his abode.

Dan watched him leaving for as long as she could see his faint form, only a few seconds. She had no intention of following him, if that is what he wanted her to do. No, Dan hadn't followed anyone for quite some time. *Art has replaced people in my life.* She had researched the subject and learned that while it is not a common occurrence--art displacing the need for human contact--it isn't unheard of.

The earth shifted imperceptibly along a fault that runs under the bench, allowing a musty smell to escape and rise in the night. It rose into Dan's nose. The smell became a picture in her brain, a thought in her mind, a word in her mouth: *Terry*. The moon glimpsed at her through a short-lived hole in the clouds: *Dot*. A breeze twisted around the tree trunk behind her and dove into her hair: *Sprat*. Right beside her, on the seat of the bench, Roy's living butt-and-thighs print glowed as if it were afire. A wail, a cry in the distance made her remember Milosh. She cried back, "Where's Willa?" Sola Resta's face appeared in the night. Was it Jill again in the Sola Resta mask? Not tonight. It was Sola Resta herself, dressed all in black and walking right toward Dan. SR stopped in front of the bench. She had put on black rain gear and was wearing her black felt hat, rendering herself quite invisible, except for her face. She stared at Dan, Dan at her. "I'm not going in that direction…but if you need help, Dan…I'll accompany you home." Dan grinned like it was the end of the world. "Thanks, Sola. I was just enjoying the night. I don't need any help. But thanks again." Sola said OK. Yet she dimpled her chin eight or ten times before continuing on her way.

· · · · ·

"Who?"

"Nubbel. Remember Nubbel? I used to see you two walking together every so often, back before Terry told him to vamoose. You remember Terry, don't you?" Milosh's upper lip wrinkled oddly both times that he said Terry's name.

"Yes, Milo." Dan wrapped her arms tautly about her middle. She was feeling decidedly uncomfortable. She had been on her way out of the building when Milosh, who was just coming in, stopped her. Dressed very informally she was, whereas he wore a dark grey sharp-edged suit that reminded Dan of the skin of a shark she had once seen in an old photograph.

Milosh smiled at Dan's nervous twitches. He also kept close watch over who was passing in or out of the lobby and who was noticing him talking to Dan. "Nubbel not only vamoosed, he seemed to just up and disappear. I hadn't seen him for a long, long time. I thought--and it's still my working explanation--that Terry put the real fear in him."

Dan decided she had better say something. *I should contribute something here, something verbal, some words of my own beside "who" and "yes" and "Milo."* She came up with a couple of *not* sentences. (More correctly speaking, -*n't* sentences.) "I haven't seen Nubbel either. I thought once or twice about going to check on him, but I don't know where he lives."

"That sounds like anemic excuse-making, Dan. It's easy enough to find out where someone lives."

Dan gazed at the empty air just beyond the tip of one individual strand of Milosh's hair. "You said you *hadn't* seen him?"

"I saw him yesterday." Milosh opened his shoulderbag to take out something. "He came whizzing by me on a bike."

"A bicycle-type bike?"

"I think his hair is longer, but otherwise he looked the same."

"Oh."

Milosh pushed a scrap of paper into Dan's hand and forced Dan's fingers closed over it. He pinched the flesh of Dan's upper arm, then turned toward the elevators and marched away.

An address written in Milosh's handwriting was the only thing on the paper. Dan tried to figure the where of the address. *Oh yeah.* She didn't recall the exact building but remembered the general area. *Deal with this after lunch, pal.* Shoving the paper into a rear pocket of her pants, Dan resumed her exit of her office building. She had brought along a sandwich and planned to eat it while sitting by some running water.

Not Chuck. Chuck was too far to go just for lunch.
Probably Dan would sit beside one of the manufactured
creeks nearby. Dan remembered Nubbel's last words to
her: "Next you'll be telling me that depression doesn't
exist." Dan passed Gawkabit Howlsey on the walk; they
exchanged glances, nothing more.

· · · · ·

*Was this piece of paper ready and waiting in Milosh's
bag for him to pass it to me?* Dan filed that question under
Deal With Later When You Have More Info, a file that
actually exists in Dan's head, a file not duplicated on her
machine. *Is the address on the paper Nubbel's?* Dan felt
fairly safe in assuming that after Milosh saw Nubbel go
by on a bicycle Milosh went to his office to look up
where Nubbel lives. While Milosh, for whatever reason
he may have had, might have done just that, that is not
how he got the address that he gave to Dan, unless he
knew more about the workings of the Name/Address
Directory than she did. Dan opened the N/A Directory
on her machine right after lunch and found the address
from Milosh listed as unoccupied.

"Might as well look up Dot's address too while
I'm at it, just to check on the directory, ha-ha." Under
that address, Dan found another UNOCCUPIED. "No
new neighbor across the way, I see."

Under *Dot Sett*, she found DECEASED.

Under *Dan Butxn*, she found her address.

Under *Willamette Washingstone*, she found no
listing.

Dan had looked for Willa under LOCAL ONLY, but everywhere else that Dan checked during the next forty-five minutes she got the same answer: NO LISTING.

With a little work and patience Dan found Nubbel's address without first knowing his last name. His last name turned out to be *Nunshe*, and his listed address was in a whole other living area than the address Milosh had pressed into Dan's hand without explanation.

• • • • •

So Dan decided to take a different way home after work. Her plan was to stroll out by that address Milosh had forced on her and then loop back around to her house. The zigzag trip would take maybe three times longer than her normal walk home. She locked her office door for the night and headed for the stairs down.

She had left behind her building and its cluster of taller structures and was crossing a more or less open area of grass, trees, and flowers when she noticed something unusual: an extra brightness. The sun wasn't down, not yet; there was still plenty of regular light available; even so, she fancied she saw a glow hovering in the air just above the grass a ways off to the side of the walk.

The transparent yet blurry volume of light--Dan assumed the glow had volume--was probably half or more the size of her office. It was a cool light, meaning a low temperature light, a light not ascribable to incandescence. *Just pure light!* Hadn't Dan read something a long time ago about another phenomenon like this? She liked the light. Merely looking at it made her feel good, made her feel peaceful and quiet inside. She stared at the light, smiling, asking herself if she knew any way at all that she could induce the big lump of glow over there to come home with her. Dan laughed at the picture in her mind of the light following her home--*by this evening's longer route no less. Or is yonder light an outside only light? A hanging-over-the-grass only light? A this-time-of-the-evening and no-place-else light?* The thought slowly seeped into Dan's head that the light was for her only. But then she sighted someone standing over on the other side of the light looking fixedly at it. Then again, Dan was not entirely sure the individual was staring at the light. *That person across the way might be looking not at the light but at me.* If Dan could have seen herself from the outside, from over where that other person was standing, she would have been even more inclined to believe that that individual was looking long at her; yes, at her; for the series of poses that Dan was assuming was strikingly peculiar.

Dan returned her thoughts to the glow. *Is this the light that Dot was talking about, "a slanting light that only occasionally visits our earth," a light that enables one to assess just how much her or his imagination is influencing how she or he sees things? Probably not, I don't feel blessed or anything. Well...actually I do, a teensy bit. But the light is definitely not "slanting."*

Dan blinked. And blinked again. The person

who had been standing over on the other side of the light had started toward her--*walking right through the light!*

Neither burning to ash in an instant nor ripening beyond the human form before Dan's eyes, that person, a man, passed unharmed through the glow and approached her. It was Nubbel. Nubbel Nunshe. *Weirder things have happened, ho-ho.* Dan looked exceedingly pleased. *Nubbel with red pants on. Nubbel with a blue shirt on. Nubbel with tall boots on. Nubbel with his bone-black hair up in a bun on the back of his head.*

"Hello there."

"Hello, Nubbel," burbled Dan's happy lips.

"Long time no see, Dan Butxn."

Dan's head bobbed about inanely, like a cork on excited water. "I've been thinking about you off and on for most of the day, Nubbel."

"How generous of you, Dan."

Dan squinched her eyes tightly closed, then opened them wide. "Was that supposed to hurt my feelings?" How could even the possibility of hurt have occurred to Dan while her glad face was beaming like a searchlight?

"No! Don't do that kind of question, Dan! Not now. Don't get all strange on me. I just meant to say that I am pleased you would think about me. And think about me more than once in a day."

Dan's huge smile slid around a corner into whimsy. "You're looking most mysterious and glamorous this evening. Where have you been all this time? Why haven't I seen you around, like I used to?"

The man's guarded reply: "Do you want the long

or the short story?"

Dan noticed Nubbel's wariness but mistook it for flirty playfulness not unlike her own. She mimicked the way he had spoken out the side of his mouth. "Probably both stories, Nubbel." Shining her eyes in a small circle around and around his iron-brown eyes, soft she added, "If that's not asking too much." She winked at him. Really, she did. "You can tell me the short one first, while we're walking somewhere."

Nubbel merely looked at Dan's face. His own face now appeared quite neutral, purposely neutral.

With much ado, Dan vertical-ized her body. She stood up as straight, as up-and-down as a plumb line. But then she let her head tumble all the way forward. With her mouth aimed straight down her body at the toes of her shoes, she said fourteen words. She said them big and round. She said them witlessly. "Would you like to come to my place to partake of my lowly fare?"

Nubbel couldn't not grin. He laughed low in his throat. "Not if you're going to talk like that."

"Did I sound a trifle slimy, my dear-ahh?"

Nubbel hesitated, then giggled, then said melodramatically, "Oh! Were you wanting to sound lecherous?" Either the coil of hair at the nape of his neck was coming undone or he had put his hair up that way, loosely. "To me, you looked and sounded more like a demented monster."

"Then it's settled. My place."

Nubbel reassumed his neutral air. He stepped a bit closer, his eyes alert to anything and everything happening on Dan's face. "I hear you have an art-type studio now."

So! He's been out of sight but not totally out of hearing range. "You're right. But there are no dinner fixings there."

"Maybe after dinner you will show me your studio?"

Dan laughed operatically from behind her hand. "Ha-ha! That I will. That I will!" Talented as an actress she wasn't.

Nubbel changed his demeanor again. He slipped to Dan's side, slid his hand up under her arm, and leaned his body against hers. "Where were you headed before you saw me, my heroine?"

Without hesitation Dan leaned her head against Nubbel's head. She pulled the slip of paper from her back pocket and handed it to him. Nubbel read the paper.

He returned all of his weight to his own two feet. He freed his head from Dan's head, dropped his hand from her arm, peered out the side of his eyes at her face. In those heeled boots he was just a touch taller than she. His voice had a wobble and a wheeze in it. "Why were you going there?" He flapped the paper.

Dan couldn't read this new expression on Nubbel's brown face. She couldn't tell if he was in distress or if he was somewhere entirely else, somewhere a long way from trouble. "Someone gave me that address without telling me why," she answered him.

"Let me guess who gave it to you."

"OK, guess."

"Milosh Veerwright."

Dan just nodded her head. *What is going on? Everyone else seems to know. Why don't I?*

Suddenly she remembered the glow, the extraordinary event that had stopped her here. *How could I have forgotten it? Indeed, how could I have forgotten it for so long a time?* Dan looked out over the grass to see it again. Gone away it was. Not there it was. *Or maybe that lump of light was a connection of some kind between Nubbel and me, a connection we no longer need.*

"That's where I live, Dan." Nubbel crammed the paper into Dan's chest pocket instead of returning it to her pants pocket.

"But that address is listed as unoccupied."

"I have it listed that way to protect my health. I keep my old address listed as my residence, but I never go there."

"What do you mean, Nubbel? What are you talking about?"

"Where is Terry, Dan?

"I don't know. He died."

"Where is Dot Sett?"

"He died, too."

Nubbel pointed his consciousness at her. "I didn't and don't want to die, too."

Something just would not click for Dan. *People I knew died.* She actually scratched her scalp. "People who *I* knew died? Is that what you are saying?"

Nubbel just nodded his head in parody of the way Dan had just nodded her head a short while before.

"But I don't know you in the same way that I knew Terry and Dot."

"Terry thought you knew me that way, Dan. And maybe someone else thinks you did or do."

"Who is this someone?"

"Willamette Washingstone."

Dan caught herself before her knees gave out. Nubbel grabbed a fistful of her shirt to steady her.

Dan mumbled, "What about Milosh?" The thoughts inside her head were blaring trumpet notes.

Nubbel let go of her. With the palm of his hand he flattened out Dan's shirt where he had wrinkled it. "What about him?"

"I knew him too."

"It wasn't quite the same with him, though. Was it, Dan?"

"No, not the same." Dan squeezed her temples hard. "Why did he give me your address?"

"I don't know that."

"Then how did you guess that he gave it to me, Nubbel?"

"I have a monitor on Security's *real* directory. So I knew that someone sneaked in yesterday and looked up my name. It was easy enough to find out who."

Dan had no trouble at all believing that Security kept a realer directory; she had just never heard anyone make mention of it before. "Why were you standing over there looking at me?"

"I followed you from your office building, Dan. I thought you would head home, but you took off in this direction. So I had to rush to catch up with you.

And you saw me."

"The light saw you."

"Huh?"

"That's a whole different story, Nubbel. At least I think it is. Maybe you can explain it to me later, maybe over dinner. Why were you following me?"

"Milosh found out my hiding place...Milosh has been seen a number of times with Dan Butxn...people who knew Dan Butxn died. A loose chain of thoughts like that led me to you. And when you left work a while ago and started directly toward my place, I got scared and clumsy. You turned your head and saw me. I froze. But then you went into a mime that, even as scared as I was, I couldn't resist. And now, I am standing here talking to you after all this time."

"And you're not too afraid of being seen with me to go to my house for dinner?"

"Your demented monster washed away my fear. In spite of everything, Dan, I feel safe when I'm with you."

Something still wasn't right. Dan didn't know what it was or who she could ask. Who could help her figure everything out? *No one. Not Milosh, not now. Certainly not Diane. And not Willa either. I can't ask for help from either Willa or Sprat--if I ever see him again.* While Dan thought it possible that she might yet see Sprat, she had pretty well accepted the probability that she would never again talk to Willa. *Roy? No, not Roy. While Milosh thinks that Terry could intimidate people like Nubbel, Roy thinks or thought that Terry was capable of murder. But it was Terry who died, not Roy.* Next, as if the possibility had just occurred to her, Dan considered asking the person standing there talking to her. *How about Nubbel? He's right here waiting. If that dynamite blast was his short story, he still has the long one to tell. I could ask him some more questions, like why oh why did he say Willamette Washingstone.* Dan called down to Her Memory and asked if she could watch again that vision she had seen on her bedroom ceiling. The requested vision was sent up quick as a flash. Attached to it were some of the associated words: "Terry…wherever he is, it's nighttime there…he's looking out a window at a dark starry sky…there's someone else, someone near to him…" Dan looked hard and yet harder but still could not see who this someone was. Was it Willa Washingstone? Dan had asked Nubbel, "Who is this someone?" He had answered, "Willamette Washingstone." *One fact lingers, however: Nubbel has a history. Depression might have gotten the upper hand and held him captive ever since I last saw him. What then should I make of his stories, short or long?* Dan recalled another scene, back in Willa's studio. *I see someone curled up like a napping cat on a bed pinched in the corner. I see Willa Washingstone noticing me peeking over at the bed again. She deadpans to me, "Greying undies." What did Willa mean by that?* For that matter, when Willa suddenly walked into Dan's ex-office two days later, what did she mean by all that *Dan-a-kill, Dan is a kill, Dan will kill, Dan did kill* stuff? Dan's thoughts winged back to Nubbel. *What if Nubbel here asks to lay down on the bed in the studio tonight? Should I tell him that the first time ever I saw Dot Sett he was lying on that very same bed? Or should I keep it a secret to protect Nubbel's health? Tell him, of course. But not until he asks. For he will ask.*

"As I said, I'm standing here talking to you after all this time. I'm standing here talking to Dan Butxn! Why is she not talking back to me?"

"Oh!" Dan shook her head violently. "I'm sorry, Nubbel, very extremely sorry." She rubbed her cheeks strongly with her fingertips. "Thank you for waiting so patiently. I was busy drowning in the implications of what you have said to me."

"Are you all right now?"

"I think so." Dan wiped her brow drolly in an attempt to lighten the mood.

Nubbel pursed his lips. "What say we go for dinner?"

"My place still?"

"I've never been inside your house, Dan, but I've always been curious about how you live, stylewise."

Dan bent way forward at the waist. "This cabbage-head's got no style. She just bulldozes through anything and everything."

Nubbel straightened Dan's bent body by lifting her chin with the back of his hand. "I doubt that's true. But true or not, I'll say nothing further about it."

"Is it a deal, Nubbel doll?"

"It's a deal, dandy Dan."

"You can call me Dan for short."

"You can call me Nub for short."

"Not Nubby?"

"Definitely not Nubby."

"How come you never told me about the Nub before?"

Nubbel bent one knee to Dan and belatedly returned her wink. (Remember: Dan winked at Nubbel just before she became the monster-with-bowed-neck who invited him to dinner.)

Dan cocked not one but two knees at Nubbel and offered her hand. Away they strolled, as if on a great adventure together.

• • • • •

Tall Dog joined them for a while.

"Did you know that dog?" asked Nubbel after Tall Dog had turned off onto another walkway. Nubbel squeezed Dan's hand and swung it ahead of and behind them as they walked.

"That was Tall Dog, Nub. She's in charge of this part of the world."

"How big a part?"

"As far as the eye can see the earth from the earth on a clear morning."

"Does she have office hours?"

"As far as I know, no. She's just there when you need her."

"Why did she appear for us, Dan? Were we in need?"

"She has been keeping me from harm, Nubbel. So she wanted to check you out. That last wag of her tail? That was her OK sign."

Nubbel let go of Dan's hand to interlace his ten fingers and hang his arms from the crown of his head. "A wag of a stray dog's tail told you it is all right for me to walk beside you?"

"You got it."

"And what if I had not checked out OK, Dan?"

"Then Tall Dog would have torn your beautiful body to ribbons and packed off the pieces, leaving behind the red pants and blue shirt but taking your boots with her to clean her teeth on after the feast."

"Gick-k!" Nubbel curled his lips and stuck out his tongue.

"Gack-k!" Dan exhibited her teeth excessively.

"Gawk-k!" said Nubbel like a long-mouthed fish blowing a bubble.

Dan screeched to a halt. "Where?" She glanced everywhere for Gawkabit Howlsey, woman in uniform.

Nubbel scurried around behind Dan to crouch low and hide. "Where what?" He looked everywhere, just as she had.

"Do you want to take a rather long detour to meet a friend of mine?" Dan raised her hand to point a finger. "That way."

"Another dog?"

"A river."

Nubbel sprang out from behind Dan to land on his feet some distance away from her. He landed standing tall and pointing a finger in the same direction she had. "There be a river out there?"

"Where else would it be? Rivers don't often change course overnight."

"You saw this river yesterday, Dan? You saw it out there?"

"No-o-o, not yesterday."

Nubbel's "beautiful body" began dancing a hula. It swished, swished itself up very close in front of Dan. The dancing stopped. Nubbel pressed his forehead to Dan's shoulder and whimpered as if surely he would be beaten for what he was about to say. "I would rather eat first and then go to see your studio."

He took a quick step backward and laughed gaily. Dan laughed, too. Truly afraid she was that Nubbel was going to die right there in front of her.

• • • • •

As Dan and Nubbel threw off their clothes, out of Dan's shirt pocket flew the piece of paper. The scrap of paper floated in the shadowy air like a bird cruising for a comfy place to land for the night. Dan and Nubbel stood dumb struck, watching. Actually, the loosely wadded paper did not settle in for the night; it perched high on the studio's wood floor, only touching the floor at three points. Then it changed. The northern stars shining in the big window turned the crumpled paper into a flower, a yellow rose.

"Have you ever been there, Dan?"

Dan glanced up from the shimmering illusion on the floor. Nubbel had sounded as if he did not in truth want her to answer his question. "To the address written on that paper, Nub?"

Nubbel planted his chin on Dan's shoulder and gripped her arm with both his hands. He gave her a thin smile. "Yes." He had taken off all his clothes except one sock. "Answer. Please."

Dan pulled the remaining sock off Nubbel's foot with her gifted toes. "No. Yes. I don't know." They were both standing entirely naked now.

"That about covers the possibilities, Dan."

"I've been in that area, certainly, though I don't remember precisely when or what for, but never to that exact address, probably." Dan touched her face to Nubbel's face. "Was that a sufficient answer?"

"You never went there while Dot Sett was using it as his studio?"

Round! Round and round! Round and round! Round and round!

Nubbel held on steadfastly to Dan and kept her on her feet while she cried for Dot, not so many tears this time, only two or three, not a great flood. The tears? Were they still entirely expressions of Dan's grief? How much of the pain that Dan still suffered was really confusion?

Dan undid Nubbel's hair and used it's length to dry her eyes and face. "Was the place empty when you started using it, Nub?" She had never thought to ask Dot where he painted before he took over the studio after Willa.

"The place was stripped absolutely bare." Nubbel petted Dan's back and offered her all the hair she needed. "Dot must have taken all of his stuff with him."

"Probably so. Probably so. I came up here not long after Willa took off, and she had left nothing behind, nothing personal; but when I came up here again and Dot was using the place, the studio was full of painter's equipment and supplies, looking much like it does now."

"Where did you meet him, Dan?"

"Dot?"

"Yes. Don't get slippery."

"It's kind of hard to say, Nub."

"In that case, let's start off with an easier question. Where were you the first time you saw him?"

See! I was right! Nubbel's going to ask! He wants to know now where I was, but next he is going ask where Dot was the first time ever I saw him. Dan stepped over to the spot on the floor and stood with her arms stiff at her sides. "Here."

Nubbel almost smiled, almost frowned. "Where was he?"

"On the bed there, that bed, asleep. Or so I thought at the time."

"Willamette Washingstone? Was she here? Was this before or after she left us?"

"Before. Yes, she was here, too." Dan pointed. "She was over there."

"Was anyone else here?"

"No one else, Nub."

"What happened?"

"He wasn't asleep. He was listening to me." Moisture started collecting in Dan's eyes. She returned to stand fairly close to Nubbel. "I didn't stay here very long. I left, thinking not much had happened, except that I finally got to see where Willa worked."

"What happened next, Dan?"

"Next?"

"Between you and Dot."

"He came to my door that same night. In the middle of the night. Woke me up from a deep sleep." Just then the moon peeked around the corner of the building to flood the studio with light. "I didn't know who or what he/it was. He handed me a box wrapped in white paper and left."

Nubbel sat down on the edge of the bed. He appeared to be studying the bed, but he could just as easily have been lost in thought. He petted the single cotton sheet laid over the mattress. His smooth, hairless chest shone in the moonlight. His left thigh gleamed like fine, polished wood.

As Dan watched Nubbel, her thoughts swung away from Dot. *Nubbel has a tap on a Security file…or he could work for Security…and wouldn't that be a fine howdy-do…no, he did not say that he has a tap, he said he has a monitor…and isn't that even more questionable? Who knows?* Not Dan for sure. People could have monitors on anything and everything, and she wouldn't know.

18

ROSES IN A CLEAR TUBE

A week passed. Seven days slipped by without incident. Dan and Nubbel had spent most of that time together up in the studio, her quietly painting, him reading or watching her or tidying up the studio or just staring out the window. Whene'er they left the studio together, it was usually to go to Dan's house to eat. They showered at Dan's, too; and twice they spent the night there. The rest of the nights they slept on the studio bed. The five mornings that Dan had to go to the office, they embraced, kissed, and affectionately bid each other *to-the-seeing-again*. Dan had not an inkling of what Nubbel did with the hours while she was at work; but he was always right there waiting for her when she returned, sitting and smiling at her when she came in the door of either the studio or her house, whichever they had prearranged.

"They just stand around shouting nasty, cruel things at each other. In public too. Anywhere they are. They look like frantic sailors on a sinking ship."

Intent on the medium-tall canvas mounted low on the easel before her, Dan hardly stirred. Her brush was loaded with red. She stared at the canvas. A brilliant red. She could have been high in the sky looking down through the clouds at...*at what?* "Who?" she finally asked. "Are you talking about us, Nub?" Although generally she stood on her thongs while painting, today Dan was sitting on the stool that Dot Sett had so often painted from. *Did Willa use this stool, too?*

"No!" Nubbel grunted contentedly and scooted back deeper into the overstuffed chair that Dan had found and packed to the studio. He liked the chair very much. "Milosh and Diane. Veerwright and Potter."

Dan, still studying the canvas and having not yet applied any of the red, hummed a short, spiraling string of *m*'s. "Sounds to me," she said pleasantly, "like they have their lives reduced to the basics, to the good parts."

Nubbel's chair sat out in front of the easel where a model might pose, except that the painter in this room didn't use models. No, Dan, like Dot before her, faced the canvas squarely and seldom looked away from the working surface. So Nubbel couldn't see Dan's face, couldn't evaluate its expression, couldn't know for certain whether Dan was joshing him. From his chair he could see only her feet and ankles and the back of the canvas she was presently transforming. Nubbel stretched out his tongue, then curled it luxuriously back into his mouth, twice, as though he were secretly licking those tasty bare feet. "You *are* a cynical dame!" he said.

Dan chuckled softly. "Someone told you I was?"

Nubbel chuckled softly. "Yes." He was positive. "But I'm not going to tell you who."

Dan peeked around the edge of the canvas for the first time in more than an hour. "How would you know about Milosh V's and Diane P's public displays?" Smiling like our heaven's brightest ball of light, Dan asked Nubbel, "You never go outside nowadays, do you?"

"You're poking round in my private time, Dan Buttinsky."

"Sorry." Dan's shining face apologized. "I will zip my thoughtless trap."

Quick, before that smiling countenance disappeared again behind the canvas, Nubbel said, "Oh, I go out every once in a while." He raised one hand. "For walks or sometimes to go to the store." The hand held up a metal object so that it could be clearly seen by both Dan and him. Not one of Dan's rods, a new one, pale silver. "This is the last of these they had in the store. The fellow said they would not be getting any more. 'Fads come and go,' he told me. We both laughed."

Dan stared at the thing in Nubbel's hand. She nearly let go of her brush.

Nubbel's eyelids closed partway down as he grinned at Dan. He got up from his chair and stepped over to stand beside her. He took the red-ready brush from her hand and replaced it with the silver rod.

Dan's mouth still hung ajar.

Nubbel carefully placed the brush on a dish on the little round table by Dan's knee and returned to his chair, his grin having grown fully as wide as his mouth would allow.

Dan grinned, too, as she turned the silver token of sexual love in her hand. *When I get home and take down that box and add this fifth rod, the box I was given will then be full. What does that mean?*

Nubbel was sitting up unusually straight and proper on the well stuffed chair. He clasped his hands tightly together. "Do you like it?"

Dan scooted her stool out to the edge of the canvas. From there she could speak directly at Nubbel without having to lean her body heavily to one side. "Yes, I certainly do."

"Have you ever seen one of those things before?"

"Maybe I will have a bit of surprise for you, Nub, when we go to the house."

"Tell me now, Dan."

"I have four others, Nubbel Nunshe, each one a different color, and a felt-lined box made to hold five of them."

"Wow!"

"I thought you might be impressed."

"They only come in five colors, Dan, according to the man in the store."

"You don't say?"

"You didn't buy some of them yourself?"

"Not a one."

"And mine will fill up your box?"

"That's the way it looks from here."

Nubbel's mouth opened, then closed, then opened again to say, "Let me guess who gave them to you, Dan." He did not blink his eyes.

Dan was not so quick with her reply this time.

Nubbel waited, tilted his head toward her.

"I remember the last time you guessed who gave me something, Nub."

"I guessed right, didn't I?"

"Yeah, because you were monitoring Security. What else and who else are you monitoring?"

Splat!

Afore Dan's heart beat even one more time, her eyes jerked away from Nubbel as her attention roared right out the window, down the side of the building, and straight to Dot Sett. *Dot's sitting at a table!* Memory with a capital *M* had sent up a richly colored moving picture, with sound. *It's the table outside, below the window, the day he waded the creek.* Dot was sitting across the table from Dan, saying to her that he had bought a whole five-pack of the rods and that the other four were up in the studio awaiting their turns. That's it; that's all Dot said. But as the lush colors of the moving picture gradually faded away, leaving till the very last Dot's hotly painted fingernails--his ten red-orange moons on the rise--Dan got the point of the unsolicited movie from Memory. *Dot gave me one more rod after that. So where are the remaining three? If he gave them to other people, that's certainly OK. But what if he didn't? What if they are still hidden somewhere here in the studio? Or what if someone stole them?* "I am not spying on you, Dan Butxn!" *What? Who?* Dan rushed out of her thoughts.

Nubbel's head was jammed back against his chair and he was grimacing with his eyes shut tight, as if he were dreaming a thorny dream. "Even though you would be the easiest person in the whole wide world to spy on." His voice was as shrill as a calliope. "And if you have more of them at your house, I have never seen them there." He yanked his feet up from the floor, jerked his head forward from the chairback, folded his legs tightly and flung his arms around his shins to hug his thighs against his stomach and chest. "I only wanted to play a guessing game with you." In his haste Nubbel set his chin on his knees so sharply that his teeth clicked. His eyes were still firmly closed.

Even Dan could see she was supposed to see she had stepped on his feelings. She popped to her feet, jumped out of her shirt and shorts, and attacked him. "Thank you, Nubbel," she yelled in a stupendous voice while helping him out of the only clothes he was wearing, a pair of torn, zipperless, cutoff coveralls of Dot's, one of several pieces of paint-splattered clothing Dan had found about the studio. "Thank you for the beautiful gift." Three complete times she yelled this. That makes a total of six thundering *thank you*'s.

Someone called from outside. No, not to complain about Dan's yelling. Dan slipped her shirt back on and went to the window. Her plush "tuffy," as Dot had once called it, kissed the cool wall below the window. *Roy.* Roy was standing in the bright sunshine down on the grass across the water from the building. He held up a picnic basket with one hand, and his other hand waved for Dan to come on down. Nubbel stepped to the window to stand beside Dan. From down below, Roy would have been able to see only that Nubbel's dark shoulders were bare. A second or two or three or four passed before Roy beckoned for him, Nub, to come down, too.

• • • • •

"Your one and only problem in this world, Dan, may be that you don't recognize the standardized woman. Her aspects. Her potentials. Her limitations." Roy laid his sandwich on his leg and plucked a blade of grass to chew on. They had decided to sit on the lawn instead of at the picnic table. "I don't know if you are freer for that or if you're crippled."

"Thanks, friend." Dan threw a twisted smile at Roy. She had meant the "friend" and had most certainly meant the contortion of her face.

She glanced at Nubbel.

Both of us waved back to Roy from the studio window. Nub and I then stood like plastic playthings, silent, side by side, gazing down at Roy. All of a sudden Nub and I spun away from the window like a pair of exuberant dancers.

Dan continued to look at Nubbel.

But Nub hadn't taken even two fleet steps before he was slipping his head and arms into and through a sleeveless shirt that would turn out to be surprisingly similar to the one Roy here is wearing. And next, as if it were all the one movement, Nub grabbed up a pair of Dot's pants that we had left thrown on the studio floor since yesterday and shimmy-shaked them up his slim legs and over his other charms, accomplishing this feat, going from being buck naked to being adequately dressed, in, I'd say, six seconds flat, a good piece of time quicker than it took me to race from the window back to where my shorts lay on the floor and to turn the shorts right side out and to get 'em back on and fastened.

Dan continued to look at Nubbel.

Nub seems to be doing all right. He doesn't appear to be

bothered by Roy's talking familiarly with me. Terry would not have handled the situation as gracefully. Dot probably wouldn't have either.

While Dan was taking what turned out to be a good gander at Nubbel, Roy looked up at her. Roy Kee immediately turned his own face and eyes to Nubbel Nunshe and said, sounding a bit like someone in the distance pounding their fists on sheet metal, "I haven't been seeing you around much."

Nubbel smiled thinly. He lowered his eyes to his sandwich.

"In fact," said Roy, "come to think of it," said Roy, his words now ringing with insincerity even though these words were undoubtedly completely true, "before you appeared up there in Dan's window a few minutes ago, I had not seen you anywhere for quite some time. Where are you living now?"

"Oh, I sort of still live at the same place, Roy."

"Sort of?" Roy encircled his neck with his hands, his own neck with his own hands, while his lips outlined a hole roughly the diameter of his thumb.

Dan came to Nubbel's rescue. "Nub has been spending some time with me, Roy."

Now that was a really stupid thing for me to say. Obviously, Roy has not seen Nubbel for a much longer time than Nubbel could even possibly have been huddling away with me.

Roy didn't press the issue. He let go of his neck. He hid his frown. One of his hands took a wild swing at a bug flying by, and the other one retrieved his sandwich.

Fresh strawberries and orange juice followed the

sandwiches and scrumptious potato salad. Roy had fixed a delectable, wholesome lunch, more than enough for three. Taking one superfine bite and sip after another, savoring each, Dan wondered what Roy would say if she were to bring up the subject of Milosh and Diane and their being together. *Kind of together.* Then Dan took to wondering about Nubbel. *Why has Nub never asked me if I want to go to see where he lives? Does he go there and lead a separate life while I'm at the office?* Next she wondered about Milosh and why he had given her that address. *Assuming that Milosh did sneak into Security's directory to check on Nubbel, did he discover there that Nubbel lives in ex-Dot's once-studio? If so, why didn't Milosh say so, instead of just handing me that piece of paper and walking away? Or does Milosh know something else, something that I still don't know about? Questions, questions.*

One of Dan's questions, the first of her wonderings in the paragraph above, got answered right then and there. "It's insulting," said Roy to no one in particular.

"What is?" asked Dan, though she knew full well what he was referring to. *Roy has a faint, different smell about him today. Roses? Maybe it's roses, if it's on his clothes. If it's on his skin, then more likely it's rosewater.*

"Diane Potter and Milosh Veerwright?" inquired Nubbel somewhat slyly.

Roy glared at Nubbel as if to ask how he knew.

Nubbel had an answer ready. "I saw you and Diane Potter together once or twice, from a distance. I thought you people made a good-looking couple."

Roy just harrumphed. Nubbel grinned, not

necessarily unkindly.

After lunch, Roy gave them both a my-forehead-touching-your-forehead goodbye--*it's rosewater*--and left rather abruptly. Dan and Nubbel returned to the studio, where Dan searched for the missing three rods while Nubbel watched her with curiosity. "Should I leave while you are doing whatever you are doing, Dan?"

"Do you know what I'm looking for?"

"No. I have no idea."

She told him what.

Nubbel climbed to his feet. "I will help you look."

They searched the studio together but did not find a one. And later, when they went to her house and Dan marched directly into the kitchen to the cupboard to get out the box of her rods, the box wasn't there.

"My guess is that Willamette Washingstone has them."

"Why do you say that, Nubbel?" Dan thought about the box and could feel her fingers touching its black felt lining that first time she opened it. The unique feel of felt made her remember Sola Resta standing out in front of ex-Terry's house nervously gripping her black felt hat two-handedly behind her back.

"Just a guess."

"How would Willa have gotten them?" Dan was all but shaking her head no. "She's been gone a long time."

"I don't know, kiddo. Have you had any

strangers in your house lately?"

Glaring at Nubbel as if to ask how he knew, Dan admitted that a while back she had come home just in time to see someone sneaking out of her house.

"Was it a female?"

"It was dark; I couldn't tell. I looked all around inside the house but didn't notice anything was missing."

"Did you specifically check for the box?"

"I don't remember, Nub."

"Could it have been a man?"

Didn't I just say that I couldn't tell whether it was a female? "Why do you ask that?"

"Just a sudden feeling. Have you noticed any new men lurking around the borders of your life? Besides me. I'm not new."

Sprat? Dan didn't want to tell Nubbel about Sprat. "Not really."

Nubbel detected her resistance and remarked on it. "I say *sort of* and you say *not really*. We must make a good-looking couple." Nubbel laughed, a little too loudly. He opened his shirt to show Dan his chest. The silver rod from him was the only one she had now.

· · · · ·

"She stumbles blindly but then moves fairly fast through the gears."

"Can you give me just a clue as to what you are talking about, Jill?"

"I wasn't talking; I was quoting."

"Quoting who about whom?"

"Actually, Dan, it wasn't a real quote. Let's call it a composite quote--if such a thing is possible, which it probably isn't."

"Well?"

"No, instead of a composite, let's call it a reduction. No, let's call it a distillation, a distillation of the impressions I have gotten over a period of time while listening to people trying to describe you, Dan, your intelligence type, your work, your manners, your sexual abilities."

"Do you make up composites/reductions/distillations like that about everyone you supposedly supervise?"

Jill Atnoon smiled nicely and leaned back in her chair. Skipping right over Dan's grey-green word, *supposedly*, with nary a look back, she said, "Yes. Yes, I do. I have a line in my head for everyone in the building."

An image, most likely produced in large part by the words Jill had just said, appeared on Dan's mind. The image was of a circle of circular paintings, each round painting in the circle being a rendering of one unique way of being disappointed in the very nature of life. "Is that why you asked me to come to your office? So that you could complain about my personality?"

"Complain? Whoa! I think you're missing the point here, Dan. Nobody's complaining. Especially not me. I long for your loving. And for you to call me Lady Atnoon again."

Dan was carefully considering what to say back

to that, when Jill began fanning the air in front of her face with both her hands. "Business!" She scolded herself. "Stick to business, girl."

"What kind of business, Jill?"

"Nothing important." Jill stood up and went to a window. She opened the window, leaned out, and waved her hand.

How smooth and perfectly formed her face and neck are.

"It has been reported to me," said Jill as she returned to her chair, "that you have partially disassembled the equipment in your office."

"That's true. I have."

"You were disturbed by the sound quality? Or by the fact that the machine talks?"

"The talking bothered me."

"You should have turned in an official request for modification."

"Oh."

"I'll take care of it for you, Dan. How about lunch?"

"Sure, if the invitation is for lunch only. I am not free after work."

"Well! Neither am I, if you want to be *that* way about it."

It was the perfect moment for a knock at the door.

Jill barked, "Come in."

The door opened and Diane Potter stepped into the room.

Jill gasped in surprise. She beamed quickly at Diane, then beamed a big big long beam at Dan.

Dan grinned crookedly, nodded her head, and said she would take a rain check on the lunch.

"Hiya, Diane."

"Hiya, Dan."

"Goodbye, Jill."

"Goodbye, Dannie."

. . . . .

"She drank up so much culture she got the jimjams. She ate up so much sweet love she went right to hell. She was burning in the hollows, smoking on the points. She had to get out of here. Can you hear me? Willa *had* to get out of here!"

The man discontinued the overworked and unprovoked hand and arm gestures and the sharp twists and turns of his body and plunked himself back down on his chair. He looked off in the opposite direction yet extended his hand to Dan. "Morris Toend. But call me Mores."

Dan shook the man's hand. Yep, it was the actor again, the actor who, in the middle of a major play production, had repeated words said by Dan to Terry. Dan had gone to see this man the morning after that performance, and here, today, Dan was once more in the man's rooms. Dan had come here this second time after overhearing someone earlier in the day saying that the actor knew Willa pretty well. Dan sat in a wraparound chair next to a matching chair occupied by Morris Toend. Mores was again cloaked entirely in black. *In fact, today's outfit could be the very one he wore in the play.* Unlike Dan's first visit to these rooms, this time the man had a voice.

"So what's it to you, Donna?"

"I'm Dan. So what's what to me?" Dan noticed she was beginning to avoid the man's eyes. She immediately stopped herself. She gazed forthrightly at the man's face.

"Why are you asking about Willa Washingstone?" Mores touched a fingertip to a corner of his mouth. "What do you want with my friend Willa?"

Dan tried not to fidget. "The most straight-out answer is that I just want to know where she is, if she is all right, and could I come see her."

"And the not-so-straight-out answer?"

"I've been hearing things about her that I would like to discuss with her."

"You would, would you?"

"Yes, I would. And I'll ask again. Can you give me any information as to her whereabouts?"

"You're with Security, aren't you?"

"Not a chance, Mores. But why would Security be interested in Willa?"

"*They've* been hearing things about her that *they* would like to discuss with her."

"Someone from Security has come here to talk to you about Willa?"

"Yes. A man whom some among us might find attractive."

"Could you describe him?"

Mores pointed at something. "I could, but I

won't." He seemed to be pointing at the side of his nose, pointing with the same finger he'd touched to his mouth. He moved the finger deliberately but confidently until the finger's tip made contact with the bulging sidewall of his nostril. Then he dropped his hand to his lap.

Why not? Why won't he describe the man? For the same reason that he has been refusing to say my name? If that finger-to-nose gesture was supposed to mean something to Dan, Dan didn't get it. Likewise with the finger-to-mouth gesture. Dan tried a different tack: she asked the question she probably should have asked in the first place. "Did he give a name?"

"Sure. But it was fake. I'm an actor. I know fake when I hear it."

"Is my name Dan or not?"

"Your name is Dan and only Dan, not Danielle."

Gotcha! And while we're still rolling, I'll hit him with the question again. "Where is Willa?"

"She killed herself last week."

Dan's head flopped back hard when her eyeballs buoyed to the ceiling.

Mores got up from his chair saying, "Are people really just people?" He ambled over to the script table to get something to put in his mouth. "Is that why we paint ourselves up to be attractive? What's the point of being attractive? It's so…so utterly mechanical! Why are we always trying to make an impression?"

• • • • •

"You are going to have to come to a decision here, Dan. The river or the dog? Which one do you want?" Dan woke up with a jolt and sat up in bed. Moonlight filled the bedroom. She had just been with Dot, walking along beside him in outer space. Way out beyond the stars, he whispered to her that he had started another family portrait. She whispered back to him that she was quite pleased to hear that. But when she then asked him in a normal voice, not a whisper, to include Tall Dog in this portrait, he came right back with an ultimatum. He was the artist, and he had decided that there could be only three elements in the picture. "You are the given, Dan. So…! If you want to include both the dog and the river, you will have to do without me. I will paint me out of the portrait."

Dan studied Nubbel's sleeping face. Nub lay unclothed on his back on top of the bedding. The moon had his body looking like a plaster statue someone had tipped over onto the park grass.

Dan got up, got dressed, and trotted to the address Milosh had given her. There was a light on inside. Dan knocked on the door. Another dream.

• • • • •

"Where was Willa when she died?"

"That is my little secret." Mores put another something in his mouth and returned to his chair.

"You mean Security doesn't know?" Dan

squinted her eyes at the side of the man's head.

Mores was gazing at a picture of himself on the wall. "They're still out looking for her, aren't they?"

When the man finally turned his face toward Dan, one of his actor-eyes was half closed. His voice was low and full of faux grit. "Why do you want to know where Willa did herself in?"

Dan squirmed on her chair. "I am also looking for a certain man who knew her."

"He has a name?"

"Sprat."

"Where did you hear that name?"

"I woke up and this man was lying on the floor behind me. He told me that's his name."

"It's a fake name."

"How can you tell without seeing the man, Mores?"

"I just can tell."

"Can you tell me where Willa died?"

Sweet as honey, Mores said, "On the chair you are sitting on."

• • • • •

"You're awake!" Nubbel tried to sit up. His body was still mostly asleep.

"Yeah," said Dan. She helped him sit up beside her. "Sorry I woke you, Nub."

"Can I fix you something or give you a massage or something?"

"No." Dan shook her head and looked at the

window. "Thanks anyway."

· · · · ·

Women from Maintenance reinstalled some of
Dan's speakers.

They hooked up speakers and positioned them
about the room but did nothing inside the machine's
cabinet. They told Dan that if her machine could not
speak before they arrived, it would still be unable to
speak; but now she could access the majority of the
music channels.

Music. "Thank you."

· · · · ·

"Why don't you get up off the floor? What is
your real name? Do you know about Willa? Is it true
about Willa? What are you doing here now?" She kept
rehearsing lists of questions to ask Sprat, if she ever saw
him.

"We see a woman walk into a room, into a
roomful of people. She doesn't speak to anyone, stays
but a minute, leaves without a goodbye. When next we
see this woman she is out on a desert alone, standing on
one certain spot in order to touch one particular cactus
flower. Next she is--where? Somewhere certainly. And
then somewhere else. She is leaving silent prints of her
life on the greater life."

Nubbel flinched at the unmistakably
uncharacteristic tone of Dan's voice. Lying on his side
near the edge of the bed with his back to Dan, he
nervously narrowed his eyes. He closed the book he
had been reading, one of Dan's, and silently lowered it
to the floor. He listened. Dan didn't say anything
more. Nubbel rolled slowly, cautiously over onto his
back. He was then lying close beside Dan with his
upper arm pressed solidly against hers. He turned his
head to look. He could see only one of her eyes. It was
looking straight up from the bed.

Dan sighed.

Nubbel spoke. "What you are saying, I assume,
dong dong, is that we are all significant, that it takes
everybody to make the world. Everything everyone
does is important. Right? That's what you were
saying?"

Wrong. No. As far as Dan knew, she wasn't
trying to say anything. She had improvised that brief
speech about an unnamed woman solely to see how it

would feel to talk that way, the way she had once heard Dot Sett talk to the big coldbox in his kitchen. Dan clearly remembered both the lecturer's voice and the carefully cocky style that Dot had employed that day when he thought he was all alone in the kitchen. Talking like her everyday self again, Dan said, "I don't know what I was saying, Nub. Don't know, don't know, don't know. *Significant* is probably the word to examine, since everyone wants everything that they do to be significant, one way or the other, by hook or by crook, by this or that."

"*This-or-that* is *his-or-hat* with a pair of *t*'s thrown in."

Dan thought, glanced sideways at Nubbel, grinned. "So it is, so it is."

Nubbel purred right back, "Now, if you're going to repeat everything tonight, Dan, let us proceed directly to the sex replay." He twisted his torso and bent his neck to position his mouth against Dan's shoulder. He curled back his lips and chewed on her shoulder. He licked her skin, chewed some more.

Dan turned her head to smell Nubbel's hair. She pushed her face still closer and kissed his forehead. "Your flower is still hungry?"

"It's one of those cactus flowers that never gets enough lonely girls dropping by to touch it."

"You're pretty quick and slick with the words tonight, Nubsy-bubsy."

"That's so easy to explain that even a wild orchard like you might understand. I had a good day all day; I had a good servicing just a while ago; I have prospects of another one real soon."

Dan jerked her face away from Nubbel's forehead to spout at the ceiling above, in a loud voice, as if she were speaking to someone in the other room, "Shoot low! Maybe the dust spurting up out in front of them will spook their horses."

"Dan!" Nubbel shivered all over. "Where did you find that crock?"

"In an old script I was reading this morning."

"One of those Wilkan Xeniat plays? Like the one out in the living room?"

"No, this play is quite a bit older than any of his."

• • • • •

¡¡START RIGHT
HERE, WOMAN, RIGHT
NOW, TODAY, MAKING IT
AN AFFAIR OF THE HEART
INSTEAD OF THE HEART
OF THE AFFAIR!!

The note, three short lines machine-printed on a full sheet of paper, hung midway between Dan's eye level and the door handle. Dan read the words but did not touch the paper, for this note was not meant for her. Someone had left the words for Diane Potter, or apparently so, assuming Diane Potter hadn't hung them on her door herself. *Double exclamation points at both the*

beginning and the end? It must be a sharp reminder of some sort
for Diane. That's how Dan read the sentence anyway.
Sharp or not, a reminder or not, the message is too
cute/pat/cloying to be from Roy. Too blurred. And maybe too-
too to be from Milosh too. But maybe not. Someone new? Or
Jill? No, surely it's not from Jill. I really don't think either Roy
or Milosh, and certainly not Jill, would leave a message like this
hanging out in the hall to be read by just any old someone who
happens by. Dan stared at the note. *Now I get it.* What
Dan *got* was that the sheet of paper fixed to Diane
Potter's blue plastic office door sorely reminded Dan of
the hateful black ink scrawl she had found one morning
on the door to Terry's office, now her office, the door
right behind her--no, the red door that would have been
behind her if it hadn't been replaced by a new, mint
green door. The penmanship of that ugly scribble on
Terry's door had looked almost certainly feminine to
Dan, while today's "START RIGHT HERE" order--*if it*
is in fact an order!--had been mechanically printed, not
handwritten, making it next to impossible for Dan to
determine whether the message had been composed and
posted by a woman or by a man. *The position of the note on*
the door gives away no gender secrets, either. Dan had little to
go on this time, but the balance scale kept wanting to
drop to the masculine side.

Never mind, old chap, Dan told herself. The
note was none of her business. She turned away,
unlocked her door, and had all but stepped into her
office when the elevator door opened. Down the hall,
standing alone in the rectangle of bluish elevator light--
or greenish or yellowish, depending on the beholder's

attitude--was Milosh. Dan didn't want Milosh to see her, and Milosh quite clearly didn't want Dan to see him. Yet their eyes unavoidably locked on each the other's. Seconds crawled by before Milosh--*timidly?*-- pointed up at the floor-number indicator above him and shook his head as if to tell Dan he had mistakenly stopped on the wrong floor. Dan stepped into her office and closed and locked the door behind her.

What is Sprat's true name? She set down her lunch bag. Fresh music wafted from the speakers. *Who has the rods? Dot's rods and my rods.* She checked for bodies lying on the floor. *Again and again I ask myself, why has Nubbel not taken me to either of the places where he lives?* She changed the music channel. *Again and again and again, why did Milosh sneak into Security's files to get Nubbel's real address and then pass the address to me the next time he saw me?* She sat down on her chair. There was a request waiting to be noticed on her machine. "Dan, please step back out into the hall."

Dan considered the request every which way, then stood up and stepped back out into the hall.

Nothing had changed in the last minute. The note was still attached to the door across the way, the hall was still empty, the elevator door was closed. Dan Butxn let another minute pass, then stomped back into her office and sat down and went to work.

• • • • •

I must have forgotten to lock it the second time, she thought when she heard the door handle turning behind her. She whipped her chair around and stood up. *What a surprise! Nubbel has come to visit me at my office.*

It wasn't exactly a visit. Not only were Nubbel's eyes big, as if with fear or awe; they looked as though he had been crying hard only a short while before. Dan closed the door and bade him sit down. "What's the matter, Nub?"

Nub mightn't have noticed that he sat himself down. His enlarged eyes stared blankly in the general direction of the window that opens. "My things--" He choked on his words.

Dan noticed dark smudges on the sleeves of his shirt. "What things?" His shoes were blackened, too.

"I went to get some more of my clothes..."

"Hmm?" Dan kneeled in front of Nubbel and held on lightly to the arms of his chair.

"...and the building was gone," said Nubbel breathlessly. He squeezed Dan's hands, then pulled her hands down to his knees.

"What do you mean? How was the building gone? Which building?" *He said he went to get some of his clothes.*

"Burned...to the ground." Nubbel spoke very slowly, carefully pronouncing each word. "It burned up...completely." He pat-patted the backs of Dan's hands with the palms of his. "The buildings on either side were not even touched. But all my things are gone!"

Dan didn't need to ask again which building. *The address from Milosh. The address listed in Security's directory. Dot's place to paint before the studio.* "When did the

---

293

building catch fire?"

"A woman that I talked to down the walk said it was late last night."

"Is anything salvageable, Nub?"

"No!" Nubbel's shoulders vibrated with the force of his reply.

"Nothing?"

"There's a Security ribbon around the mess, but I ducked under it..." He had held back the tears for as long as he could. Nubbel's eyes filled and overflowed. "There was nothing to save, Dan. Nothing at all! Just masses of gunk. Hardly anything was even recognizable."

Dan hurried to ask, before her fear of tears incapacitated her, "What caused the fire?"

"How would I know?" Nubbel threw Dan's hands away from his knees and set his flooding eyes well above her head. "All I saw was black desolation!"

• • • • •

"And baby makes three, in my blue heaven."

Dan didn't look away from her machine. "What's that song you're singing, Nub?"

Neither did Nubbel turn his head to look at her. Sitting and staring out the office window, he had not moved from that chair for close to an hour. The volume of his voice rose and fell and rose and fell. "It's an old-timer. From long before our time."

The up-and-down, up-and-down in his voice was so noticeable that Dan did look. She glanced back over her shoulder at him. His head was turned away from her, and she couldn't see much of his face.

Dan returned her face to her machine. "I don't think I've ever heard it before, Nubbel."

"That's no big loss. It's not much of a song."

Now he sounds plain bored. No, he's probably just tired. The blow of the fire has worn him down. This time Dan turned not just her head but her entire body to better see Nubbel. He had turned to look at her, too; so she briefly caught his eyes; but he quickly turned back away. *He looks simply exhausted.* "It may have seemed more relevant back when it was popular, Nub."

"Undoubtedly so," he mumbled, a tough, bitter mouthful.

Dan glanced back at her work.

"Can we go to the studio or to the house pretty soon?" That rushed question had come out Nubbel's mouth as a whine, a cry of distress. Did he hear how he sounded? He pushed his elbows together and pressed his palms to his cheeks, perhaps trying to lower the pitch of his voice. "I am not very comfortable here."

"Sure. Real quick."

"I can go by myself, Dan."

"No way, Jose. Me gotta go, too."

• • • • •

"What about where you lived before?" Dan held on gently to Nub's arm.

"My old address? I never go there, Dan."

"I know. I understand that. But did you leave

anything there?"

"Some furniture. And a few odds and ends."
Nubbel was talking a bit more fluidly now. "I left stuff
scattered here and there where it could be seen from the
outside. With the automatic timer turned on for the
lights, I hoped the place would look like I still live
there." His voice was nowhere near normal sounding
yet, yet it had stopped bottoming out and the little sharp
peaks were starting to round off. "But otherwise,
nothing. No, there is nothing personal of mine there,
Dan."

"What are you going to do?"

"I don't know. Can I stay with you a while
longer?"

"Sure you can."

Walking and talking on their way home--to
Dan's house--Nubbel and Dan were seen together by a
number of people. It was lunchtime and people were
out and about. A woman ran to catch up with them.
When Dan stopped to see what the woman wanted, the
woman asked Nubbel if she could speak with him for a
moment. Nubbel followed the woman off to the side
of the walk. Dan stared at the sky, at a tree or two. She
wondered how Tall Dog was doing. When Nubbel
returned to her side, his face was flushed. They walked
the rest of the way to Dan's house in silence.

Depression. Nubbel had shown no overt signs of
being depressed; not one hint of depression had he
displayed in all the days since Dan spotted him watching
her from beyond a strange glow. *Not until this morning in
my office, that is. The fire changed all that.* By the time they

reached the house Nubbel was clearly much worse than Dan had ever seen him. *Wait! He has lost precious ground all right, but maybe not entirely on account of the fire. For a while after we left the office, it seemed he was getting over the trauma of losing everything overnight. Until that woman stopped him and told him something, his attitude seemed to be improving. What did that woman tell him?* Whether it was the fire or the woman, or the fire and the woman, something changed something drastically in Nubbel. For the rest of that afternoon he looked like a misshapen, overstuffed doll, a beat-up, bloated rag-baby. He sat like a dried turd or he moped about the house, dull, dejected, listless. When Dan spoke to him, if he answered at all, he only mumble-grumbled at the nearest wall.

Afternoon dragged into evening. Dan gave up and said she was going to the studio. But before she could turn away from him to leave the house, Nubbel's eyes came alive. He glared up at Dan from the couch. Dan didn't know what to do. She just stood there before Nubbel in the sudden heat of his stare.

Finally she said, "What?"

Nubbel threw off the heavy cloak of dejection and sprang to his feet. "Willamette Washingstone is dead."

"I know."

"I know you know. Why didn't you tell me?"

Dan felt her face and neck redden. She and Nubbel were standing very close to each other, facing each other. "I don't know why, Nub."

"You don't trust me!"

"That's not it."

"What is *it* then?"

"Probably--"

Dan didn't go on with whatever, if anything, she was about to say. She lowered her eyes. She turned her body clear around, in a complete circle. "I don't know what is going on, Nubby."

"Leave off with the *Nubby*! Going on with what?"

"Is the world as peculiar as it seems to me, or am I a fruitcake?"

"The world is peculiar. You are a fruitcake."

"Thank you, Nub. I do feel much better now."

Nubbel kneeled to pick up something from the floor. Dan didn't look to see what. Nubbel straightened back up and whacked Dan hard on her shoulder with his shoe. He barely parted his lips to say, "Remember something, Dan Butxn!"

Dan covered both her shoulders with her hands. *Good thing he isn't wearing his boots today.* "Yes?"

"I am on your side. If I could find a way to do it, I would attach myself permanently to you."

Dan felt stupid with her hands protecting her shoulders. She dropped them to her sides. Her hands.

"Any questions, Dan?"

Dan did not move or speak.

"Feel free to ask me anything you want to."

"Did you burn down your place, Nub?"

"No."

"Do you work for Security?"

"No."

"Were you really afraid someone might kill you?"

"Yes."

• • • • •

Please take notice of Dan's last question, how it's worded. She asked Nubbel if he was afraid someone might kill him. She did not ask him if he was afraid someone might *try to* kill him. Also note the first word of the question: *Were*. She did not ask, "*Are* you really afraid…?"

• • • • •

She was perched, sitting on her hunkers, at the edge of Chuck. As she gazed in reverie out over the water, the sky immediately above her filled with loves. (A gathering of loves is often mistaken for a covey of clouds, the type of clouds produced by a localized change in air pressure.) Dan crouched beside the big male only a few feet from where she had been sitting on the sloping muddy beach when Milosh sneaked up behind her right after Terry died. Nubbel was there, too, visiting with Chuck. This was Nub's first trip to the river. He sat upstream of Dan atop a sheer bank, the bank on which Dan and Dot had stood arm-in-arm, hanging over the rushing water. Tall Dog was there, lying not far from Nubbel. The dog lay on the very spot where Dot and Dan were lying when Dot told Dan his name. Nubbel had not forced Dan to choose three out of four; they were all there: Tall Dog, Chuck, Dan, Nubbel. A new family portrait that would hang forever in four minds.

The painting on Dan's living room wall? It was still there, still hanging over the couch. Dan loved it. Nubbel said he loved it and acted as if he truly did. No one looked in through Dan's front window from the window across the way anymore/yet, but people passing by on the walk occasionally glanced in; they seemed to like the painting. And what about Chuck? The group picture painted by Dot had never been carried to the river so that Chuck might gaze leisurely at himself and his two human friends.

"Death walks quick."

Dan's face jerked up from the river. "What?" She started to rise from her squat. "What did you say, Nub?" She wasn't shouting, but she knew she had to talk fairly loud to be heard over Chuck's mighty movement. Nubbel wasn't there. He wasn't where he was sitting just seconds before, what seemed like just seconds before. Five hundred years had passed, and Dan was someone else. The river was much the same. The bank was still there. But Nub wasn't.

www.ingramcontent.com/pod-product-compliance
Lightning Source LLC
Chambersburg PA
CBHW031110030726
47496CB00002BA/476